HENRY JAMES'
Shorter Masterpieces
VOLUME 1

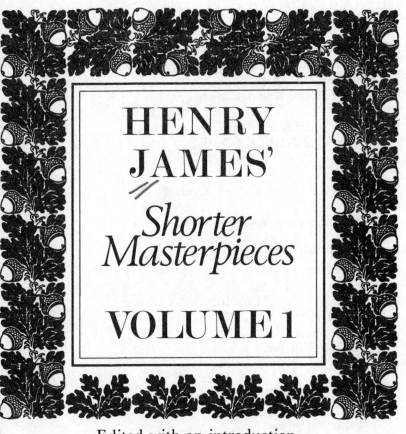

HENRY JAMES'

Shorter Masterpieces

VOLUME 1

Edited with an introduction
and notes by

Peter Rawlings

Fitzwilliam College
University of Cambridge

THE HARVESTER PRESS · SUSSEX
BARNES & NOBLE BOOKS · NEW JERSEY

First published in Great Britain in 1984 by
THE HARVESTER PRESS LIMITED
Publisher: John Spiers
16 Ship Street, Brighton, Sussex

and in the USA by
BARNES & NOBLE BOOKS
81 Adams Drive, Totowa, New Jersey 07512

© Editorial material, Peter Rawlings, 1984

British Library Cataloguing in Publication Data

James, Henry, 1843-1916
  Henry James' shorter masterpieces.
  Vol. 1
  I. Title   II. Rawlings, Peter
  813'.4[F]   PS2110

  ISBN 0-7108-0668-X
  ISBN 0-7108-0673-6 Pbk

BARNES & NOBLE BOOKS
ISBN 0-389-20502-8
ISBN 0-389-20504-4 Pbk

Printed and bound in Great Britain by
Whitstable Litho Ltd., Whitstable, Kent

CONTENTS

ACKNOWLEDGEMENTS

I SHOULD like to thank Mrs Jean M. Gooder for her valuable advice and Dr Eric Warner for his warm and vigorous encouragement throughout this project. I am particularly grateful to Mr Stephen Clark for his careful suggestions and reservations and to Mr Philip McGenity, Mr David Brown, and Mr Bob Cochrane for reading drafts of the introduction My greatest debt is to Mrs Patricia Rawlings who knows the cost of this work.

Acknowledgements are due to the University of Chicago Press and Messrs Charles Scribner's Sons for quotations from *The Notebooks of Henry James* and the Prefaces to the New York Edition.

BIOGRAPHICAL NOTE

HENRY JAMES was born in New York on 15 April 1843 and died in London on 28 February 1916 less than a year after becoming a naturalised British subject. The family moved to Europe in 1855 where James was educated, desultorily, in Geneva, London, Paris, and Boulogne. 1858 saw the James family in Newport, Rhode Island, 1859 in Geneva and Bonn, and 1860 back in Newport. Henry followed his brother William (to become an eminent psychologist and philosopher) to Harvard, passing an unlikely term at Harvard Law School in 1862-3; their parents eventually migrated to Boston and then to Cambridge in 1864. This was also the year of James' first story and reviews. He embarked on a 'grand tour' of England, France, and Italy in 1869 but returned occasionally to America. He settled in London in 1876 there to remain, apart from regular visits to France and Italy in particular and two late trips to America, until moving to the relative seclusion of Rye, Sussex, in 1898.

James, who never married, had a ferocious capacity for work. He wrote twenty-two novels (two uncompleted), 112 tales, twelve plays, a vast quantity of travel essays and criticism of all kinds, and a bewildering number of letters. A characteristic concern in the 1870s and through into the 1880s — notably in *Roderick Hudson* (1875), *The American* (1877), *The Europeans*, and 'Daisy Miller' (both 1878) — was with the so-called 'international theme': the confrontation of American and European values. Although there was an oblique return to this theme in later novels — particularly in *The Ambassadors*

vii

(1903) — *The Portrait of a Lady* (1881) can be seen as the culmination of a phase with which James had grown tired.

The Bostonians (1886), *The Princess Casamassima* (1886), and *The Tragic Muse* (1890) are among James' most heavily furnished works and, as he acknowledged in the case of *The Princess Casamassima*, owe a little to the documentary ambience of 'Naturalism'. During the 1890s the *mise-en-scène* of James' fiction became very much that of London and to an extent its *demi-monde*. This latter aspect is presaged in 'A London Life' (1888), one of James' finest stories, and perhaps reaches its zenith in the difficult but brilliant *What Maisie Knew* (1897) and *The Awkward Age* (1899). In the first half of the 1890s James was intensively occupied with the writing of plays and with the theatre, a large proportion of the tales of this period considering questions of the artist and society. At the level of popular success the plays were a complete failure.

The complexities of the later work are notorious; and many a reader has echoed William James' exasperated 'Say it *out* for God's sake ... and have done with it'. But earlier in that letter (4 May 1907) *The American Scene* (1907) is described as 'in its peculiar way ... *supremely* great'. And that comment seems appropriate to James' work as a whole.

INTRODUCTION

I

THE PRINCIPAL aim of this volume and its companion is to make available a selection of tales written by Henry James in the 1890s which in most cases have been relatively inaccessible for some time. Although uneven in quality, few of these tales flinch under the glare of the word 'masterpiece' and some bask in such a light. (James used the word 'tales' generally for his short fiction and tended to reserve 'short story' for relatively uncomplicated tales of considerably less than 10,000 words. His preference, as with 'The Coxon Fund', was for the longer form of what he called the *nouvelle* with its greater scope for the development of character and plot.)

It is natural to consider James within the context of great writers of tales, especially fellow Americans such as Poe, Hawthorne, and Melville. He also read and admired some of the European lions: Mérimée, Flaubert, Turgenev, and Maupassant in particular. Among English writers he had long been attracted to the work of Robert Louis Stevenson and was taken up, even if momentarily and with qualifications, by that great gush of enthusiasm for Kipling in the 1890s.

James shared characteristics with these writers. But what is distinctive about his work is the extent to which it is concerned with reflections on events rather than with the events themselves. There are plots and intrigues, of a breathless kind in a story like 'The Figure in the Carpet', but the focus is usually on a character reporting, often the narrator, and not so much on what is being reported.

One consequence of this is that at first sight these tales occasionally seem to be a little inert. But they require and repay careful rereadings if there is to be a penetration to what James called in 'The Next Time' their 'shyer secrets' and 'second line of defence'. And though they sometimes lack the immediacy of certain types of depicted action and excitement, they luxuriate in gentle ironies, surprises of a subtle kind, and tones which range from those of broad comedy to deep pathos.

Immediacy is not an effect for which James generally calculated and in fact the conflict between artistic integrity and the compromising pressures of popular taste is often at the heart of these stories. The 1890s saw questions of art and society fiercely debated at a time when art was increasingly keen in some quarters to distance itself from the market-place. It is clear that for a writer like James there were going to be difficulties. He was hardly an 'aesthete', let alone decadent, but he had always been nervous about the associations of the novel with middle-class and commercial values and the way in which they interfered with its status as art. His tales in this period are practically all concerned directly or indirectly with the rôle of the artist and his work in society.

Many of the traditional associations of the novel were with the market-place and the demands of its consumers. Shorter forms released a writer such as James from some of the problems of the novel in this context and not least from the obligation to be primarily 'realistic'. The naturally smaller scope of the short story meant that there could be less emphasis on a need for it simply to be transparent on to reality and more on its own art. It had become a commonplace to talk of the short story's 'lyric' qualities, to stress its expressive and not its representational aspects. And the frequent use of a first-person narrator in shorter fiction created a greater potential for an intenser kind of subjectivity. James had written stories from the outset; but he wrote a good many more of them than usual in the 1890s and no novels at all between 1890 and 1896.

The particular complexion of James' situation was coloured by disastrous attempts to write for the theatre in the first half of the 1890s. He was disappointed at being poorly read, and exhausted (an additional incentive for turning more to tales) by three of his longest novels — *The Bostonians* and *The Princess Casamassima*, both published in 1886, and *The Tragic Muse*, 1890 — all of which were relatively unsuccessful. James wanted to be read but was alert to the market's compromising pressures on art. And when he did compromise, as he felt he was doing in the plays and succeeded in doing to an extent in the heavily melodramatic novel *The Other House* (1896), the results were often spectacularly bad.

James, then, longed for success, but for success on his own artistic terms. The terms for the literary product, however, were generally dictated not by the writer but by men such as Loder, Pinhorn, and Bousefield (their names speak volumes), and those, like Beston in 'John Delavoy' (volume II), whose only duty was to please their 'subscribers and shareholders'.

The commercial and literary world is a very real one in these tales despite their focus on the consciousness, usually the artistic consciousness, of their characters. In fact the specific concern is often with how this consciousness fares when brought into contact with the market-place. And the medium of contact is the work of art itself. In varying degrees these tales are acutely concerned with questions which impinge on their own form. It is not just that works are ill-read and under-valued (or valued on the wrong basis). There is the problem of that gap between the author's imaginative intention and its execution and the entanglement of this with those more general difficulties and compromises involved in embodying the purity of an idea in a form which inevitably partakes of the material world and its values.

II

'BROOKSMITH' IS ONE of James' few genuinely short stories — only 'A Problem' (1868) and 'The Real Right Thing' (1899) are shorter — and James admired above all its unity and brevity. The exclusive quality of Mr Offord's *salon*, and his paternal concern, spoils Brooksmith: 'to what was this sensitive young man of thirty-five, of the servile class, being educated?' After Offord's death Brooksmith, who has that string of burdensome dependents which never seem far away in James' tales in the 1890s (particularly from Frank Saltram in 'The Coxon Fund' and Ralph Limbert in 'The Next Time'), finds his position with 'large City people too dull for endurance' and is even less satisfied with the next house: a 'world of cheerful commonplace and conscious gentility . . . of hideous florid plate and ponderous order and thin conversation'. Eventually Brooksmith disappears — suicide is suggested — and for the narrator 'the great and romantic fact was Brooksmith's final evasion of his fate' when it earlier seemed that on being forced to leave the *salon* he had accepted 'the mercenary prose of butlerhood' and 'given up the struggle for the poetry'.

As the literary metaphors of 'prose' and 'poetry' imply, there is more to 'Brooksmith' than the delicate portrayal of a butler with a 'deep and shy refinement' and his plight when cast into the mercenary world. The tale is much concerned with questions of literary and social form and their often precarious and even unique conditions. Mr Offord's 'circle' was 'essentially composed' on principles of stringent selection and contained only 'such visitors as Brooksmith allowed to come up'. The narrator recounts his initial perplexity over the perfection of the *salon* in London of all places: 'there was an art in it all, and how was the art so hidden?' As the teller of the tale he exercises his imagination to come to the conclusion that 'Brooksmith, in short, was the artist!'. We are never quite sure how far the narrator's imagination extends. He, for instance, is responsible for construing what might have been Brooksmith's merely abandoning his sordid responsibilities as a 'great and romantic fact'.

The narrator is the teller and writer of the tale. Our confinement to his point of view, to his focus on Brooksmith, suggests the extent to which he skilfully constructs a work of art out of Brooksmith's life not least by a creative interpretation of events. This aspect of the tale is crucial because the relationship between the narrator and Brooksmith then becomes an analogue of that between a writer and his subject and, more particularly, of that between a writer and a reader who plays no small part in establishing by selection the form of his 'reading' experience.

Offord's death breaks up the *salon* and demonstrates the tenuous and contingent network of interdependencies which allows Brooksmith to exercise his kind of art as a sensitive and privileged listener within a circle which he also composes. But there can be no 'prime minister' without a 'sovereign' and this is the suggested nature of the relationship between Brooksmith and a Mr Offord and others whose anecdotes, quotations, and lively discussions are the objects of his composition. In the narrator's view it seems that Brooksmith is now prepared to compromise his art to the point of its extinction in the vulgar world. He has Brooksmith renounce this option though, and the consequence of this, Offord's *salon* and his patronage being as distant as the pastoral delights of Arcadia, is death.

The 'ghost' of Brooksmith remains with the narrator who, after all, although socially more privileged than the butler, has lost the elevated retreat of the *salon* and that sense of community conducive to art. The figure of a writer, enigmatic and some-times a journalist of a kind, is a prevalent one in James' tales of the 1890s. He is often in the guise of a narrator watching other writers and artists and reflecting in the process on the conditions of art and the impossibility of succeeding, without compromise, with the 'essentially composed' as opposed to the prosaically loose.

'The Chaperon', like 'Brooksmith' has its setting in the London social world and deals, if more indirectly, with questions of its own form, of literary and social tradition. But the social circle from which Mrs Tramore is excluded, and Mrs Tramore herself, bears little resemblance to that coterie over which Brooksmith presided and much more to the vulgar world in which he finds himself. Rose in particular is under no illusions as to its nature whilst being at the same time unwilling to resist the challenge it presents.

This story belongs to a group of James' works which includes 'A London Life' (1888), *What Maisie Knew* (1897), and *The Awkward Age* (1899), and which is part of a sub-genre whose chief characteristic is indicated by the title of Fanny Burney's *Evelina; or The History of a Young Lady's Entrance into the World* (1778). This novel, and to an extent Jane Austen's *Mansfield Park* (1814) among others, has roots in the tradition of the courtesy book with its function of educating the young in the principles of social behaviour. What distinguishes the group to which 'The Chaperon' belongs from a novel such as James' *The Portrait of a Lady* (1881) is its concern, to varying degrees and in different ways, with London, and especially its *demi-monde* and the possibilities and consequences of adultery and divorce.

A keynote of James' work with a London *milieu* in this period is struck in 'The Chaperon': there is 'the stale, slightly sweet taste of the London season when the London season is overripe and spoiling' and 'Homburg' is a place 'where London was trying to wash away some of its stains'. Rose Tramore's mother is described as being 'nothing but a tinted and stippled surface'; and yet the language in which London is depicted hints at rather more than the shallow nature of society which emerges in the process of Rose's attempts to reintegrate her mother. The satirical, even parodic element is clear: it is usually the mother who introduces the daughter into society of course. But this is part of the way in which the courtesy book tradition was invigorated by the novel; the young have begun to educate their elders as early as in *Mansfield Park* and there are strains of this theme in James' 'The Pupil' (1891) and *What Maisie Knew*.

Rose, then, is engaged in a game — 'her purpose was a pious game, but it was still essentially a game' — in which she was to outwit such skilful players as Gwendolen Vesey and Lady Maresfield. She learns the rules for this game not from courtesy books but from 'the new American books; she wanted to see how girls got on by themselves'. (James had made his popular reputation by writing stories such as 'Daisy Miller' on this theme.) And this gives her, for instance, a superiority over Captain Jay who 'had not read the funny American books'. She extends her reading skills to the world at large — there are often phrases such as 'in reading him' and 'she could read that this was what her mother would have liked' — and allows herself to become, with Mrs Tramore, a performer in a 'drama' arranged by Mrs Vesey and Lady Maresfield and which they, and 'the dowagers, the old dragons with prominent fangs and glittering scales', totally misinterpret.

Rose, in keeping with aspects of the pervasive 'new woman' of the 1890s, takes on society in an independent way not least because she sees men as being 'dull and mean'. But the question which arises at the close is how far Captain Jay has manipulated the situation so that he can marry Rose; her mother now being back in society with the Mrs Donovans. The extent to which Rose the outwitter has been outwitted, perhaps intentionally, is not clear. Appropriately, the tale concludes with a circular dialogue in which each credits the other with launching Mrs Tramore.

The next story, 'Nona Vincent', is directly concerned with drama and the theatre and was written in the air of the play-version of *The American* (1890). It appeared shortly after that play ended a run of seventy performances (begun in Southport on 3 January 1891) in London and the provinces. The play was comparatively successful but James, as a reading of most of his plays shows, was not to be a Wilde, a Shaw, nor an Ibsen.

James had previously dramatised 'Daisy Miller' but it was rejected by the Madison Square Theatre management in 1882 because although 'beautifully written' it was too 'literary'. James seemed to lose his judgement when it came to his plays and always maintained that the managers had behaved like 'asses and sharpers'. His own experiences in the theatre provide some of the material for this story and it is interesting that Loder, the theatre manager, by virtue of his 'veiled and shrouded' appearance to Wayworth is associated with that 'danger' which there is in the 'world of art, and still more in the world of commerce'.

'Nona Vincent' is partly concerned with the compromises which have to be made if a scrupulous art has to pay its way and Mrs Alsager's marriage is itself a version of the compromise envisaged between drama and the theatre. Her drawing-room, as in 'Brooksmith', is a 'harbour of refuge from' the 'storms'. But that drawing-room and the liberty and leisure which allow Mrs Alsager to throw herself into the 'things of the soul' are only made possible by a 'prodigiously vulgar' husband, a 'massive personality in the City' who 'owned half a big newspaper and the whole of a great many other things'. In a story rich in imagery, the Alsagers have their counterparts in that used to express the relation between drama and the theatre: 'a jewel, dim at the best, hidden in a dunghill, a taper burning low in an air thick with vulgarity'.

Wayworth's problem, from a city and newspaper point of view at any rate, is that he is too concerned with a 'Form' for which there is no demand. If Brooksmith's inability to find such a demand outside Offord's *salon* leads ultimately to renunciation and death, the immediate threat to Wayworth is also to his livelihood. One safe but ludicrous haven is in 'writing for a biographical dictionary little lives of celebrities he had never heard of' as 'he couldn't smuggle style into a dictionary'.

Wayworth is alert to the 'fearful amount' of concession necessary in the theatre but still maintains, in a theory of composition exercised by Brooksmith, that the 'dramatic form' could have a purity based on the 'incorruptibility of line and law' and stringent selection: what he calls 'throwing over the cargo to save the ship'. James was later to make much more vigorously the distinction here between the artistic purity of drama as opposed to the commercial greed of the theatre itself with its compromising pressures. In the end Wayworth's play succeeds; but in such a unique and peculiar way as to augur badly for James' own play-writing venture.

The stress here is on the purity of conception and the satisfaction of composition as distinct from the inevitable compromises and misunderstandings which arise when the play is introduced into the theatre, when an attempt is made to execute the intention. The 'joy of the artist' for Wayworth lies in the 'polishing' rather than in 'the compromise of practice'. The 'pure art', in Mrs Alsager's terms, is in the 'working out of the thing itself'. This distinction between pure art and its compromise in practice is a significant one throughout James' tales collected here. It arises to an extent in 'The Middle Years' but its most penetrating treatment is in 'The Great Good Place' (volume II).

A consequence of this distinction is that for Wayworth the most intense excitement is generated by the rehearsals rather than by the play, by the process and not by the product (although one attraction of the play form for James was its nature as a compromise between process and product). It is Mrs Alsager who embodies the ideal aspect of art and she is similar in this respect to Brooksmith. A further similarity is that she is also the subject of the play, or the model for its central character of Nona Vincent at least, as well as a vital spectator of it. Mrs Alsager is described as Wayworth's 'ideal public' and the significance of this, given that this was a juxtaposition as sharp as the jewel and the dunghill for James, is that she amounts to a public of only one. The most successful 'productions' of the play are Wayworth's readings of it to Mrs Alsager in her drawing-room. The implications of this, as with the unique nature of Mr Offord's circle and its breaking up, are profoundly pessimistic for James' expectations of the likely size of any ideal as opposed to real audience and readership.

Several of the writers in these tales, notably Paraday in 'The Death of the Lion', have few readers; and at the centre of 'The Middle Years' is the problem experienced even by a careful reader in understanding a writer's work. What makes Mrs Alsager peculiarly ideal is that she is able to exercise her taste despite, in fact with the aid of, her commercial boor of a husband.

Wayworth's 'Form' then is not a particularly viable product in the market and this problem is compounded by the difficulties he has in 'realising' it outside of Mrs Alsager's drawing-room: 'his form had now become quite an ultimate idea for him'. At this level the problem is how to realise or embody an intention. More accurately, how to do so with a minimum degree of concession to those less imaginative than the artist, including actors. The implication seems to be that there will always be a discrepancy between such intention and a performance unless there can be some ideal fusion of artistic, imaginative temperaments. The gap between intention and performance can be narrowed at a rehearsal because of the 'executive' presence of the author. It is only narrowed completely here, however, by some kind of mystical, supernatural process whereby Mrs Alsager, the inspirational model for or germinating seed of Nona Vincent, communes with her interpreter, Violet Grey. The consequence of this is the creation of the character of Nona Vincent on the stage by Violet Grey and in a dream to Wayworth. This resolution of the difficulties can hardly be possible generally and we are left to draw our own conclusions about the nature of the plays which Wayworth continues to write after marrying Violet Grey. It is worth adding that an important sub-text of the whole tale is the alternative, significantly illicit, of Wayworth communing more permanently with the ideal by way of an adulterous relationship with Mrs Alsager.

'The Middle Years', in which there are clear similarities of theme with 'Nona Vincent', appeared just a few weeks after James' fiftieth birthday in 1893. Not the least of its memorable qualities is the tone of gentle pathos. To an even greater extent than in 'Nona Vincent' there is a communion here, an artistic communion of a kind, which both creates the conditions for and is a consequence of a deeper dependency.

Dencombe is a dying writer who accidentally encounters a Dr Hugh reading his latest work: 'The Middle Years'. Earlier in the story Dencombe reads it over himself and sees that 'the result produced in his little book was somehow a result beyond his conscious intention'. Later he is 'amused once more at the fine, full way with which an intention could be missed': even Dr Hugh 'with all his intelligence, on a first perusal' has failed 'to find a deeper meaning'.

The situation at this point is a little like that in 'Nona Vincent' when Wayworth is trying to communicate the intended character of Nona to Violet Grey. There is a rehearsal of a kind in 'The Middle Years'; an attempt, at least, to convey intention by telling Dr Hugh what has been 'tried for'. Wayworth's explanations in 'Nona Vincent' are not enough; that mystical communion is necessary. A corresponding compound, without the supernatural element, is mixed here: 'the interest of knowing the great author had made the young man begin 'The Middle Years' afresh, and would help him to find a deeper meaning in its pages'.

The context of this situation is Dencombe's own sense of that discrepancy between his rereading of 'The Middle Years' and his conscious intention. The implications for general reading and its potential are again profoundly pessimistic. It would be difficult to see how any reader — especially given the failure of the careful, sensitive, and recursive Dr Hugh — could detect a deeper meaning which even for the author is unstable in relation to his intention.

And what Dencombe sees as being unavailable to the general reader is not only any deeper meaning but, in a paradox also sharply present in 'The Figure in the Carpet' (volume II), the nature of the art which has concealed art: when reading over ' "The Middle Years" ' 'his difficulties were still there, but what was also there, to his perception, though probably alas! to nobody's else, was the art that in most cases had surmounted them'. The premium, as in 'The Figure in the Carpet', is on an imaginative, creative reading which corresponds to the creative nature of the writing. Only a reader familiar with the processes of creation — perhaps only a writer, the writer — can detect the art, can see the composing in the composition.

If the art is not visible then the artist remains practically inconspicuous and what makes this situation bleak is that only the writer can detect this art because the evidence for composition — composition, certainly for James, depending not least on a process of establishing perspectives by careful selection — must include a knowledge of the originating idea and a history of its germination. Hence the importance here and in 'Nona Vincent' — and later between Corvick and Vereker in 'The Figure in the Carpet', and in 'The Great Good Place' — of a communion with sources of creation. The longing in the face of fatal illness is for a second chance, the opportunity for a 'last manner', perhaps for a more conspicuous artistry. Possibly, had Dencombe lived, he would (like James) have supplied prefaces to his works outlining the history of their conception and germination. There is, then, a resonating ambiguity to Dencombe's 'the pearl is the unwritten — the pearl is the unalloyed, the *rest*, the lost!' especially when set against 'the last thing he ever arrived at was a form final for himself'.

Throughout 'The Middle Years' there is an intriguing management of the point of view and the way in which it shifts between Dencombe's imaginative constructions and the interpretations of a prosaic narrator. Dencombe's initial view of the opening scene on the beach, for instance, is flatly contradicted by the narrator. Alternative perspectives are also established by Dr Hugh's own accounts of his situation and by our brief contact with Miss Vernham through relatively unmediated dialogue. There is a correspondence between this oscillating point of view, where certainties are few and paraphrase is perilous, and Dencombe's anxieties about the stability of his own work and the nature of the way in which it is perceived. One answer is that there is no answer and that, as Dr Hugh says, '"if you've doubted, if you've despaired, you've always 'done' it"'. Or as Dencombe movingly expresses it: '"We work in the dark — we do what we can — we give what we have. Our doubt is our passion and our passion is our task. The rest is the madness of art"'.

Paraday, in 'The Death of the Lion', like Wayworth and Dencombe, has difficulties in realising his intention. But the nature of its obstruction is treated here in terms of broad comedy. The relation between the life of a writer and his work was one which James pondered frequently, being only too well aware that an interest in the 'life' was often paid for by a neglect of the work. He imbibed some of the subjective air of the late nineteenth century and seemed sometimes to subscribe in a careful way to the idea that style is an expression of the man, the artist. But there is hardly a licence here for using a synthesis of a writer's work and fragmentary evidence of his life, often problematically selected, to 'interpret' that work and then the 'life' in what becomes a pernicious form of the vicious circle.

In 'The Death of the Lion' Mr Morrow, when presented with 'two volumes of Paraday's new book' and told '"his life's here"', pointedly asks '"Do you mean to say that no other source of information should be open to us?"'. The reply broadly hints, as in the case with parts of 'The Middle Years', at the way in which the work should be read: '"None other till this particular one — by far the most copious — has been quite exhausted. Have you exhausted it, my dear sir?"'.

Much of the high comedy of 'The Death of the Lion' arises from the fact that hardly anyone does read Paraday's work. At Prestidge 'there is supposed to be a copy of his last book in the house ... and every one is telling every one where they put it last. I'm sure it's rather smudgy about the twentieth page'. Paraday, originally protected by his obscurity, finds it impossible in the hands of a social circle presided over by (oh for a Brooksmith!) a 'Mrs Weeks Wimbush, wife of the boundless brewer and proprietess of the universal menagerie' to find the 'lone isle in a tepid sea' necessary to an execution of 'the written scheme of another book'.

Paraday is both helpless and implicated in his demise. He is the victim of popularity — 'the first lesson of his greatness has been precisely that he can't do what he likes' — but does have a 'talent' for talking nonsense which is a 'prodigious success'. And at London dinners 'he took his profit where it seemed most to crowd upon him, having in his pocket the portable sophistries about the nature of the artist's task'. He partly justifies his situation in terms of having the opportunity to observe life richly for his work: the 'phantasmogoric town was probably after all less of a battlefield than the haunted study'.

The more abstract considerations in both 'Nona Vincent' and 'The Middle Years' of the problems involved in realising intention, or the way in which there are obstructions between intention and execution, are riotously rehearsed in a concrete way here. Even Paraday's death hardly turns the tale to tragedy. Some of the humour arises out of the 1890s context: there is a good deal of satire on the words 'new' (its application being much in vogue at the end of the nineteenth century) and 'modern'. Aspects of 1890s sexuality — 'the larger latitude' —

and the fashion of writers adopting pseudonyms of the opposite sex are comically treated: 'in the age we live in one gets lost among the genders and the pronouns'. James was nervous about his work appearing in such a decadent organ as the *Yellow Book* (see the *Note on the Texts*) and much of this tale can be seen as a satire on aspects of the kind of company it might have kept there.

There are gentle ironies worth considering in the text itself, and mainly centring on the narrator. He begins with an account of his 'change of heart', his decision not to write the kind of article on Paraday wanted by Pinhorn. But we are later told, in a cliché betraying the popular kind of writer the narrator has become, that 'these meagre notes are essentially private, so that if they see the light the insidious forces that, as my story itself shows, make at present for publicity will have overmastered my precautions'.

Our reading this story is evidence for this second change of heart. The narrator writes to the American admirer of Paraday's: 'I want to monopolise Paraday in order that he may push me on'. In other words, genuine as his desire to protect Paraday from the likes of Mrs Wimbush is, he has (and Rose Tramore is a relevant comparison) to play her at her own game. The rivalries and jealousies are quite explicitly stated. What is implied by the close, and partly to be inferred from his 'sometimes I believe her, but I have quite ceased to believe myself', is that the narrator has himself succumbed to the distracting lure of 'success'. The search for the lost manuscript becomes rather nominal; but the whole episode provides the narrator with a story that would not have disgraced Mr Pinhorn's pages.

In 'The Coxon Fund', Frank Saltram is also a man of huge intentions unrealised. Yet, protected from it as we are, there is an impression of big talk, perhaps stimulated by alcohol, in the drawing-room. Saltram is rarely there to give his lectures; but there is some kind of communication in the privacy of the drawing-room. Communication with a wider audience is again fraught with difficulties.

'The Coxon Fund', which James called a *nouvelle*, is much the longest of any of the stories in this volume and at one point in his notebook he considers that the subject might well expand to 100,000 words. But it already seems a little attenuated and occasionally like one of the views the narrator has of Frank Saltram: 'wherever you touched him you found equally little firmness'. This arises partly from this deliberate strategy of indirect presentation, of adopting, as the notebook has it, a 'formula for the presentation' in '20,000 words' (it became 24,000) that involved making it into an '*Impression* — as one of Sargent's pictures is an impression. That is, I must do it from my own point of view — that of an imagined observer, participator, chronicler'. And Frank Saltram is to be 'an implied and suggested thing'. Perhaps the best application of this method comes in that scene which was envisaged as being '*one whole brief section* devoted to an impressionism of the beauty of his personal genius and the kindling effect of his talk' (*Notebooks*, pp.160, 161; see *A Guide to Further Reading* in this volume). This scene, beginning with the narrator finding Saltram on a bench 'unbuttoned and fatigued', is undoubtedly moving. And there is the kind of communion — 'I was conscious of what I owed him' — we saw in 'Nona Vincent' and in 'The Middle Years'.

The problem here, though, is whether this scene is enough — given our general view before and after it of some kind of 'parasite', a 'fat philosopher', who is as like as not drunk, neglects his domestic responsibilities, and is full of grand designs at other people's expense — to make plausible Ruth Anvoy's sacrifice of her marriage and the Coxon fund. The marriage might easily be discounted; George Gravener comes across as a kind of fortune-hunter with a neat turn of phrase. But it is difficult to avoid seeing Ruth Anvoy as anything other than duped. One of the dramatic points of the story is clearly intended to be Saltram's transcendence of the question of whether his ' want of virtue' is mitigated by his greatness. It is this want of virtue that Ruth Anvoy puts aside in the melodramatic business of the letter. There is much dark hinting at its nature coupled with the device of a secretive narrator: 'the innumerable facets of the big drama — which is yet to be reported' and 'what he confessed was more than I shall venture to confess to-day' are typical. The indirect presentation of Saltram is meant to make it difficult for us to judge him and perhaps to suggest that Saltram, and the artist in general, is beyond the pale of such judgement. The point is that our impression of Saltram's qualities is not strong enough to reverse the judgements of him that are made by the characters in the story.

The loose inspiration for Frank Saltram, according to James in his notebook and in his Preface to the New York Edition, was provided by a reading of a book by J. Dyke Campbell on Coleridge. James became 'infinitely struck with the suggest-iveness of S.T.C.'s figure' and the type with its 'rare, anomalous, magnificent, interesting, curious, tremendously suggestive character, vices and all' and the great 'Coleridge-quality', that of being 'a splendid, an incomparable *talker*' (*Notebooks*, p.152). The Preface tells us that the character of Frank Saltram 'pretends' to be 'no more than a dim reflexion and above all a free rearrangement' of the type suggested by Coleridge (*The Art of the Novel*, p.229; there are full references in *A Guide to Further Reading*). The conflict between the attempt to convey Saltram's qualities and the satirical treatment of his failings is never really resolved. Nor is it sufficiently clear whether or not such irresolution is intended.

As a whole, then, these tales are deeply concerned with the tenuous position of the artist in society and the likelihood that both he and his work will be vulgarised or misunderstood in the market-place. 'The Chaperon' is not so directly connected with these issues but it does suggest the compromising nature of the world into which Mrs Tramore is reintegrated. The particular problem of the artist here is often how to embody successfully his imaginative intention in a form which can be understood and which by its nature has the stability of a product as opposed to the creative instability of a process. 'Nona Vincent' seems to rule out the possibility of a dramatic solution and illustrates the extent to which these difficulties are intensified by the way in which men such as Loder and Pinhorn handle the product when it comes on to the market. Frank Saltram's intention is rarely transferred from the drawing-room to the lecture-hall, and there are also obstructions, if comical, between intention and execution in 'The Death of the Lion'. The implications of that tale, though, are serious enough: a writer's achieving success spells the end of creative work. In 'Nona Vincent' and 'Brooksmith' in particular, the pessimistic implication is that artistic communion unsullied by the vulgar pressures of the market can only take place on unique occasions and in fragile contexts. The tales in the second volume of this edition continue to consider the compromises involved in executing artistic intentions and, specifically, the possibility of the artist abandoning the attempt at execution altogether.

Peter Rawlings

BROOKSMITH

WE are scattered now, the friends of the late Mr Oliver
Offord; but whenever we chance to meet I think we are conscious of a certain esoteric respect for each other. "Yes, you
too have been in Arcadia," we seem not too grumpily to
allow. When I pass the house in Mansfield Street I remember
that Arcadia was there. I don't know who has it now, and I
don't want to know; it's enough to be so sure that if I should
ring the bell there would be no such luck for me as that
Brooksmith should open the door. Mr Offord, the most agreeable, the most lovable of bachelors, was a retired diplomatist,
living on his pension, confined by his infirmities to his fireside and delighted to be found there any afternoon in the year
by such visitors as Brooksmith allowed to come up. Brooksmith was his butler and his most intimate friend, to whom we
all stood, or I should say sat, in the same relation in which the
subject of the sovereign finds himself to the prime minister.
By having been for years, in foreign lands, the most delightful
Englishman any one had ever known, Mr Offord had, in my
opinion, rendered signal service to his country. But I suppose
he had been too much liked—liked even by those who didn't
like *it*—so that as people of that sort never get titles or dota-
tions for the horrid things they have *not* done, his principal
reward was simply that we went to see him.

Oh, we went perpetually, and it was not our fault if he was
not overwhelmed with this particular honour. Any visitor who
came once came again—to come merely once was a slight
which nobody, I am sure, had ever put upon him. His circle,
therefore, was essentially composed of *habitués*, who were

1

habitués for each other as well as for him, as those of a happy
salon should be. I remember vividly every element of the
place, down to the intensely Londonish look of the grey
opposite houses, in the gap of the white curtains of the high
windows, and the exact spot where, on a particular afternoon,
I put down my tea-cup for Brooksmith, lingering an instant,
to gather it up as if he were plucking a flower. Mr Offord's
drawing-room was indeed Brooksmith's garden, his pruned
and tended human *parterre*, and if we all flourished there and
grew well in our places it was largely owing to his supervision.

Many persons have heard much, though most have doubtless seen little, of the famous institution of the *salon*, and many
are born to the depression of knowing that this finest flower of
social life refuses to bloom where the English tongue is
spoken. The explanation is usually that our women have not
the skill to cultivate it—the art to direct, between suggestive
shores, the course of the stream of talk. My affectionate, my
pious memory of Mr Offord contradicts this induction only, I
fear, more insidiously to confirm it. The very sallow and
slightly smoked drawing-room in which he spent so large a
portion of the last years of his life certainly deserved the distinguished name; but on the other hand it could not be said at
all to owe its stamp to the soft pressure of the indispensable
sex. The dear man had indeed been capable of one of those
sacrifices to which women are deemed peculiarly apt; he had
recognised (under the influence, in some degree, it is true, of
physical infirmity), that if you wished people to find you at
home you must manage not to be out. He had in short
accepted the fact which many dabblers in the social art are slow
to learn, that you must really, as they say, take a line and that
the only way to be at home is to stay at home. Finally his own
fireside had become a summary of his habits. Why should he
ever have left it?—since this would have been leaving what
was notoriously pleasantest in London, the compact charmed
cluster (thinning away indeed into casual couples), round the

fine old last century chimney-piece which, with the exception of the remarkable collection of miniatures, was the best thing the place contained. Mr Offord was not rich; he had nothing but his pension and the use for life of the somewhat super-annuated house.

When I am reminded by some uncomfortable contrast of to-day how perfectly we were all handled there I ask myself once more what had been the secret of such perfection. One had taken it for granted at the time, for anything that is supremely good produces more acceptance than surprise. I felt we were all happy, but I didn't consider how our happiness was managed. And yet there were questions to be asked, questions that strike me as singularly obvious now that there is nobody to answer them. Mr Offord had solved the in-soluble; he had, without feminine help (save in the sense that ladies were dying to come to him and he saved the lives of several), established a *salon;* but I might have guessed that there was a method in his madness—a law in his success. He had not hit it off by a mere fluke. There was an art in it all, and how was the art so hidden? Who, indeed, if it came to that, was the occult artist? Launching this inquiry the other day, I had already got hold of the tail of my reply. I was helped by the very wonder of some of the conditions that came back to me—those that used to seem as natural as sun-shine in a fine climate.

How was it, for instance, that we never were a crowd, never either too many or too few, always the right people *with* the right people (there must really have been no wrong people at all), always coming and going, never sticking fast nor overstaying, yet never popping in or out with an in-decorous familiarity? How was it that we all sat where we wanted and moved when we wanted and met whom we wanted and escaped whom we wanted; joining, according to the accident of inclination, the general circle or falling in with a single talker on a convenient sofa? Why were all the sofas so convenient, the accidents so happy, the talkers so ready, the listeners so willing, the subjects presented to you in a rotation as quickly fore-ordained as the courses at dinner? A dearth of topics would have been as unheard of as a lapse in the service. These speculations couldn't fail to lead me to the fundamental truth that Brooksmith had been somehow at the bottom of the mystery. If he had not established the *salon* at least he had carried it on. Brooksmith, in short, was the artist!

We felt this, covertly, at the time, without formulating it, and were conscious, as an ordered and prosperous community, of his evenhanded justice, untainted with flunkeyism. He had none of that vulgarity—his touch was infinitely fine. The delicacy of it was clear to me on the first occasion my eyes rested, as they were so often to rest again, on the domestic revealed, in the turbid light of the street, by the opening of the house-door. I saw on the spot that though he had plenty of school he carried it without arrogance—he had remained articulate and human. *L'Ecole Anglaise*, Mr Offord used to call him, laughing, when, later, it happened more than once that we had some conversation about him. But I remember accusing Mr Offord of not doing him quite ideal justice. That he was not one of the giants of the school, however, my old friend, who really understood him perfectly and was devoted to him, as I shall show, quite admitted; which doubtless poor Brooksmith had himself felt, to his cost, when his value in the market was originally determined. The utility of his class in general is estimated by the foot and the inch, and poor Brooksmith had only about five feet two to put into circulation. He acknowledged the inadequacy of this provision, and I am sure was penetrated with the everlasting fitness of the relation between service and stature. If *he* had been Mr Offord he certainly would have found Brooksmith wanting, and indeed the laxity of his employer on this score was one of many things which he had had to condone and to which he had at last indulgently adapted himself.

I remember the old man's saying to me: "Oh, my servants, if they can live with me a fortnight they can live with me for ever. But it's the first fortnight that tries 'em." It was in the first fortnight, for instance, that Brooksmith had had to learn that he was exposed to being addressed as "my dear fellow" and "my poor child." Strange and deep must such a probation have been to him, and he doubtless emerged from it tempered and purified. This was written to a certain extent in his appearance; in his spare, brisk little person, in his cloistered white face and extraordinarily polished hair, which told of responsibility, looked as if it were kept up to the same high standard as the plate; in his small, clear, anxious eyes, even in the permitted, though not exactly encouraged tuft on his chin. "He thinks me rather mad, but I've broken him in, and now he likes the place, he likes the company," said the old man. I embraced this fully after I had become aware that Brooksmith's main characteristic was a deep and shy refinement, though I remember I was rather puzzled when, on another occasion, Mr Offord remarked: "What he likes is the talk—mingling in the conversation." I was conscious that I had never seen Brooksmith permit himself this freedom, but I guessed in a moment that what Mr Offord alluded to was a participation more intense than any speech could have represented—that of being perpetually present on a hundred legitimate pretexts, errands, necessities, and breathing the very atmosphere of criticism, the famous criticism of life. "Quite an education, sir, isn't it, sir?" he said to me one day at the foot of the stairs, when he was letting me out; and I have always remembered the words and the tone as the first sign of the quickening drama of poor Brooksmith's fate. It was indeed an education, but to what was this sensitive young man of thirty-five, of the servile class, being educated?

Practically and inevitably, for the time, to companionship, to the perpetual, the even exaggerated reference and appeal of a person brought to dependence by his time of life and his

8:B

infirmities and always addicted moreover (this was the exaggeration) to the art of giving you pleasure by letting you do things for him. There were certain things Mr Offord was capable of pretending he liked you to do, even when he didn't, if he thought *you* liked them. If it happened that you didn't either (this was rare, but it might be), of course there were cross-purposes; but Brooksmith was there to prevent their going very far. This was precisely the way he acted as moderator: he averted misunderstandings or cleared them up. He had been capable, strange as it may appear, of acquiring for this purpose an insight into the French tongue, which was often used at Mr Offord's; for besides being habitual to most of the foreigners, and they were many, who haunted the place or arrived with letters (letters often requiring a little worried consideration, of which Brooksmith always had cognisance), it had really become the primary language of the master of the house. I don't know if all the *malentendus* were in French, but almost all the explanations were, and this didn't a bit prevent Brooksmith from following them. I know Mr Offord used to read passages to him from Montaigne and Saint-Simon, for he read perpetually when he was alone—when they were alone, I should say—and Brooksmith was always about. Perhaps you'll say no wonder Mr Offord's butler regarded him as "rather mad." However, if I'm not sure what he thought about Montaigne I'm convinced he admired Saint-Simon. A certain feeling for letters must have rubbed off on him from the mere handling of his master's books, which he was always carrying to and fro and putting back in their places.

I often noticed that if an anecdote or a quotation, much more a lively discussion, was going forward, he would, if busy with the fire or the curtains, the lamp or the tea, find a pretext for remaining in the room till the point should be reached. If his purpose was to catch it you were not discreet to call him off, and I shall never forget a look, a hard, stony stare (I caught it in its passage), which, one day when there were a good many people in the room, he fastened upon the footman who was helping him in the service and who, in an undertone, had asked him some irrelevant question. It was the only manifestation of harshness that I ever observed on Brooksmith's part, and at first I wondered what was the matter. Then I became conscious that Mr Offord was relating a very curious anecdote, never before perhaps made so public, and imparted to the narrator by an eye-witness of the fact, bearing upon Lord Byron's life in Italy. Nothing would induce me to reproduce it here; but Brooksmith had been in danger of losing it. If I ever should venture to reproduce it I shall feel how much I lose in not having my fellow-auditor to refer to.

The first day Mr Offord's door was closed was therefore a dark date in contemporary history. It was raining hard and my umbrella was wet, but Brooksmith took it from me exactly as if this were a preliminary for going upstairs. I observed however that instead of putting it away he held it poised and trickling over the rug, and then I became aware that he was looking at me with deep, acknowledging eyes—his air of universal responsibility. I immediately understood; there was scarcely need of the question and the answer that passed between us. When I did understand that the old man had given up, for the first time, though only for the occasion, I exclaimed dolefully: "What a difference it will make—and to how many people!"

"I shall be one of them, sir!" said Brooksmith; and that was the beginning of the end.

Mr Offord came down again, but the spell was broken, and the great sign of it was that the conversation was, for the first time, not directed. It wandered and stumbled, a little frightened, like a lost child—it had let go the nurse's hand. "The worst of it is that now we shall talk about my health—*c'est la fin de tout*," Mr Offord said, when he reappeared; and then I recognised what a sign of change that would be—for he had never tolerated anything so provincial. The talk became ours, in a word—not his; and as ours, even when *he* talked, it could only be inferior. In this form it was a distress to Brooksmith, whose attention now wandered from it altogether: he had so much closer a vision of his master's intimate conditions than our superficialities represented. There were better hours, and he was more in and out of the room, but I could see that he was conscious that the great institution was falling to pieces. He seemed to wish to take counsel with me about it, to feel responsible for its going on in some form or other. When for the second period—the first had lasted several days—he had to tell me that our old friend didn't receive, I half expected to hear him say after a moment: "Do you think I ought to, sir, in his place?"—as he might have asked me, with the return of autumn, if I thought he had better light the drawing-room fire.

He had a resigned philosophic sense of what his guests—our guests, as I came to regard them in our colloquies—would expect. His feeling was that he wouldn't absolutely have approved of himself as a substitute for the host; but he was so saturated with the religion of habit that he would have made, for our friends, the necessary sacrifice to the divinity. He would take them on a little further, till they could look about them. I think I saw him also mentally confronted with the opportunity to deal—for once in his life—with some of his own dumb preferences, his limitations of sympathy, *weeding* a little, in prospect, and returning to a purer tradition. It was not unknown to me that he considered that toward the end of Mr Offord's career a certain laxity of selection had crept in.

At last it came to be the case that we all found the closed door more often than the open one; but even when it was closed Brooksmith managed a crack for me to squeeze through; so that practically I never turned away without having paid a visit. The difference simply came to be that the visit was to Brooksmith. It took place in the hall, at the familiar

foot of the stairs, and we didn't sit down—at least Brooksmith didn't; moreover it was devoted wholly to one topic
and always had the air of being already over—beginning, as
it were, at the end. But it was always interesting—it always
gave me something to think about. It is true that the subject
of my meditation was ever the same—ever "It's all very well,
but what *will* become of Brooksmith?" Even my private
answer to this question left me still unsatisfied. No doubt Mr
Offord would provide for him, but *what* would he provide?
that was the great point. He couldn't provide society; and
society had become a necessity of Brooksmith's nature. I must
add that he never showed a symptom of what I may call sordid solicitude—anxiety on his own account. He was rather
livid and intensely grave, as befitted a man before whose eyes
the "shade of that which once was great" was passing away.
He had the solemnity of a person winding up, under depressing circumstances, a long established and celebrated business;
he was a kind of social executor or liquidator. But his manner
seemed to testify exclusively to the uncertainty of *our* future.
I couldn't in those days have afforded it—I lived in two rooms
in Jermyn Street and didn't "keep a man;" but even if my
income had permitted I shouldn't have ventured to say to
Brooksmith (emulating Mr Offord), "My dear fellow, I'll
take you on." The whole tone of our intercourse was so
much more an implication that it was *I* who should now want
a lift. Indeed there was a tacit assurance in Brooksmith's whole
attitude that he would have me on his mind.

One of the most assiduous members of our circle had been
Lady Kenyon, and I remember his telling me one day that her
ladyship had, in spite of her own infirmities, lately much
aggravated, been in person to inquire. In answer to this I
remarked that she would feel it more than any one. Brooksmith was silent a moment; at the end of which he said, in a
certain tone (there is no reproducing some of his tones), "I'll
go and see her." I went to see her myself, and I learned that

he had waited upon her; but when I said to her, in the form of a joke but with a core of earnest, that when all was over some of us ought to combine, to club together to set Brooksmith up on his own account, she replied a trifle disappointingly: "Do you mean in a public-house?" I looked at her in a way that I think Brooksmith himself would have approved, and then I answered: "Yes, the Offord Arms." What I had meant, of course, was that, for the love of art itself, we ought to look to it that such a peculiar faculty and so much acquired experience should not be wasted. I really think that if we had caused a few black-edged cards to be struck off and circulated —"Mr Brooksmith will continue to receive on the old premises from four to seven; business carried on as usual during the alterations"—the majority of us would have rallied.

Several times he took me upstairs—always by his own proposal—and our dear old friend, in bed, in a curious flowered and brocaded *casaque* which made him, especially as his head was tied up in a handkerchief to match, look, to my imagination, like the dying Voltaire, held for ten minutes a sadly shrunken little *salon*. I felt indeed each time, as if I were attending the last *coucher* of some social sovereign. He was royally whimsical about his sufferings and not at all concerned—quite as if the Constitution provided for the case—about his successor. He glided over *our* sufferings charmingly, and none of his jokes—it was a gallant abstention, some of them would have been so easy—were at our expense. Now and again, I confess, there was one at Brooksmith's, but so pathetically sociable as to make the excellent man look at me in a way that seemed to say: "Do exchange a glance with me, or I sha'n't be able to stand it." What he was not able to stand was not what Mr Offord said about him, but what he wasn't able to say in return. His notion of conversation, for himself, was giving you the convenience of speaking to him; and when he went to "see" Lady Kenyon, for instance, it was to carry her the tribute of his receptive silence. Where would the speech of his betters have been if proper service had been a manifestation of sound? In that case the fundamental difference would have had to be shown by *their* dumbness, and many of them, poor things, were dumb enough without that provision. Brooksmith took an unfailing interest in the preservation of the fundamental difference; it was the thing he had most on his conscience.

What had become of it, however, when Mr Offord passed away like any inferior person—was relegated to eternal stillness like a butler upstairs? His aspect for several days after the expected event may be imagined, and the multiplication by funereal observance of the things he didn't say. When everything was over—it was late the same day—I knocked at the door of the house of mourning as I so often had done before. I could never call on Mr Offord again, but I had come, literally, to call on Brooksmith. I wanted to ask him if there was anything I could do for him, tainted with vagueness as this inquiry could only be. My wild dream of taking him into my own service had died away: my service was not worth his being taken into. My offer to him could only be to help him to find another place, and yet there was an indelicacy, as it were, in taking for granted that his thoughts would immediately be fixed on another. I had a hope that he would be able to give his life a different form—though certainly not the form, the frequent result of such bereavements, of his setting up a little shop. That would have been dreadful; for I should have wished to further any enterprise that he might embark in, yet how could I have brought myself to go and pay him shillings and take back coppers over a counter? My visit then was simply an intended compliment. He took it as such, gratefully and with all the tact in the world. He knew I really couldn't help him and that I knew he knew I couldn't; but we discussed the situation—with a good deal of elegant generality—at the foot of the stairs, in the hall already dismantled, where I had so often discussed other situations with him. The executors were in possession, as was still more apparent when he made me pass for a few minutes into the dining-room, where various objects were muffled up for removal.

Two definite facts, however, he had to communicate; one being that he was to leave the house for ever that night (servants, for some mysterious reason, seem always to depart by night), and the other—he mentioned it only at the last, with hesitation—that he had already been informed his late master had left him a legacy of eighty pounds. "I'm very glad," I said, and Brooksmith rejoined: "It was so like him to think of me." This was all that passed between us on the subject, and I know nothing of his judgment of Mr Offord's memento. Eighty pounds are always eighty pounds, and no one has ever left *me* an equal sum; but, all the same, for Brooksmith, I was disappointed. I don't know what I had expected— in short I was disappointed. Eighty pounds might stock a little shop—a *very* little shop; but, I repeat, I couldn't bear to think of that. I asked my friend if he had been able to save a little, and he replied: "No, sir; I have had to do things." I didn't inquire what things he had had to do; they were his own affair, and I took his word for them as assentingly as if he had had the greatness of an ancient house to keep up; especially as there was something in his manner that seemed to convey a prospect of further sacrifice.

"I shall have to turn round a bit, sir—I shall have to look about me," he said; and then he added, indulgently, magnanimously: "If you should happen to hear of anything for me——"

I couldn't let him finish; this was, in its essence, too much in the really grand manner. It would be a help to my getting him off my mind to be able to pretend I *could* find the right place, and that help he wished to give me, for it was doubtless painful to him to see me in so false a position. I interposed with a few words to the effect that I was well aware that wherever he should go, whatever he should do, he would miss our old friend terribly—miss him even more than I should, having been with him so much more. This led him to make the speech that I have always remembered as the very text of the whole episode.

"Oh, sir, it's sad for *you*, very sad, indeed, and for a great many gentlemen and ladies; that it is, sir. But for me, sir, it is, if I may say so, still graver even than that: it's just the loss of something that was everything. For me, sir," he went on, with rising tears, "he was just *all*, if you know what I mean, sir. You have others, sir, I daresay—not that I would have you understand me to speak of them as in any way tantamount. But you have the pleasures of society, sir; if it's only in talking about him, sir, as I daresay you do freely—for all his blessed memory has to fear from it—with gentlemen and ladies who have had the same honour. That's not for me, sir, and I have to keep my associations to myself. Mr Offord was *my* society, and now I have no more. You go back to conversation, sir, after all, and I go back to my place," Brooksmith stammered, without exaggeration irony or dramatic bitterness, but with a flat, unstudied veracity and his hand on the knob of the street-door. He turned it to let me out and then he added: "I just go downstairs, sir, again, and I stay there."

"My poor child," I replied, in my emotion, quite as Mr Offord used to speak, "my dear fellow, leave it to me; we'll look after you, we'll all do something for you."

"Ah, if you could give me some one *like* him! But there ain't two in the world," said Brooksmith as we parted.

He had given me his address—the place where he would be to be heard of. For a long time I had no occasion to make use of the information; for he proved indeed, on trial, a very difficult case. In a word the people who knew him and had known Mr Offord, didn't want to take him, and yet I couldn't bear to try to thrust him among people who didn't know him. I spoke to many of our old friends about him, and I found them all governed by the odd mixture of feelings of which I myself was conscious, and disposed, further, to entertain a suspicion that he was "spoiled," with which I then would have nothing to do. In plain terms a certain embarrassment, a sensible awkwardness, when they thought of it, attached to the idea of using him as a menial: they had met him so often in society. Many of them would have asked him, and did ask him, or rather did ask me to ask him, to come and see them; but a mere visiting-list was not what I wanted for him. He was too short for people who were very particular; nevertheless I heard of an opening in a diplomatic household which led me to write him a note, though I was looking much less for something grand than for something human. Five days later I heard from him. The secretary's wife had decided, after keeping him waiting till then, that she couldn't take a servant out of a house in which there had not been a lady. The note had a P.S.: "It's a good job there wasn't, sir, such a lady as some."

A week later he came to see me and told me he was "suited"—committed to some highly respectable people (they were something very large in the City), who lived on the Bayswater side of the Park. "I daresay it will be rather poor, sir," he admitted; "but I've seen the fireworks, haven't I, sir?—it can't be fireworks *every* night. After Mansfield Street there ain't much choice." There was a certain amount, however, it seemed; for the following year, going one day to call on a country cousin, a lady of a certain age who was spending a fortnight in town with some friends of her own, a family unknown to me and resident in Chester Square, the door of the house was opened, to my surprise and gratification, by Brooksmith in person. When I came out I had some conversation with him, from which I gathered that he had found the large City people too dull for endurance, and I guessed, though he didn't say it, that he had found them vulgar as well. I don't know what judgment he would have passed on his actual patrons if my relative had not been their friend; but under the circumstances he abstained from comment.

None was necessary, however, for before the lady in question brought her visit to a close they honoured me with an invitation to dinner, which I accepted. There was a largeish party on the occasion, but I confess I thought of Brooksmith rather more than of the seated company. They required no depth of attention—they were all referable to usual, irredeemable, inevitable types. It was the world of cheerful commonplace and conscious gentility and prosperous density, a full-fed, material, insular world, a world of hideous florid plate and ponderous order and thin conversation. There was not a word said about Byron. Nothing would have induced me to look at Brooksmith in the course of the repast, and I felt sure that not even my overturning the wine would have induced him to meet my eye. We were in intellectual sympathy—we felt, as regards each other, a kind of social responsibility. In short we had been in Arcadia together, and we had both come to *this!* No wonder we were ashamed to be confronted. When he helped on my overcoat, as I was going away, we parted, for the first time since the earliest days in Mansfield Street, in silence. I thought he looked lean and wasted, and I guessed that his new place was not more "human" than his previous one. There was plenty of beef and beer, but there was no reciprocity. The question for him to have asked before accepting the position would have been not "How many footmen are kept?" but "How much imagination?"

The next time I went to the house—I confess it was not very soon—I encountered his successor, a personage who evidently enjoyed the good fortune of never having quitted his natural level. Could any be higher? he seemed to ask—over the heads of three footmen and even of some visitors. He made me feel as if Brooksmith were dead; but I didn't dare to inquire—I couldn't have borne his "I haven't the least idea, sir." I despatched a note to the address Brooksmith had given me after Mr Offord's death, but I received no answer. Six months later, however, I was favoured with a visit from an elderly, dreary, dingy person, who introduced herself to me as Mr Brooksmith's aunt and from whom I learned that he was out of place and out of health and had allowed her to come and say to me that if I could spare half-an-hour to look in at him he would take it as a rare honour.

I went the next day—his messenger had given me a new address—and found my friend lodged in a short sordid street in Marylebone, one of those corners of London that wear the last expression of sickly meanness. The room into which I was shown was above the small establishment of a dyer and cleaner who had inflated kid gloves and discoloured shawls in his shop-front. There was a great deal of grimy infant life up and down the place, and there was a hot, moist smell within, as of the "boiling" of dirty linen. Brooksmith sat with a blanket over his legs at a clean little window, where, from behind stiff bluish-white curtains, he could look across at a huckster's and a tinsmith's and a small greasy public-house. He had passed through an illness and was convalescent, and his mother, as well as his aunt, was in attendance on him. I liked the mother, who was bland and intensely humble, but I didn't much fancy the aunt, whom I connected, perhaps unjustly, with the opposite public-house (she seemed somehow to be greasy with the same grease), and whose furtive eye followed every movement of my hand, as if to see if it were not going into my pocket. It didn't take this direction—I couldn't, unsolicited, put myself at that sort of ease with Brooksmith. Several times the door of the room opened, and mysterious old women peeped in and shuffled back again. I don't know who they were; poor Brooksmith seemed encompassed with vague, prying, beery females.

He was vague himself, and evidently weak, and much embarrassed, and not an allusion was made between us to Mansfield Street. The vision of the *salon* of which he had been an ornament hovered before me, however, by contrast, sufficiently. He assured me that he was really getting better, and his mother remarked that he would come round if he could only get his spirits up. The aunt echoed this opinion, and I became more sure that in her own case she knew where to go for such a purpose. I'm afraid I was rather weak with my old friend, for I neglected the opportunity, so exceptionally good, to rebuke the levity which had led him to throw up honourable positions—fine, stiff, steady berths, with morning prayers, as I knew, attached to one of them—in Bayswater and Belgravia. Very likely his reasons had been profane and sentimental; he didn't want morning prayers, he wanted to be somebody's dear fellow; but I couldn't be the person to rebuke him. He shuffled these episodes out of sight—I saw that he had no wish to discuss them. I perceived further, strangely enough, that it would probably be a questionable pleasure for him to see me again: he doubted now even of my power to condone his aberrations. He didn't wish to have to explain; and his behaviour, in future, was likely to need explanation. When I bade him farewell he looked at me a moment with eyes that said everything: "How can I talk about those exquisite years in this place, before these people, with the old women poking their heads in? It was very good of you to come to see me—it wasn't my idea; *she* brought you. We've said everything; it's over; you'll lose all patience with me, and I'd rather you shouldn't see the rest." I sent him some money, in a letter, the next day, but I saw the rest only in the light of a barren sequel.

A whole year after my visit to him I became aware once, in dining out, that Brooksmith was one of the several servants who hovered behind our chairs. He had not opened the door of the house to me, and I had not recognised him in the cluster of retainers in the hall. This time I tried to catch his eye, but he never gave me a chance, and when he handed me a dish I could only be careful to thank him audibly. Indeed I partook of two *entrées* of which I had my doubts, subsequently converted into certainties, in order not to snub him. He looked well enough in health, but much older, and wore, in an exceptionally marked degree, the glazed and expressionless mask of the British domestic *de race*. I saw with dismay that if I had not known him I should have taken him, on the showing of his countenance, for an extravagant illustration of irresponsive servile gloom. I said to myself that he had become a reactionary, gone over to the Philistines, thrown himself into religion, the religion of his "place," like a foreign lady *sur le retour*. I divined moreover that he was only engaged for the evening—he had become a mere waiter, had joined the band of the white-waistcoated who "go out." There was something pathetic in this fact, and it was a terrible vulgarisation of Brooksmith. It was the mercenary prose of butlerhood; he had given up the struggle for the poetry. If reciprocity was what he had missed, where was the reciprocity now? Only in the bottoms of the wine-glasses and the five shillings (or whatever they get), clapped into his hand by the permanent man. However, I supposed he had taken up a precarious branch of his profession because after all it sent him less downstairs. His relations with London society were more superficial, but they were of course more various. As I went away, on this occasion, I looked out for him eagerly among the four or five attendants whose perpendicular persons, fluting the walls of London passages, are supposed to lubricate the process of departure; but he was not on duty. I asked one of the others if he were not in the house, and received the prompt answer: "Just left, sir. Anything I can do for you, sir?" I wanted to say "Please give him my kind regards;" but I abstained; I didn't want to compromise him, and I never came across him again.

Often and often, in dining out, I looked for him, sometimes accepting invitations on purpose to multiply the chances of my meeting him. But always in vain; so that as I met many other members of the casual class over and over again, I at last adopted the theory that he always procured a list of expected guests beforehand and kept away from the banquets which he thus learned I was to grace. At last I gave up hope, and one day, at the end of three years, I received another visit from his aunt. She was drearier and dingier, almost squalid, and she was in great tribulation and want. Her sister, Mrs Brooksmith, had been dead a year, and three months later her nephew had disappeared. He had always looked after her a bit—since her troubles; I never knew what her troubles had been—and now she hadn't so much as a petticoat to pawn. She had also a niece, to whom she had been everything, before her troubles, but the niece had treated her most shameful. These were details; the great and romantic fact was Brooksmith's final evasion of his fate. He had gone out to wait one evening, as usual, in a white waistcoat she had done up for him with her own hands, being due at a large party up Kensington way. But he had never come home again, and had never arrived at the large party, or at any party that any one could make out. No trace of him had come to light—no gleam of the white waistcoat had pierced the obscurity of his doom. This news was a sharp shock to me, for I had my ideas about his real destination. His aged relative had promptly, as she said, guessed the worst. Somehow and somewhere he had got out of the way altogether, and now I trust that, with characteristic deliberation, he is changing the plates of the immortal gods. As my depressing visitant also said, he never *had* got his spirits up. I was fortunately able to dismiss her with her own somewhat improved. But the dim ghost of poor Brooksmith is one of those that I see. He had indeed been spoiled.

3rd
Person

THE CHAPERON

I

AN old lady, in a high drawing-room, had had her chair moved close to the fire, where she sat knitting and warming her knees. She was dressed in deep mourning; her face had a faded nobleness, tempered, however, by the somewhat illiberal compression assumed by her lips in obedience to something that was passing in her mind. She was far from the lamp, but though her eyes were fixed upon her active needles she was not looking at them. What she really saw was quite another train of affairs. The room was spacious and dim; the thick London fog had oozed into it even through its superior defences. It was full of dusky, massive, valuable things. The old lady sat motionless save for the regularity of her clicking needles, which seemed as personal to her and as expressive as prolonged fingers. If she was thinking something out, she was thinking it thoroughly.

When she looked up, on the entrance of a girl of twenty, it might have been guessed that the appearance of this young lady was not an interruption of her meditation, but rather a contribution to it. The young lady, who was charming to behold, was also in deep mourning, which had a freshness, if mourning can be fresh, an air of having been lately put on. She went straight to the bell beside the chimney-piece and pulled it, while in her other hand she held a sealed and directed letter. Her companion glanced in silence at the letter; then she looked still harder at her work. The girl hovered near the fire-place, without speaking, and after a due, a dignified interval the butler appeared in response to the bell. The time had been sufficient to make the silence between the ladies seem long.

20

The younger one asked the butler to see that her letter should be posted; and after he had gone out she moved vaguely about the room, as if to give her grandmother—for such was the elder personage—a chance to begin a colloquy of which she herself preferred not to strike the first note. As equally with herself her companion was on the face of it capable of holding out, the tension, though it was already late in the evening, might have lasted long. But the old lady after a little appeared to recognise, a trifle ungraciously, the girl's superior resources.

"Have you written to your mother?"

"Yes, but only a few lines, to tell her I shall come and see her in the morning."

"Is that all you've got to say?" asked the grandmother.

"I don't quite know what you want me to say."

"I want you to say that you've made up your mind."

"Yes, I've done that, granny."

"You intend to respect your father's wishes?"

"It depends upon what you mean by respecting them. I do justice to the feelings by which they were dictated."

"What do you mean by justice?" the old lady retorted.

The girl was silent a moment; then she said: "You'll see my idea of it."

"I see it already! You'll go and live with her."

"I shall talk the situation over with her to-morrow and tell her that I think that will be best."

"Best for her, no doubt!"

"What's best for her is best for me."

"And for your brother and sister?" As the girl made no reply to this her grandmother went on: "What's best for them is that you should acknowledge some responsibility in regard to them and, considering how young they are, try and do something for them."

"They must do as I've done—they must act for themselves. They have their means now, and they're free."

"Free? They're mere children."

"Let me remind you that Eric is older than I."

"He doesn't like his mother," said the old lady, as if that were an answer.

"I never said he did. And she adores him."

"Oh, your mother's adorations!"

"Don't abuse her now," the girl rejoined, after a pause.

The old lady forbore to abuse her, but she made up for it the next moment by saying: "It will be dreadful for Edith."

"What will be dreadful?"

"Your desertion of her."

"The desertion's on her side."

"Her consideration for her father does her honour."

"Of course I'm a brute, *n'en parlons plus*," said the girl. "We must go our respective ways," she added, in a tone of extreme wisdom and philosophy.

Her grandmother straightened out her knitting and began to roll it up. "Be so good as to ring for my maid," she said, after a minute. The young lady rang, and there was another wait and another conscious hush. Before the maid came her mistress remarked: "Of course then you'll not come to *me*, you know."

"What do you mean by 'coming' to you?"

"I can't receive you on that footing."

"She'll not come *with* me, if you mean that."

"I don't mean that," said the old lady, getting up as her maid came in. This attendant took her work from her, gave her an arm and helped her out of the room, while Rose Tramore, standing before the fire and looking into it, faced the idea that her grandmother's door would now under all circumstances be closed to her. She lost no time however in brooding over this anomaly: it only added energy to her determination to act. All she could do to-night was to go to bed, for she felt utterly weary. She had been living, in imagination, in a prospective struggle, and it had left her as exhausted as a real fight. Moreover this was the culmination of a crisis, of weeks of suspense, of a long, hard strain. Her father had been laid in his grave five days before, and that morning his will had been read. In the afternoon she had got Edith off to St Leonard's with their aunt Julia, and then she had had a wretched talk with Eric. Lastly, she had made up her mind to act in opposition to the formidable will, to a clause which embodied if not exactly a provision, a recommendation singularly emphatic. She went to bed and slept the sleep of the just.

"Oh, my dear, how charming! I must take another house!" It was in these words that her mother responded to the announcement Rose had just formally made and with which she had vaguely expected to produce a certain dignity of effect. In the way of emotion there was apparently no effect at all, and the girl was wise enough to know that this was not simply on account of the general line of non-allusion taken by the extremely pretty woman before her, who looked like her elder sister. Mrs Tramore had never manifested, to her daughter, the slightest consciousness that her position was peculiar; but the recollection of something more than that fine policy was required to explain such a failure to appreciate Rose's sacrifice. It was simply a fresh reminder that she had never appreciated anything, that she was nothing but a tinted and stippled surface. Her situation was peculiar indeed. She had been the heroine of a scandal which had grown dim only because, in the eyes of the London world, it paled in the lurid light of the contemporaneous. That attention had been fixed on it for several days, fifteen years before; there had been a high relish of the vivid evidence as to his wife's misconduct with which, in the divorce-court, Charles Tramore had judged well to regale a cynical public. The case was pronounced awfully bad, and he obtained his decree. The folly of the wife had been inconceivable, in spite of other examples: she had quitted her children, she had followed the "other fellow" abroad. The other fellow hadn't married her, not having had time: he had lost his life in the Mediterranean by the capsizing of a boat, before the prohibitory term had expired.

Mrs Tramore had striven to extract from this accident something of the austerity of widowhood; but her mourning only made her deviation more public, she was a widow whose husband was awkwardly alive. She had not prowled about the Continent on the classic lines; she had come back to London to take her chance. But London would give her no chance, would have nothing to say to her; as many persons had remarked, you could never tell how London would behave. It would not receive Mrs Tramore again on any terms, and when she was spoken of, which now was not often, it was inveterately said of her that she went nowhere. Apparently she had not the qualities for which London compounds; though in the cases in which it does compound you may often wonder what these qualities are. She had not at any rate been successful: her lover was dead, her husband was liked and her children were pitied, for in payment for a topic London will parenthetically pity. It was thought interesting and magnanimous that Charles Tramore had not married again. The disadvantage to his children of the miserable story was thus left uncorrected, and this, rather oddly, was counted as *his* sacrifice. His mother, whose arrangements were elaborate, looked after them a great deal, and they enjoyed a mixture of laxity and discipline under the roof of their aunt, Miss Tramore, who was independent, having, for reasons that the two ladies had exhaustively discussed, determined to lead her own life. She had set up a home at St Leonard's, and that contracted shore had played a considerable part in the upbringing of the little Tramores. They knew about their mother, as the phrase was, but they didn't know her; which was naturally deemed more pathetic for them than for her. She had a house in Chester Square and an income and a victoria—it served all purposes, as she never went out in the evening—and flowers on her window-sills, and a remarkable appearance of youth. The income was supposed to be in part the result of a bequest from the man for whose sake she had committed the error of her life, and in the appearance of youth there was a slightly impertinent implication that it was a sort of afterglow of the same connection.

Her children, as they grew older, fortunately showed signs of some individuality of disposition. Edith, the second girl, clung to her aunt Julia; Eric, the son, clung frantically to polo; while Rose, the elder daughter, appeared to cling mainly to herself. Collectively, of course, they clung to their father, whose attitude in the family group, however, was casual and intermittent. He was charming and vague; he was like a clever actor who often didn't come to rehearsal. Fortune, which but for that one stroke had been generous to him, had provided him with deputies and trouble-takers, as well as with whimsical opinions, and a reputation for excellent taste, and whist at his club, and perpetual cigars on morocco sofas, and a beautiful absence of purpose. Nature had thrown in a remarkably fine hand, which he sometimes passed over his children's heads when they were glossy from the nursery brush. On Rose's eighteenth birthday he said to her that she might go to see her mother, on condition that her visits should be limited to an hour each time and to four in the year. She was to go alone; the other children were not included in the arrangement. This was the result of a visit that he himself had paid his repudiated wife at her urgent request, their only encounter during the fifteen years. The girl knew as much as this from her aunt Julia, who was full of tell-tale secrecies. She availed herself eagerly of the license, and in course of the period that elapsed before her father's death she spent with Mrs Tramore exactly eight hours by the watch. Her father, who was as inconsistent and disappointing as he was amiable, spoke to her of her mother only once afterwards. This occasion had been the sequel of her first visit, and he had made no use of it to ask what she thought of the personality in Chester Square or how she liked it. He had only said "Did she take you out?" and when Rose answered "Yes, she put me straight into a carriage and drove me up and down Bond Street," had rejoined sharply "See that that never occurs again." It never did, but once was enough, every one they knew having happened to be in Bond Street at that particular hour.

After this the periodical interview took place in private, in Mrs Tramore's beautiful little wasted drawing-room. Rose knew that, rare as these occasions were, her mother would not have kept her "all to herself" had there been anybody she could have shown her to. But in the poor lady's social void there was no one; she had after all her own correctness and she consistently preferred isolation to inferior contacts. So her daughter was subjected only to the maternal; it was not necessary to be definite in qualifying that. The girl had by this time a collection of ideas, gathered by impenetrable processes; she had tasted, in the ostracism of her ambiguous parent, of the acrid fruit of the tree of knowledge. She not only had an approximate vision of what every one had done, but she had a private judgment for each case. She had a particular vision of her father, which did not interfere with his being dear to her, but which was directly concerned in her resolution, after his death, to do the special thing he had expressed the wish she should not do. In the general estimate her grandmother and her grandmother's money had their place, and the strong probability that any enjoyment of the latter commodity would now be withheld from her. It included Edith's marked inclination to receive the law, and doubtless eventually a more substantial memento, from Miss Tramore, and opened the question whether her own course might not contribute to make her sister's appear heartless. The answer to this question however would depend on the success that might attend her own, which would very possibly be small. Eric's attitude was eminently simple; he didn't care to know people who didn't know *his* people. If his mother should ever get back into society perhaps he would take her up. Rose Tramore had decided to do what she could to bring this consummation about; and strangely enough—so mixed were her superstitions and her heresies—a large part of her motive lay in the value she attached to such a consecration.

Of her mother intrinsically she thought very little now, and if her eyes were fixed on a special achievement it was much more for the sake of that achievement and to satisfy a latent energy that was in her than because her heart was wrung by this sufferer. Her heart had not been wrung at all, though she had quite held it out for the experience. Her purpose was a pious game, but it was still essentially a game. Among the ideas I have mentioned she had her idea of triumph. She had caught the inevitable note, the pitch, on her very first visit to Chester Square. She had arrived there in intense excitement, and her excitement was left on her hands in a manner that reminded her of a difficult air she had once heard sung at the opera when no one applauded the performer. That flatness had made her sick, and so did this, in another way. A part of her agitation proceeded from the fact that her aunt Julia had told her, in the manner of a burst of confidence, something she was not to repeat, that she was in appearance the very image of the lady in Chester Square. The motive that prompted this declaration was between aunt Julia and her conscience; but it was a great emotion to the girl to find her entertainer so beautiful. She was tall and exquisitely slim; she had hair more exactly to Rose Tramore's taste than any other she had ever seen, even to every detail in the way it was dressed, and a complexion and a figure of the kind that are always spoken of as "lovely." Her eyes were irresistible, and so were her clothes, though the clothes were perhaps a little more precisely the right thing than the eyes. Her appearance was marked to her daughter's sense by the highest distinction; though it may be mentioned that this had never been the opinion of all the world. It was a revelation to Rose that she herself might look a little like that.

She knew however that aunt Julia had not seen her deposed sister-in-law for a long time, and she had a general impression that Mrs Tramore was to-day a more complete production—for instance as regarded her air of youth—than she had ever been. There was no excitement on her side—that was all her visitor's; there was no emotion—that was excluded by the plan, to say nothing of conditions more primal. Rose had from the first a glimpse of her mother's plan. It was to mention nothing and imply nothing, neither to acknowledge, to explain nor to extenuate. She would leave everything to her child; with her child she was secure. She only wanted to get back into society; she would leave even that to her child, whom she treated not as a high-strung and heroic daughter, a creature of exaltation, of devotion, but as a new, charming, clever, useful friend, a little younger than herself. Already on that first day she had talked about dressmakers. Of course, poor thing, it was to be remembered that in her circumstances there were not many things she *could* talk about. "She wants to go out again; that's the only thing in the wide world she wants," Rose had promptly, compendiously said to herself. There had been a sequel to this observation, uttered, in intense engrossment, in her own room half an hour before she had, on the important evening, made known her decision to her grandmother: "Then I'll *take* her out!"

"She'll drag you down, she'll drag you down!" Julia Tramore permitted herself to remark to her niece, the next day, in a tone of feverish prophecy.

As the girl's own theory was that all the dragging there might be would be upward, and moreover administered by herself, she could look at her aunt with a cold and inscrutable eye.

"Very well, then, I shall be out of your sight, from the pinnacle you occupy, and I sha'n't trouble you."

"Do you reproach me for my disinterested exertions, for the way I've toiled over you, the way I've lived for you?" Miss Tramore demanded.

"Don't reproach *me* for being kind to my mother and I won't reproach you for anything."

"She'll keep you out of everything—she'll make you miss everything," Miss Tramore continued.

"Then she'll make me miss a great deal that's odious," said the girl.

"You're too young for such extravagances," her aunt declared.

"And yet Edith, who is younger than I, seems to be too old for them: how do you arrange that? My mother's society will make me older," Rose replied.

"Don't speak to me of your mother; you *have* no mother."

"Then if I'm an orphan I must settle things for myself."

"Do you justify her, do you approve of her?" cried Miss Tramore, who was inferior to her niece in capacity for retort and whose limitations made the girl appear pert.

Rose looked at her a moment in silence; then she said, turning away: "I think she's charming."

"And do you propose to become charming in the same manner?"

"Her manner is perfect; it would be an excellent model. But I can't discuss my mother with you."

"You'll have to discuss her with some other people!" Miss Tramore proclaimed, going out of the room.

Rose wondered whether this were a general or a particular vaticination. There was something her aunt might have meant by it, but her aunt rarely meant the best thing she might have meant. Miss Tramore had come up from St Leonard's in response to a telegram from her own parent, for an occasion like the present brought with it, for a few hours, a certain relaxation of their dissent. "Do what you can to stop her," the old lady had said; but her daughter found that the most she could do was not much. They both had a baffled sense that Rose had thought the question out a good deal further than they; and this was particularly irritating to Mrs Tramore, as consciously the cleverer of the two. A question thought out as far as *she* could think it had always appeared to her to have performed its human uses; she had never encountered a ghost emerging from that extinction. Their great contention was that Rose would cut herself off; and certainly if she wasn't afraid of that she wasn't afraid of anything. Julia Tramore could only tell her mother how little the girl was afraid. She was already prepared to leave the house, taking with her the possessions, or her share of them, that had accumulated there during her father's illness. There had been a going and coming of her maid, a thumping about of boxes, an ordering of four-wheelers; it appeared to old Mrs Tramore that something of the objectionableness, the indecency, of her granddaughter's prospective connection had already gathered about the place. It was a violation of the decorum of bereavement which was still fresh there, and from the indignant gloom of the mistress of the house you might have inferred not so much that the daughter was about to depart as that the mother was about to arrive. There had been no conversation on the dreadful sub-ject at luncheon; for at luncheon at Mrs Tramore's (her son never came to it) there were always, even after funerals and other miseries, stray guests of both sexes whose policy it was to be cheerful and superficial. Rose had sat down as if nothing had happened—nothing worse, that is, than her father's death; but no one had spoken of anything that any one else was thinking of.

Before she left the house a servant brought her a message from her grandmother—the old lady desired to see her in the drawing-room. She had on her bonnet, and she went down as if she were about to step into her cab. Mrs Tramore sat there with her eternal knitting, from which she forebore even to raise her eyes as, after a silence that seemed to express the ful-ness of her reprobation, while Rose stood motionless, she began: "I wonder if you really understand what you're doing."

8:F

"I think so. I'm not so stupid."

"I never thought you were; but I don't know what to make of you now. You're giving up everything."

The girl was tempted to inquire whether her grandmother called herself "everything"; but she checked this question, answering instead that she knew she was giving up much.

"You're taking a step of which you will feel the effect to the end of your days," Mrs Tramore went on.

"In a good conscience, I heartily hope," said Rose.

"Your father's conscience was good enough for his mother; it ought to be good enough for his daughter."

Rose sat down—she could afford to—as if she wished to be very attentive and were still accessible to argument. But this demonstration only ushered in, after a moment, the surprising words "I don't think papa had any conscience."

"What in the name of all that's unnatural do you mean?" Mrs Tramore cried, over her glasses. "The dearest and best creature that ever lived!"

"He was kind, he had charming impulses, he was delightful. But he never reflected."

Mrs Tramore stared, as if at a language she had never heard, a farrago, a *galimatias*. Her life was made up of items, but she had never had to deal, intellectually, with a fine shade. Then while her needles, which had paused an instant, began to fly again, she rejoined: "Do you know what you are, my dear? You're a dreadful little prig. Where do you pick up such talk?"

"Of course I don't mean to judge between them," Rose pursued. "I can only judge between my mother and myself. Papa couldn't judge for me." And with this she got up.

"One would think you were horrid. I never thought so before."

"Thank you for that."

"You're embarking on a struggle with society," continued Mrs Tramore, indulging in an unusual flight of oratory. "Society will put you in your place."

"Hasn't it too many other things to do?" asked the girl.

This question had an ingenuity which led her grandmother to meet it with a merely provisional and somewhat sketchy answer. "Your ignorance would be melancholy if your behaviour were not so insane."

"Oh, no; I know perfectly what she'll do!" Rose replied, almost gaily. "She'll drag me down."

"She won't even do that," the old lady declared contradictiously. "She'll keep you forever in the same dull hole."

"I shall come and see *you*, granny, when I want something more lively."

"You may come if you like, but you'll come no further than the door. If you leave this house now you don't enter it again."

Rose hesitated a moment. "Do you really mean that?"

"You may judge whether I choose such a time to joke."

"Good-bye, then," said the girl.

"Good-bye."

Rose quitted the room successfully enough; but on the other side of the door, on the landing, she sank into a chair and buried her face in her hands. She had burst into tears, and she sobbed there for a moment, trying hard to recover herself, so as to go downstairs without showing any traces of emotion, passing before the servants and again perhaps before aunt Julia. Mrs Tramore was too old to cry; she could only drop her knitting and, for a long time, sit with her head bowed and her eyes closed.

Rose had reckoned justly with her aunt Julia; there were no footmen, but this vigilant virgin was posted at the foot of the stairs. She offered no challenge however; she only said: "There's some one in the parlour who wants to see you." The girl demanded a name, but Miss Tramore only mouthed inaudibly and winked and waved. Rose instantly reflected that there was only one man in the world her aunt would look such deep things about. "Captain Jay?" her own eyes asked, while

Miss Tramore's were those of a conspirator: they were, for a moment, the only embarrassed eyes Rose had encountered that day. They contributed to make aunt Julia's further response evasive, after her niece inquired if she had communicated in advance with this visitor. Miss Tramore merely said that he had been upstairs with her mother—hadn't she mentioned it?—and had been waiting for her. She thought herself acute in not putting the question of the girl's seeing him before her as a favour to him or to herself; she presented it as a duty, and wound up with the proposition: "It's not fair to him, it's not kind, not to let him speak to you before you go."

"What does he want to say?" Rose demanded.

"Go in and find out."

She really knew, for she had found out before; but after standing uncertain an instant she went in. "The parlour" was the name that had always been borne by a spacious sitting-room downstairs, an apartment occupied by her father during his frequent phases of residence in Hill Street—episodes increasingly frequent after his house in the country had, in consequence, as Rose perfectly knew, of his spending too much money, been disposed of at a sacrifice which he always characterised as horrid. He had been left with the place in Hertfordshire and his mother with the London house, on the general understanding that they would change about; but during the last years the community had grown more rigid, mainly at his mother's expense. The parlour was full of his memory and his habits and his things—his books and pictures and *bibelots*, objects that belonged now to Eric. Rose had sat in it for hours since his death; it was the place in which she could still be nearest to him. But she felt far from him as Captain Jay rose erect on her opening the door. This was a very different presence. He had not liked Captain Jay. She herself had, but not enough to make a great complication of her father's coldness. This afternoon however she foresaw complications. At the very outset for instance she was not pleased with his having arranged such a surprise for her with her grandmother and her aunt. It was probably aunt Julia who had sent for him; her grandmother wouldn't have done it. It placed him immediately on their side, and Rose was almost as disappointed at this as if she had not known it was quite where he would naturally be. He had never paid her a special visit, but if that was what he wished to do why shouldn't he have waited till she should be under her mother's roof? She knew the reason, but she had an angry prospect of enjoyment in making him express it. She liked him enough, after all, if it were measured by the idea of what she could make him do.

In Bertram Jay the elements were surprisingly mingled; you would have gone astray, in reading him, if you had counted on finding the complements of some of his qualities. He would not however have struck you in the least as incomplete, for in every case in which you didn't find the complement you would have found the contradiction. He was in the Royal Engineers, and was tall, lean and high-shouldered. He looked every inch a soldier, yet there were people who considered that he had missed his vocation in not becoming a parson. He took a public interest in the spiritual life of the army. Other persons still, on closer observation, would have felt that his most appropriate field was neither the army nor the church, but simply the world—the social, successful, worldly world. If he had a sword in one hand and a Bible in the other he had a Court Guide concealed somewhere about his person. His profile was hard and handsome, his eyes were both cold and kind, his dark straight hair was imperturbably smooth and prematurely streaked with grey. There was nothing in existence that he didn't take seriously. He had a first-rate power of work and an ambition as minutely organised as a German plan of invasion. His only real recreation was to go to church, but he went to parties when he had time. If he was in love with Rose Tramore this was distracting to him only in the same sense as his religion, and it was included in that department of his extremely sub-divided life. His religion indeed was of an encroaching, annexing sort. Seen from in front he looked diffident and blank, but he was capable of exposing himself in a way (to speak only of the paths of peace) wholly inconsistent with shyness. He had a passion for instance for open-air speaking, but was not thought on the whole to excel in it unless he could help himself out with a hymn. In conversation he kept his eyes on you with a kind of colourless candour, as if he had not understood what you were saying and, in a fashion that made many people turn red, waited before answering. This was only because he was considering their remarks in more relations than they had intended. He had in his face no expression whatever save the one just mentioned, and was, in his profession, already very distinguished.

He had seen Rose Tramore for the first time on a Sunday of the previous March, at a house in the country at which she was staying with her father, and five weeks later he had made her, by letter, an offer of marriage. She showed her father the letter of course, and he told her that it would give him great pleasure that she should send Captain Jay about his business. "My dear child," he said, "we must really have some one who will be better fun than that." Rose had declined the honour, very considerately and kindly, but not simply because her father wished it. She didn't herself wish to detach this flower from the stem, though when the young man wrote again, to express the hope that he *might* hope—so long was he willing to wait—and ask if he might not still sometimes see her, she answered even more indulgently than at first. She had shown her father her former letter, but she didn't show him this one; she only told him what it contained, submitting to him also that of her correspondent. Captain Jay moreover wrote to Mr Tramore, who replied sociably, but so vaguely that he almost neglected the subject under discussion—a communication that made poor Bertram ponder long. He could never get to

the bottom of the superficial, and all the proprieties and con-
ventions of life were profound to him. Fortunately for him old
Mrs Tramore liked him, he was satisfactory to her long-
sightedness; so that a relation was established under cover of
which he still occasionally presented himself in Hill Street—
presented himself nominally to the mistress of the house. He
had had scruples about the veracity of his visits, but he had
disposed of them; he had scruples about so many things that
he had had to invent a general way, to dig a central drain.
Julia Tramore happened to meet him when she came up to
town, and she took a view of him more benevolent than her
usual estimate of people encouraged by her mother. The fear
of agreeing with that lady was a motive, but there was a
stronger one, in this particular case, in the fear of agreeing
with her niece, who had rejected him. His situation might be
held to have improved when Mr Tramore was taken so gravely
ill that with regard to his recovery those about him left their
eyes to speak for their lips; and in the light of the poor gentleman's recent death it was doubtless better than it had ever
been.

He was only a quarter of an hour with the girl, but this gave
him time to take the measure of it. After he had spoken to her
about her bereavement, very much as an especially mild
missionary might have spoken to a beautiful Polynesian, he
let her know that he had learned from her companions the
very strong step she was about to take. This led to their spending together ten minutes which, to her mind, threw more light
on his character than anything that had ever passed between
them. She had always felt with him as if she were standing on
an edge, looking down into something decidedly deep. To-
day the impression of the perpendicular shaft was there, but
it was rather an abyss of confusion and disorder than the large
bright space in which she had figured everything as ranged
and pigeon-holed, presenting the appearance of the labelled
shelves and drawers at a chemist's. He discussed without an

invitation to discuss, he appealed without a right to appeal. He was nothing but a suitor tolerated after dismissal, but he took strangely for granted a participation in her affairs. He assumed all sorts of things that made her draw back. He implied that there was everything now to assist them in arriving at an agreement, since she had never informed him that he was positively objectionable; but that this symmetry would be spoiled if she should not be willing to take a little longer to think of certain consequences. She was greatly disconcerted when she saw what consequences he meant and at his reminding her of them. What on earth was the use of a lover if he was to speak only like one's grandmother and one's aunt? He struck her as much in love with her and as particularly careful at the same time as to what he might say. He never mentioned her mother; he only alluded, indirectly but earnestly, to the "step." He disapproved of it altogether, took an unexpectedly prudent, politic view of it. He evidently also believed that she would be dragged down; in other words that she would not be asked out. It was his idea that her mother would contaminate her, so that he should find himself interested in a young person discredited and virtually unmarriageable. All this was more obvious to him than the consideration that a daughter should be merciful. Where was his religion if he understood mercy so little, and where were his talent and his courage if he were so miserably afraid of trumpery social penalties? Rose's heart sank when she reflected that a man supposed to be first-rate hadn't guessed that rather than not do what she could for her mother she would give up all the Engineers in the world. She became aware that she probably would have been moved to place her hand in his on the spot if he had come to her saying "Your idea is the right one; put it through at every cost." She couldn't discuss this with him, though he impressed her as having too much at stake for her to treat him with mere disdain. She sickened at the revelation that a gentleman could see so much in mere vulgarities of opinion, and though she uttered as few words as possible, conversing only in sad smiles and headshakes and in intercepted movements toward the door, she happened, in some unguarded lapse from her reticence, to use the expression that she was disappointed in him. He caught at it and, seeming to drop his field-glass, pressed upon her with nearer, tenderer eyes.

"Can I be so happy as to believe, then, that you had thought of me with some confidence, with some faith?"

"If you didn't suppose so, what is the sense of this visit?" Rose asked.

"One can be faithful without reciprocity," said the young man. "I regard you in a light which makes me want to protect you even if I have nothing to gain by it."

"Yet you speak as if you thought you might keep me for yourself."

"For *yourself.* I don't want you to suffer."

"Nor to suffer yourself by my doing so," said Rose, looking down.

"Ah, if you would only marry me next month!" he broke out inconsequently.

"And give up going to mamma?" Rose waited to see if he would say "What need that matter? Can't your mother come to us?" But he said nothing of the sort; he only answered—

"She surely would be sorry to interfere with the exercise of any other affection which I might have the bliss of believing that you are now free, in however small a degree, to entertain."

Rose knew that her mother wouldn't be sorry at all; but she contented herself with rejoining, her hand on the door: "Good-bye. I sha'n't suffer. I'm not afraid."

"You don't know how terrible, how cruel, the world can be."

"Yes, I do know. I know everything!"

The declaration sprang from her lips in a tone which made

him look at her as he had never looked before, as if he saw
something new in her face, as if he had never yet known her.
He hadn't displeased her so much but that she would like to
give him that impression, and since she felt that she was doing
so she lingered an instant for the purpose. It enabled her to see,
further, that he turned red; then to become aware that a carriage had stopped at the door. Captain Jay's eyes, from where he
stood, fell upon this arrival, and the nature of their glance made
Rose step forward to look. Her mother sat there, brilliant, conspicuous, in the eternal victoria, and the footman was already
sounding the knocker. It had been no part of the arrangement
that she should come to fetch her; it had been out of the question—a stroke in such bad taste as would have put Rose in
the wrong. The girl had never dreamed of it, but somehow,
suddenly, perversely, she was glad of it now; she even hoped
that her grandmother and her aunt were looking out upstairs.

"My mother has come for me. Good-bye," she repeated;
but this time her visitor had got between her and the door.

"Listen to me before you go. I will give you a life's devotion," the young man pleaded. He really barred the way.

She wondered whether her grandmother had told him that
if her flight were not prevented she would forfeit money.
Then, vividly, it came over her that this would be what he
was occupied with. "I shall never think of you—let me go!"
she cried, with passion.

Captain Jay opened the door, but Rose didn't see his face,
and in a moment she was out of the house. Aunt Julia, who
was sure to have been hovering, had taken flight before the
profanity of the knock.

"Heavens, dear, where did you get your mourning?" the
lady in the victoria asked of her daughter as they drove away.

II

LADY MARESFIELD had given her boy a push in his plump back and had said to him, "Go and speak to her now; it's your chance." She had for a long time wanted this scion to make himself audible to Rose Tramore, but the opportunity was not easy to come by. The case was complicated. Lady Maresfield had four daughters, of whom only one was married. It so happened moreover that this one, Mrs Vaughan-Vesey, the only person in the world her mother was afraid of, was the most to be reckoned with. The Honourable Guy was in appearance all his mother's child, though he was really a simpler soul. He was large and pink; large, that is, as to everything but the eyes, which were diminishing points, and pink as to everything but the hair, which was comparable, faintly, to the hue of the richer rose. He had also, it must be conceded, very small neat teeth, which made his smile look like a young lady's. He had no wish to resemble any such person, but he was perpetually smiling, and he smiled more than ever as he approached Rose Tramore, who, looking altogether, to his mind, as a pretty girl should, and wearing a soft white opera-cloak over a softer black dress, leaned alone against the wall of the vestibule at Covent Garden while, a few paces off, an old gentleman engaged her mother in conversation. Madame Patti had been singing, and they were all waiting for their carriages. To their ears at present came a vociferation of names and a rattle of wheels. The air, through banging doors, entered in damp, warm gusts, heavy with the stale, slightly sweet taste of the London season when the London season is overripe and spoiling.

Guy Mangler had only three minutes to reëstablish an interrupted acquaintance with our young lady. He reminded her that he had danced with her the year before, and he mentioned that he knew her brother. His mother had lately been to see old Mrs Tramore, but this he did not mention, not being aware of it. That visit had produced, on Lady Maresfield's part, a private crisis, engendered ideas. One of them was that the grandmother in Hill Street had really forgiven the wilful girl much more than she admitted. Another was that there would still be some money for Rose when the others should come into theirs. Still another was that the others would come into theirs at no distant date; the old lady was so visibly going to pieces. There were several more besides, as for instance that Rose had already fifteen hundred a year from her father. The figure had been betrayed in Hill Street; it was part of the proof of Mrs Tramore's decrepitude. Then there was an equal amount that her mother had to dispose of and on which the girl could absolutely count, though of course it might involve much waiting, as the mother, a person of gross insensibility, evidently wouldn't die of cold-shouldering. Equally definite, to do it justice, was the conception that Rose was in truth remarkably good looking, and that what she had undertaken to do showed, and would show even should it fail, cleverness of the right sort. Cleverness of the right sort was exactly the quality that Lady Maresfield prefigured as indispensable in a young lady to whom she should marry her second son, over whose own deficiencies she flung the veil of a maternal theory that *his* cleverness was of a sort that was wrong. Those who knew him less well were content to wish that he might not conceal it for such a scruple. This enumeration of his mother's views does not exhaust the list, and it was in obedience to one too profound to be uttered even by the historian that, after a very brief delay, she decided to move across the crowded lobby. Her daughter Bessie was the only one with her; Maggie was dining with the Vaughan-Veseys, and Fanny was not of an age. Mrs Tramore the younger showed only an admirable back—her face was to her old gentleman—and Bessie had drifted to some other people; so that it was comparatively easy for Lady Maresfield to say to Rose, in a moment: "My dear child, are you never coming to see us?"

"We shall be delighted to come if you'll ask us," Rose smiled.

Lady Maresfield had been prepared for the plural number, and she was a woman whom it took many plurals to disconcert. "I'm sure Guy is longing for another dance with you," she rejoined, with the most unblinking irrelevance.

"I'm afraid we're not dancing again quite yet," said Rose, glancing at her mother's exposed shoulders, but speaking as if they were muffled in crape.

Lady Maresfield leaned her head on one side and seemed almost wistful. "Not even at my sister's ball? She's to have something next week. She'll write to you."

Rose Tramore, on the spot, looking bright but vague, turned three or four things over in her mind. She remembered that the sister of her interlocutress was the proverbially rich Mrs Bray, a bankeress or a breweress or a builderess, who had so big a house that she couldn't fill it unless she opened her doors, or her mouth, very wide. Rose had learnt more about London society during these lonely months with her mother than she had ever picked up in Hill Street. The younger Mrs Tramore was a mine of *commérages*, and she had no need to go out to bring home the latest intelligence. At any rate Mrs Bray might serve as the end of a wedge. "Oh, I dare say we might think of that," Rose said. "It would be very kind of your sister."

"Guy'll think of it, won't you, Guy?" asked Lady Maresfield.

"Rather!" Guy responded, with an intonation as fine as if he had learnt it at a music hall; while at the same moment the name of his mother's carriage was bawled through the place. Mrs Tramore had parted with her old gentleman; she turned again to her daughter. Nothing occurred but what always occurred, which was exactly this absence of everything—a universal lapse. She didn't exist, even for a second, to any recognising eye. The people who looked at her—of course there were plenty of those—were only the people who didn't exist for hers. Lady Maresfield surged away on her son's arm.

It was this noble matron herself who wrote, the next day, inclosing a card of invitation from Mrs Bray and expressing the hope that Rose would come and dine and let her ladyship take her. She should have only one of her own girls; Gwendolen Vesey was to take the other. Rose handed both the note and the card in silence to her mother; the latter exhibited only the name of Miss Tramore. "You had much better go, dear," her mother said; in answer to which Miss Tramore slowly tore up the documents, looking with clear, meditative eyes out of the window. Her mother always said "You had better go"—there had been other incidents—and Rose had never even once taken account of the observation. She would make no first advances, only plenty of second ones, and, condoning no discrimination, would treat no omission as venial. She would keep all concessions till afterwards; then she would make them one by one. Fighting society was quite as hard as her grandmother had said it would be; but there was a tension in it which made the dreariness vibrate—the dreariness of such a winter as she had just passed. Her companion had cried at the end of it, and she had cried all through; only her tears had been private, while her mother's had fallen once for all, at luncheon on the bleak Easter Monday—produced by the way a silent survey of the deadly square brought home to her that every creature but themselves was out of town and having tremendous fun. Rose felt that it was useless to attempt to explain simply by her mourning this severity of solitude; for if people didn't go to parties (at least a few didn't) for six months after their father died, this was the very time other people took for coming to see them. It was not too much to say that during this first winter of Rose's period with her mother she had no communication whatever with the world. It had the effect of making her take to reading the new American books: she wanted to see how girls got on by themselves. She had never read so much before, and there was a legitimate indifference in it when topics failed with her mother. They often failed after the first days, and then, while she bent over instructive volumes, this lady, dressed as if for an impending function, sat on the sofa and watched her. Rose was not embarrassed by such an appearance, for she could reflect that, a little before, her companion had not even a girl who had taken refuge in queer researches to look at. She was moreover used to her mother's attitude by this time. She had her own description of it: it was the attitude of waiting for the carriage. If they didn't go out it was not that Mrs Tramore was not ready in time, and Rose had even an alarmed prevision of their some day always arriving first. Mrs Tramore's conversation at such moments was abrupt, inconsequent and personal. She sat on the edge of sofas and chairs and glanced occasionally at the fit of her gloves (she was perpetually gloved, and the fit was a thing it was melancholy to see wasted), as people do who are expecting guests to dinner. Rose used almost to fancy herself at times a perfunctory husband on the other side of the fire.

What she was not yet used to—there was still a charm in it—was her mother's extraordinary tact. During the years they lived together they never had a discussion; a circumstance all the more remarkable since if the girl had a reason for sparing her companion (that of being sorry for her) Mrs Tramore had none for sparing her child. She only showed in doing so a happy instinct—the happiest thing about her. She took in perfection a course which represented everything and covered everything; she utterly abjured all authority. She testified to her abjuration in hourly ingenious, touching ways. In this manner nothing had to be talked over, which was a mercy all round. The tears on Easter Monday were merely a

nervous gust, to help show she was not a Christmas doll from
the Burlington Arcade; and there was no lifting up of the
repentant Magdalen, no uttered remorse for the former
abandonment of children. Of the way she could treat her
children her demeanour to this one was an example; it was an
uninterrupted appeal to her eldest daughter for direction. She
took the law from Rose in every circumstance, and if you had
noticed these ladies without knowing their history you would
have wondered what tie was fine enough to make maturity so
respectful to youth. No mother was ever so filial as Mrs
Tramore, and there had never been such a difference of position between sisters. Not that the elder one fawned, which
would have been fearful; she only renounced—whatever she
had to renounce. If the amount was not much she at any rate
made no scene over it. Her hand was so light that Rose said
of her secretly, in vague glances at the past, "No wonder
people liked her!" She never characterised the old element of
interference with her mother's respectability more definitely
than as "people." They were people, it was true, for whom
gentleness must have been everything and who didn't demand
a variety of interests. The desire to "go out" was the one
passion that even a closer acquaintance with her parent
revealed to Rose Tramore. She marvelled at its strength, in
the light of the poor lady's history: there was comedy enough
in this unquenchable flame on the part of a woman who had
known such misery. She had drunk deep of every dishonour,
but the bitter cup had left her with a taste for lighted candles,
for squeezing up staircases and hooking herself to the human
elbow. Rose had a vision of the future years in which this
taste would grow with restored exercise—of her mother, in a
long-tailed dress, jogging on and on and on, jogging further
and further from her sins, through a century of the "Morning
Post" and down the fashionable avenue of time. She herself
would then be very old—she herself would be dead. Mrs Tramore would cover a span of life for which such an allowance

of sin was small. The girl could laugh indeed now at that theory of her being dragged down. If one thing were more present to her than another it was the very desolation of their propriety. As she glanced at her companion, it sometimes seemed to her that if she had been a bad woman she would have been worse than that. There were compensations for being "cut" which Mrs Tramore too much neglected.

The lonely old lady in Hill Street—Rose thought of her that way now—was the one person to whom she was ready to say that she would come to her on any terms. She wrote this to her three times over, and she knocked still oftener at her door. But the old lady answered no letters; if Rose had remained in Hill Street it would have been her own function to answer them; and at the door, the butler, whom the girl had known for ten years, considered her, when he told her his mistress was not at home, quite as he might have considered a young person who had come about a place and of whose eligibility he took a negative view. That was Rose's one pang, that she probably appeared rather heartless. Her aunt Julia had gone to Florence with Edith for the winter, on purpose to make her appear more so; for Miss Tramore was still the person most scandalised by her secession. Edith and she, doubtless, often talked over in Florence the destitution of the aged victim in Hill Street. Eric never came to see his sister, because, being full both of family and of personal feeling, he thought she really ought to have stayed with his grandmother. If she had had such an appurtenance all to herself she might have done what she liked with it; but he couldn't forgive such a want of consideration for anything of his. There were moments when Rose would have been ready to take her hand from the plough and insist upon reintegration, if only the fierce voice of the old house had allowed people to look her up. But she read, ever so clearly, that her grandmother had made this a question of loyalty to seventy years of virtue. Mrs Tramore's forlornness didn't prevent her

8:G

drawing-room from being a very public place, in which Rose could hear certain words reverberate: "Leave her alone; it's the only way to see how long she'll hold out." The old woman's visitors were people who didn't wish to quarrel, and the girl was conscious that if they had not let her alone—that is if they had come to her from her grandmother—she might perhaps not have held out. She had no friends quite of her own; she had not been brought up to have them, and it would not have been easy in a house which two such persons as her father and his mother divided between them. Her father disapproved of crude intimacies, and all the intimacies of youth were crude. He had married at five-and-twenty and could testify to such a truth. Rose felt that she shared even Captain Jay with her grandmother; she had seen what *he* was worth. Moreover, she had spoken to him at that last moment in Hill Street in a way which, taken with her former refusal, made it impossible that he should come near her again. She hoped he went to see his protectress: he could be a kind of substitute and administer comfort.

It so happened, however, that the day after she threw Lady Maresfield's invitation into the waste-paper basket she received a visit from a certain Mrs Donovan, whom she had occasionally seen in Hill Street. She vaguely knew this lady for a busybody, but she was in a situation which even busybodies might alleviate. Mrs Donovan was poor, but honest— so scrupulously honest that she was perpetually returning visits she had never received. She was always clad in weatherbeaten sealskin, and had an odd air of being prepared for the worst, which was borne out by her denying that she was Irish. She was of the English Donovans.

"Dear child, won't you go out with me?" she asked.

Rose looked at her a moment and then rang the bell. She spoke of something else, without answering the question, and when the servant came she said: "Please tell Mrs Tramore that Mrs Donovan has come to see her."

"Oh, that'll be delightful; only you mustn't tell your grandmother!" the visitor exclaimed.

"Tell her what?"

"That I come to see your mamma."

"You don't," said Rose.

"Sure I hoped you'd introduce me!" cried Mrs Donovan, compromising herself in her embarrassment.

"It's not necessary; you knew her once."

"Indeed and I've known every one once," the visitor confessed.

Mrs Tramore, when she came in, was charming and exactly right; she greeted Mrs Donovan as if she had met her the week before last, giving her daughter such a new illustration of her tact that Rose again had the idea that it was no wonder "people" had liked her. The girl grudged Mrs Donovan so fresh a morsel as a description of her mother at home, rejoicing that she would be inconvenienced by having to keep the story out of Hill Street. Her mother went away before Mrs Donovan departed, and Rose was touched by guessing her reason—the thought that since even this circuitous personage had been moved to come, the two might, if left together, invent some remedy. Rose waited to see what Mrs Donovan had in fact invented.

"You won't come out with me then?"

"Come out with you?"

"My daughters are married. You know I'm a lone woman. It would be an immense pleasure to me to have so charming a creature as yourself to present to the world."

"I go out with my mother," said Rose, after a moment.

"Yes, but sometimes when she's not inclined?"

"She goes everywhere she wants to go," Rose continued, uttering the biggest fib of her life and only regretting it should be wasted on Mrs Donovan.

"Ah, but do you go everywhere *you* want?" the lady asked sociably.

"One goes even to places one hates. Every one does that."

"Oh, what *I* go through!" this social martyr cried. Then she laid a persuasive hand on the girl's arm. "Let me show you at a few places first, and then we'll see. I'll bring them all here."

"I don't think I understand you," replied Rose, though in Mrs Donovan's words she perfectly saw her own theory of the case reflected. For a quarter of a minute she asked herself whether she might not, after all, do so much evil that good might come. Mrs Donovan would take her out the next day, and be thankful enough to annex such an attraction as a pretty girl. Various consequences would ensue and the long delay would be shortened; her mother's drawing-room would resound with the clatter of teacups.

"Mrs Bray's having some big thing next week; come with me there and I'll show you what I mane," Mrs Donovan pleaded.

"I see what you mane," Rose answered, brushing away her temptation and getting up. "I'm much obliged to you."

"You know you're wrong, my dear," said her interlocutress, with angry little eyes.

"I'm not going to Mrs Bray's."

"I'll get you a kyard; it'll only cost me a penny stamp."

"I've got one," said the girl, smiling.

"Do you mean a penny stamp?" Mrs Donovan, especially at departure, always observed all the forms of amity. "You can't do it alone, my darling," she declared.

"Shall they call you a cab?" Rose asked.

"I'll pick one up. I choose my horse. You know you require your start," her visitor went on.

"Excuse my mother," was Rose's only reply.

"Don't mention it. Come to me when you need me. You'll find me in the Red Book."

"It's awfully kind of you."

Mrs Donovan lingered a moment on the threshold. "Who will you *have* now, my child?" she appealed.

"I won't have any one!" Rose turned away, blushing for

her. "She came on speculation," she said afterwards to Mrs Tramore.

Her mother looked at her a moment in silence. "You can do it if you like, you know."

Rose made no direct answer to this observation; she remarked instead: "See what our quiet life allows us to escape."

"We don't escape it. She has been here an hour."

"Once in twenty years! We might meet her three times a day."

"Oh, I'd take her with the rest!" sighed Mrs Tramore; while her daughter recognised that what her companion wanted to do was just what Mrs Donovan was doing. Mrs Donovan's life was her ideal.

On a Sunday, ten days later, Rose went to see one of her old governesses, of whom she had lost sight for some time and who had written to her that she was in London, unoccupied and ill. This was just the sort of relation into which she could throw herself now with inordinate zeal; the idea of it, however, not preventing a foretaste of the queer expression in the excellent lady's face when she should mention with whom she was living. While she smiled at this picture she threw in another joke, asking herself if Miss Hack could be held in any degree to constitute the nucleus of a circle. She would come to see her, in any event—come the more the further she was dragged down. Sunday was always a difficult day with the two ladies—the afternoons made it so apparent that they were not frequented. Her mother, it is true, was comprised in the habits of two or three old gentlemen—she had for a long time avoided male friends of less than seventy —who disliked each other enough to make the room, when they were there at once, crack with pressure. Rose sat for a long time with Miss Hack, doing conscientious justice to the conception that there could be troubles in the world worse than her own; and when she came back her mother was alone, but with a story to tell of a long visit from Mr Guy

Mangler, who had waited and waited for her return. "He's in love with you; he's coming again on Tuesday," Mrs Tramore announced.

"Did he say so?"

"That he's coming back on Tuesday?"

"No, that he's in love with me."

"He didn't need, when he stayed two hours."

"With you? It's you he's in love with, mamma!"

"That will do as well," laughed Mrs Tramore. "For all the use we shall make of him!" she added in a moment.

"We shall make great use of him. His mother sent him."

"Oh, she'll never come!"

"Then *he* sha'n't," said Rose. Yet he was admitted on the Tuesday, and after she had given him his tea Mrs Tramore left the young people alone. Rose wished she hadn't—she herself had another view. At any rate she disliked her mother's view, which she had easily guessed. Mr Mangler did nothing but say how charming he thought his hostess of the Sunday, and what a tremendously jolly visit he had had. He didn't remark in so many words "I had no idea your mother was such a good sort"; but this was the spirit of his simple discourse. Rose liked it at first—a little of it gratified her; then she thought there was too much of it for good taste. She had to reflect that one does what one can and that Mr Mangler probably thought he was delicate. He wished to convey that he desired to make up to her for the injustice of society. Why shouldn't her mother receive gracefully, she asked (not audibly) and who had ever said she didn't? Mr Mangler had a great deal to say about the disappointment of his own parent over Miss Tramore's not having come to dine with them the night of his aunt's ball.

"Lady Maresfield knows why I didn't come," Rose answered at last.

"Ah, now, but *I* don't, you know; can't you tell *me*?" asked the young man.

"It doesn't matter, if your mother's clear about it."

"Oh, but why make such an awful mystery of it, when I'm dying to know?"

He talked about this, he chaffed her about it for the rest of his visit: he had at last found a topic after his own heart. If her mother considered that he might be the emblem of their redemption he was an engine of the most primitive construction. He stayed and stayed; he struck Rose as on the point of bringing out something for which he had not quite, as he would have said, the cheek. Sometimes she thought he was going to begin: "By the way, my mother told me to propose to you." At other moments he seemed charged with the admission: "I say, of course I really know what you're trying to do for her," nodding at the door: "therefore hadn't we better speak of it frankly, so that I can help you with my mother, and more particularly with my sister Gwendolen, who's the difficult one? The fact is, you see, they won't do anything for nothing. If you'll accept me they'll call, but they won't call without something 'down.'" Mr Mangler departed without their speaking frankly, and Rose Tramore had a hot hour during which she almost entertained, vindictively, the project of "accepting" the limpid youth until after she should have got her mother into circulation. The cream of the vision was that she might break with him later. She could read that this was what her mother would have liked, but the next time he came the door was closed to him, and the next and the next.

In August there was nothing to do but to go abroad, with the sense on Rose's part that the battle was still all to fight; for a round of country visits was not in prospect, and English watering-places constituted one of the few subjects on which the girl had heard her mother express herself with disgust. Continental autumns had been indeed for years, one of the various forms of Mrs Tramore's atonement, but Rose could only infer that such fruit as they had borne was bitter. The stony stare of Belgravia could be practised at Homburg; and somehow it was inveterately only gentlemen who sat next to her at the *table d'hôte* at Cadenabbia. Gentlemen had never been of any use to Mrs Tramore for getting back into society; they had only helped her effectually to get out of it. She once dropped, to her daughter, in a moralising mood, the remark that it was astonishing how many of them one could know without its doing one any good. Fifty of them—even very clever ones—represented a value inferior to that of one stupid woman. Rose wondered at the offhand way in which her mother could talk of fifty clever men; it seemed to her that the whole world couldn't contain such a number. She had a sombre sense that mankind must be dull and mean. These cogitations took place in a cold hotel, in an eternal Swiss rain, and they had a flat echo in the transalpine valleys, as the lonely ladies went vaguely down to the Italian lakes and cities. Rose guided their course, at moments, with a kind of aimless ferocity; she moved abruptly, feeling vulgar and hating their life, though destitute of any definite vision of another life that would have been open to her. She had set herself a task and she clung to it; but she appeared to herself despicably idle. She had succeeded in not going to Homburg waters, where London was trying to wash away some of its stains; that would be too staring an advertisement of their situation. The main difference in situations to her now was the difference of being more or less pitied, at the best an intolerable danger; so that the places she preferred were the unsuspicious ones. She wanted to triumph with contempt, not with submission.

One morning in September, coming with her mother out of the marble church at Milan, she perceived that a gentleman who had just passed her on his way into the cathedral and whose face she had not noticed, had quickly raised his hat, with a suppressed ejaculation. She involuntarily glanced back; the gentleman had paused, again uncovering, and Captain Jay stood saluting her in the Italian sunshine. "Oh, good-morning!" she said, and walked on, pursuing her course; her mother was a little in front. She overtook her in a moment, with an unreasonable sense, like a gust of cold air, that men were worse than ever, for Captain Jay had apparently moved into the church. Her mother turned as they met, and suddenly, as she looked back, an expression of peculiar sweetness came into this lady's eyes. It made Rose's take the same direction and rest a second time on Captain Jay, who was planted just where he had stood a minute before. He immediately came forward, asking Rose with great gravity if he might speak to her a moment, while Mrs Tramore went her way again. He had the expression of a man who wished to say something very important; yet his next words were simple enough and consisted of the remark that he had not seen her for a year.

"Is it really so much as that?" asked Rose.

"Very nearly. I would have looked you up, but in the first place I have been very little in London, and in the second I believed it wouldn't have done any good."

"You should have put that first," said the girl. "It wouldn't have done any good."

He was silent over this a moment, in his customary deciphering way; but the view he took of it did not prevent him from inquiring, as she slowly followed her mother, if he mightn't walk with her now. She answered with a laugh that it wouldn't do any good but that he might do as he liked. He replied without the slightest manifestation of levity that it would do more good than if he didn't, and they strolled together, with Mrs Tramore well before them, across the big, amusing piazza, where the front of the cathedral makes a sort of builded light. He asked a question or two and he explained his own presence: having a month's holiday, the first clear time for several years, he had just popped over the Alps. He inquired if Rose had recent news of the old lady in Hill Street, and it was the only tortuous thing she had ever heard him say.

"I have had no communication of any kind from her since

I parted with you under her roof. Hasn't she mentioned that?" said Rose.

"I haven't seen her."

"I thought you were such great friends."

Bertram Jay hesitated a moment. "Well, not so much now."

"What has she done to you?" Rose demanded.

He fidgeted a little, as if he were thinking of something that made him unconscious of her question; then, with mild violence, he brought out the inquiry: "Miss Tramore, are you happy?"

She was startled by the words, for she on her side had been reflecting—reflecting that he had broken with her grandmother and that this pointed to a reason. It suggested at least that he wouldn't now be so much like a mouthpiece for that cold ancestral tone. She turned off his question—said it never was a fair one, as you gave yourself away however you answered it. When he repeated "You give yourself away?" as if he didn't understand, she remembered that he had not read the funny American books. This brought them to a silence, for she had enlightened him only by another laugh, and he was evidently preparing another question, which he wished carefully to disconnect from the former. Presently, just as they were coming near Mrs Tramore, it arrived in the words "Is this lady your mother?" On Rose's assenting, with the addition that she was travelling with her, he said: "Will you be so kind as to introduce me to her?" They were so close to Mrs Tramore that she probably heard, but she floated away with a single stroke of her paddle and an inattentive poise of her head. It was a striking exhibition of the famous tact, for Rose delayed to answer, which was exactly what might have made her mother wish to turn; and indeed when at last the girl spoke she only said to her companion:

"Why do you ask me that?"

"Because I desire the pleasure of making her acquaintance."

Rose had stopped, and in the middle of the square they stood looking at each other. "Do you remember what you said to me the last time I saw you?"

"Oh, don't speak of that!"

"It's better to speak of it now than to speak of it later."

Bertram Jay looked round him, as if to see whether any one would hear; but the bright foreignness gave him a sense of safety, and he unexpectedly exclaimed:

"Miss Tramore, I love you more than ever!"

"Then you ought to have come to see us," declared the girl, quickly walking on.

"You treated me the last time as if I were positively offensive to you."

"So I did, but you know my reason."

"Because I protested against the course you were taking? I did, I did!" the young man rang out, as if he still, a little, stuck to that.

His tone made Rose say gaily: "Perhaps you do so yet?"

"I can't tell till I've seen more of your circumstances," he replied with eminent honesty.

The girl stared; her light laugh filled the air. "And it's in order to see more of them and judge that you wish to make my mother's acquaintance?"

He coloured at this and he evaded; then he broke out with a confused "Miss Tramore, let me stay with you a little!" which made her stop again.

"Your company will do us great honour, but there must be a rigid condition attached to our acceptance of it."

"Kindly mention it," said Captain Jay, staring at the façade of the cathedral.

"You don't take us on trial."

"On trial?"

"You don't make an observation to me—not a single one, ever, ever!—on the matter that, in Hill Street, we had our last words about."

Captain Jay appeared to be counting the thousand pinnacles of the church. "I think you really must be right," he remarked at last.

"There you are!" cried Rose Tramore, and walked rapidly away.

He caught up with her, he laid his hand upon her arm to stay her. "If you're going to Venice, let me go to Venice with you!"

"You don't even understand my condition."

"I'm sure you're right, then: you must be right about everything."

"That's not in the least true, and I don't care a fig whether you're sure or not. Please let me go."

He had barred her way, he kept her longer. "I'll go and speak to your mother myself!"

Even in the midst of another emotion she was amused at the air of audacity accompanying this declaration. Poor Captain Jay might have been on the point of marching up to a battery. She looked at him a moment; then she said: "You'll be disappointed!"

"Disappointed?"

"She's much more proper than grandmamma, because she's much more amiable!"

"Dear Miss Tramore—dear Miss Tramore!" the young man murmured helplessly.

"You'll see for yourself. Only there's another condition," Rose went on.

"Another?" he cried, with discouragement and alarm.

"You must understand thoroughly, before you throw in your lot with us even for a few days, what our position really is."

"Is it very bad?" asked Bertram Jay artlessly.

"No one has anything to do with us, no one speaks to us, no one looks at us."

"Really?" stared the young man.

"We've no social existence, we're utterly despised."

"Oh, Miss Tramore!" Captain Jay interposed. He added quickly, vaguely, and with a want of presence of mind of which he as quickly felt ashamed: "Do none of your family—?" The question collapsed; the brilliant girl was looking at him.

"We're extraordinarily happy," she threw out.

"Now that's all I wanted to know!" he exclaimed, with a kind of exaggerated cheery reproach, walking on with her briskly to overtake her mother.

He was not dining at their inn, but he insisted on coming that evening to their *table d'hôte*. He sat next Mrs Tramore, and in the evening he accompanied them gallantly to the opera, at a third-rate theatre where they were almost the only ladies in the boxes. The next day they went together by rail to the Charterhouse of Pavia, and while he strolled with the girl, as they waited for the homeward train, he said to her candidly: "Your mother's remarkably pretty." She remembered the words and the feeling they gave her: they were the first note of a new era. The feeling was somewhat that of an anxious, gratified matron who has "presented" her child and is thinking of the matrimonial market. Men might be of no use, as Mrs Tramore said, yet it was from this moment Rose dated the rosy dawn of her confidence that her *protégée* would go off; and when later, in crowded assemblies, the phrase, or something like it behind a hat or a fan, fell repeatedly on her anxious ear, "Your mother *is* in beauty!" or "I've never seen her look better!" she had a faint vision of the yellow sunshine and the afternoon shadows on the dusty Italian platform.

Mrs Tramore's behaviour at this period was a revelation of her native understanding of delicate situations. She needed no account of this one from her daughter—it was one of the things for which she had a scent; and there was a kind of loyalty to the rules of a game in the silent sweetness with which she smoothed the path of Bertram Jay. It was clear that she was in her element in fostering the exercise of the

affections, and if she ever spoke without thinking twice it is
probable that she would have exclaimed, with some gaiety,
"Oh, I know all about *love!*" Rose could see that she thought
their companion would be a help, in spite of his being no dis-
penser of patronage. The key to the gates of fashion had not
been placed in his hand, and no one had ever heard of the
ladies of his family, who lived in some vague hollow of the
Yorkshire moors; but none the less he might administer a
muscular push. Yes indeed, men in general were broken reeds,
but Captain Jay was peculiarly representative. Respectability
was the woman's maximum, as honour was the man's, but this
distinguished young soldier inspired more than one kind of
confidence. Rose had a great deal of attention for the use to
which his respectability was put; and there mingled with this
attention some amusement and much compassion. She saw
that after a couple of days he decidedly liked her mother, and
that he was yet not in the least aware of it. He took for
granted that he believed in her but little; notwithstanding
which he would have trusted her with anything except Rose
herself. His trusting her with Rose would come very soon.
He never spoke to her daughter about her qualities of character, but two or three of them (and indeed these were all the
poor lady had, and they made the best show) were what he
had in mind in praising her appearance. When he remarked:
"What attention Mrs Tramore seems to attract everywhere!"
he meant: "What a beautifully simple nature it is!" and when
he said: "There's something extraordinarily harmonious in
the colours she wears," it signified: "Upon my word, I never
saw such a sweet temper in my life!" She lost one of her
boxes at Verona, and made the prettiest joke of it to Captain
Jay. When Rose saw this she said to herself, "Next season we
shall have only to choose." Rose knew what was in the box.

By the time they reached Venice (they had stopped at half
a dozen little old romantic cities in the most frolicsome
æsthetic way) she liked their companion better than she had

ever liked him before. She did him the justice to recognise that if he was not quite honest with himself he was at least wholly honest with *her*. She reckoned up everything he had been since he joined them, and put upon it all an interpretation so favourable to his devotion that, catching herself in the act of glossing over one or two episodes that had not struck her at the time as disinterested she exclaimed, beneath her breath, "Look out—you're falling in love!" But if he liked correctness wasn't he quite right? Could any one possibly like it more than *she* did? And if he had protested against her throwing in her lot with her mother, this was not because of the benefit conferred but because of the injury received. He exaggerated that injury, but this was the privilege of a lover perfectly willing to be selfish on behalf of his mistress. He might have wanted her grandmother's money for her, but if he had given her up on first discovering that she was throwing away her chance of it (oh, this was *her* doing too!) he had given up her grandmother as much: not keeping well with the old woman, as some men would have done; not waiting to see how the perverse experiment would turn out and appeasing her, if it should promise tolerably, with a view to future operations. He had had a simple-minded, evangelical, lurid view of what the girl he loved would find herself in for. She could see this now—she could see it from his present bewilderment and mystification, and she liked him and pitied him, with the kindest smile, for the original *naïveté* as well as for the actual meekness. No wonder he hadn't known what she was in for, since he now didn't even know what he was in for himself. Were there not moments when he thought his companions almost unnaturally good, almost suspiciously safe? He had lost all power to verify that sketch of their isolation and *déclassement* to which she had treated him on the great square at Milan. The last thing he noticed was that they were neglected, and he had never, for himself, had such an impression of society.

It could scarcely be enhanced even by the apparition of a large, fair, hot, red-haired young man, carrying a lady's fan in his hand, who suddenly stood before their little party as, on the third evening after their arrival in Venice, it partook of ices at one of the tables before the celebrated Café Florian. The lamplit Venetian dusk appeared to have revealed them to this gentleman as he sat with other friends at a neighbouring table, and he had sprung up, with unsophisticated glee, to shake hands with Mrs Tramore and her daughter. Rose recalled him to her mother, who looked at first as though she didn't remember him but presently bestowed a sufficiently gracious smile on Mr Guy Mangler. He gave with youthful candour the history of his movements and indicated the whereabouts of his family: he was with his mother and sisters; they had met the Bob Veseys, who had taken Lord Whiteroy's yacht and were going to Constantinople. His mother and the girls, poor things, were at the Grand Hotel, but he was on the yacht with the Veseys, where they had Lord Whiteroy's cook. Wasn't the food in Venice filthy, and wouldn't they come and look at the yacht? She wasn't very fast, but she was awfully jolly. His mother might have come if she would, but she wouldn't at first, and now, when she wanted to, there were other people, who naturally wouldn't turn out for her. Mr Mangler sat down; he alluded with artless resentment to the way, in July, the door of his friends had been closed to him. He was going to Constantinople, but he didn't care—if *they* were going anywhere; meanwhile his mother hoped awfully they would look her up.

Lady Maresfield, if she had given her son any such message, which Rose disbelieved, entertained her hope in a manner compatible with her sitting for half an hour, surrounded by her little retinue, without glancing in the direction of Mrs Tramore. The girl, however, was aware that this was not a good enough instance of their humiliation; inasmuch as it was rather she who, on the occasion of their last contact, had held off from Lady Maresfield. She was a little ashamed now of not having answered the note in which this affable personage ignored her mother. She couldn't help perceiving indeed a dim movement on the part of some of the other members of the group; she made out an attitude of observation in the high-plumed head of Mrs Vaughan-Vesey. Mrs Vesey, perhaps, might have been looking at Captain Jay, for as this gentleman walked back to the hotel with our young lady (they were at the "Britannia," and young Mangler, who clung to them, went in front with Mrs Tramore) he revealed to Rose that he had some acquaintance with Lady Maresfield's eldest daughter, though he didn't know and didn't particularly want to know, her ladyship. He expressed himself with more acerbity than she had ever heard him use (Christian charity so generally governed his speech) about the young donkey who had been prattling to them. They separated at the door of the hotel. Mrs Tramore had got rid of Mr Mangler, and Bertram Jay was in other quarters.

"If you know Mrs Vesey, why didn't you go and speak to her? I'm sure she saw you," Rose said.

Captain Jay replied even more circumspectly than usual. "Because I didn't want to leave you."

"Well, you can go now; you're free," Rose rejoined.

"Thank you. I shall never go again."

"That won't be civil," said Rose.

"I don't care to be civil. I don't like her."

"Why don't you like her?"

"You ask too many questions."

"I know I do," the girl acknowledged.

Captain Jay had already shaken hands with her, but at this he put out his hand again. "She's too worldly," he murmured, while he held Rose Tramore's a moment.

"Ah, you dear!" Rose exclaimed almost audibly as, with her mother, she turned away.

The next morning, upon the Grand Canal, the gondola of

8:H

our three friends encountered a stately barge which, though it contained several persons, seemed pervaded mainly by one majestic presence. During the instant the gondolas were passing each other it was impossible either for Rose Tramore or for her companions not to become conscious that this distinguished identity had markedly inclined itself—a circumstance commemorated the next moment, almost within earshot of the other boat, by the most spontaneous cry that had issued for many a day from the lips of Mrs Tramore. "Fancy, my dear, Lady Maresfield has bowed to us!"

"We ought to have returned it," Rose answered; but she looked at Bertram Jay, who was opposite to her. He blushed, and she blushed, and during this moment was born a deeper understanding than had yet existed between these associated spirits. It had something to do with their going together that afternoon, without her mother, to look at certain out-of-the-way pictures as to which Ruskin had inspired her with a desire to see sincerely. Mrs Tramore expressed the wish to stay at home, and the motive of this wish—a finer shade than any that even Ruskin had ever found a phrase for—was not translated into misrepresenting words by either the mother or the daughter. At San Giovanni in Bragora the girl and her companion came upon Mrs Vaughan-Vesey, who, with one of her sisters, was also endeavouring to do the earnest thing. She did it to Rose, she did it to Captain Jay, as well as to Gianbellini; she was a handsome, long-necked, aquiline person, of a different type from the rest of her family, and she did it remarkably well. She secured our friends—it was her own expression—for luncheon, on the morrow, on the yacht, and she made it public to Rose that she would come that afternoon to invite her mother. When the girl returned to the hotel, Mrs Tramore mentioned, before Captain Jay, who had come up to their sitting-room, that Lady Maresfield had called. "She stayed a long time—at least it seemed long!" laughed Mrs Tramore.

The poor lady could laugh freely now; yet there was some grimness in a colloquy that she had with her daughter after Bertram Jay had departed. Before this happened Mrs Vesey's card, scrawled over in pencil and referring to the morrow's luncheon, was brought up to Mrs Tramore.

"They mean it all as a bribe," said the principal recipient of these civilities.

"As a bribe?" Rose repeated.

"She wants to marry you to that boy; they've seen Captain Jay and they're frightened."

"Well, dear mamma, I can't take Mr Mangler for a husband."

"Of course not. But oughtn't we to go to the luncheon?"

"Certainly we'll go to the luncheon," Rose said; and when the affair took place, on the morrow, she could feel for the first time that she was taking her mother out. This appearance was somehow brought home to every one else, and it was really the agent of her success. For it is of the essence of this simple history that, in the first place, her success dated from Mrs Vesey's Venetian *déjeuner*, and in the second reposed, by a subtle social logic, on the very anomaly that had made it dubious. There is always a chance in things, and Rose Tramore's chance was in the fact that Gwendolen Vesey was, as some one had said, awfully modern, an immense improvement on the exploded science of her mother, and capable of seeing what a "draw" there would be in the comedy, if properly brought out, of the reversed positions of Mrs Tramore and Mrs Tramore's diplomatic daughter. With a first-rate managerial eye she perceived that people would flock into any room—and all the more into one of hers—to see Rose bring in her dreadful mother. She treated the cream of English society to this thrilling spectacle later in the autumn, when she once more "secured" both the performers for a week at Brimble. It made a hit on the spot, the very first evening—the girl was felt to play her part so well. The rumour of the performance spread; every one wanted to see it. It was an entertainment of which, that winter in the country, and the next season in town, persons of taste desired to give their friends the freshness. The thing was to make the Tramores come late, after every one had arrived. They were engaged for a fixed hour, like the American imitator and the Patagonian contralto. Mrs Vesey had been the first to say the girl was awfully original, but that became the general view.

Gwendolen Vesey had with her mother one of the few quarrels in which Lady Maresfield had really stood up to such an antagonist (the elder woman had to recognise in general in whose veins it was that the blood of the Manglers flowed) on account of this very circumstance of her attaching more importance to Miss Tramore's originality ("Her originality be hanged!" her ladyship had gone so far as unintelligently to exclaim) than to the prospects of the unfortunate Guy. Mrs Vesey actually lost sight of these pressing problems in her admiration of the way the mother and the daughter, or rather the daughter and the mother (it was slightly confusing) "drew." It was Lady Maresfield's version of the case that the brazen girl (she was shockingly coarse) had treated poor Guy abominably. At any rate it was made known, just after Easter, that Miss Tramore was to be married to Captain Jay. The marriage was not to take place till the summer; but Rose felt that before this the field would practically be won. There had been some bad moments, there had been several warm corners and a certain number of cold shoulders and closed doors and stony stares; but the breach was effectually made—the rest was only a question of time. Mrs Tramore could be trusted to keep what she had gained, and it was the dowagers, the old dragons with prominent fangs and glittering scales, whom the trick had already mainly caught. By this time there were several houses into which the liberated lady had crept alone. Her daughter had been expected with her, but they couldn't turn her out because the girl had stayed behind, and she was fast acquiring a new identity, that of a parental connection with the heroine of such a romantic story. She was at least the next best thing to her daughter, and Rose foresaw the day when she would be valued principally as a memento of one of the prettiest episodes in the annals of London. At a big official party, in June, Rose had the joy of introducing Eric to his mother. She was a little sorry it was an official party—there were some other such queer people there; but Eric called, observing the shade, the next day but one.

No observer, probably, would have been acute enough to fix exactly the moment at which the girl ceased to take out her mother and began to be taken out by her. A later phase was more distinguishable—that at which Rose forbore to inflict on her companion a duality that might become oppressive. She began to economise her force, she went only when the particular effect was required. Her marriage was delayed by the period of mourning consequent upon the death of her grandmother, who, the younger Mrs Tramore averred, was killed by the rumour of her own new birth. She was the only one of the dragons who had not been tamed. Julia Tramore knew the truth about this—she was determined such things should not kill *her*. She would live to do something—she hardly knew what. The provisions of her mother's will were published in the "Illustrated News"; from which it appeared that everything that was not to go to Eric and to Julia was to go to the fortunate Edith. Miss Tramore makes no secret of her own intentions as regards this favourite. Edith is not pretty, but Lady Maresfield is waiting for her; she is determined Gwendolen Vesey shall not get hold of her. Mrs Vesey however takes no interest in her at all. She is whimsical, as befits a woman of her fashion; but there are two persons she is still very fond of, the delightful Bertram Jays. The fondness of this pair, it must be added, is not wholly expended in return. They are extremely united, but their life is more domestic than might have been expected from the preliminary signs. It owes a portion of its concentration to the fact that Mrs Tramore has now so many places to go to that she has almost no time to come to her daughter's. She is, under her son-in-law's roof, a brilliant but a rare apparition, and the other day he remarked upon the circumstance to his wife.

"If it hadn't been for you," she replied, smiling, "she might have had her regular place at our fireside."

"Good heavens, how did I prevent it?" cried Captain Jay, with all the consciousness of virtue.

"You ordered it otherwise, you goose!" And she says, in the same spirit, whenever her husband commends her (which he does, sometimes, extravagantly) for the way she launched her mother: "Nonsense, my dear—practically it was *you!*"

NONA VINCENT

I

"I WONDERED whether you wouldn't read it to me," said
Mrs Alsager, as they lingered a little near the fire before he
took leave. She looked down at the fire sideways, drawing her
dress away from it and making her proposal with a shy sincerity that added to her charm. Her charm was always great
for Allan Wayworth, and the whole air of her house, which
was simply a sort of distillation of herself, so soothing, so
beguiling that he always made several false starts before
departure. He had spent some such good hours there, had
forgotten, in her warm, golden drawing-room, so much of the
loneliness and so many of the worries of his life, that it had
come to be the immediate answer to his longings, the cure for
his aches, the harbour of refuge from his storms. His tribula-
tions were not unprecedented, and some of his advantages, if
of a usual kind, were marked in degree, inasmuch as he was
very clever for one so young, and very independent for one so
poor. He was eight-and-twenty, but he had lived a good deal
and was full of ambitions and curiosities and disappointments.
The opportunity to talk of some of these in Grosvenor Place
corrected perceptibly the immense inconvenience of London.
This inconvenience took for him principally the line of insensibility to Allan Wayworth's literary form. He had a
literary form, or he thought he had, and her intelligent recognition of the circumstance was the sweetest consolation Mrs
Alsager could have administered. She was even more literary
and more artistic than he, inasmuch as he could often work off
his overflow (this was his occupation, his profession), while
the generous woman, abounding in happy thoughts, but

68

inedited and unpublished, stood there in the rising tide like
the nymph of a fountain in the plash of the marble basin.

The year before, in a big newspapery house, he had found
himself next her at dinner, and they had converted the intensely material hour into a feast of reason. There was no
motive for her asking him to come to see her but that she
liked him, which it was the more agreeable to him to perceive
as he perceived at the same time that she was exquisite. She
was enviably free to act upon her likings, and it made Wayworth feel less unsuccessful to infer that for the moment he
happened to be one of them. He kept the revelation to himself, and indeed there was nothing to turn his head in the
kindness of a kind woman. Mrs Alsager occupied so completely the ground of possession that she would have been
condemned to inaction had it not been for the principle of
giving. Her husband, who was twenty years her senior, a
massive personality in the City and a heavy one at home
(wherever he stood, or even sat, he was monumental), owned
half a big newspaper and the whole of a great many other
things. He admired his wife, though she bore no children, and
liked her to have other tastes than his, as that seemed to give a
greater acreage to their life. His own appetites went so far he
could scarcely see the boundary, and his theory was to trust her
to push the limits of hers, so that between them the pair should
astound by their consumption. His ideas were prodigiously
vulgar, but some of them had the good fortune to be carried
out by a person of perfect delicacy. Her delicacy made her
play strange tricks with them, but he never found this out. She
attenuated him without his knowing it, for what he mainly
thought was that he had aggrandised *her*. Without her he really
would have been bigger still, and society, breathing more
freely, was practically under an obligation to her which, to do
it justice, it acknowledged by an attitude of mystified respect.
She felt a tremulous need to throw her liberty and her leisure
into the things of the soul—the most beautiful things she

knew. She found them, when she gave time to seeking, in a hundred places, and particularly in a dim and sacred region—the region of active pity—over her entrance into which she dropped curtains so thick that it would have been an impertinence to lift them. But she cultivated other beneficent passions, and if she cherished the dream of something fine the moments at which it most seemed to her to come true were when she saw beauty plucked flower-like in the garden of art. She loved the perfect work—she had the artistic chord. This chord could vibrate only to the touch of another, so that appreciation, in her spirit, had the added intensity of regret. She could understand the joy of creation, and she thought it scarcely enough to be told that she herself created happiness. She would have liked, at any rate, to choose her way; but it was just here that her liberty failed her. She had not the voice—she had only the vision. The only envy she was capable of was directed to those who, as she said, could do something.

As everything in her, however, turned to gentleness, she was admirably hospitable to such people as a class. She believed Allan Wayworth could do something, and she liked to hear him talk of the ways in which he meant to show it. He talked of them almost to no one else—she spoiled him for other listeners. With her fair bloom and her quiet grace she was indeed an ideal public, and if she had ever confided to him that she would have liked to scribble (she had in fact not mentioned it to a creature), he would have been in a perfect position for asking her why a woman whose face had so much expression should not have felt that she achieved. How in the world could she express better? There was less than that in Shakespeare and Beethoven. She had never been more generous than when, in compliance with her invitation, which I have recorded, he brought his play to read to her. He had spoken of it to her before, and one dark November afternoon, when her red fireside was more than ever an escape from the place and the season, he had broken out as he came in—"I've done it, I've done it!" She made him tell her all about it—she took an interest really minute and asked questions delightfully apt. She had spoken from the first as if he were on the point of being acted, making him jump, with her participation, all sorts of dreary intervals. She liked the theatre as she liked all the arts of expression, and he had known her to go all the way to Paris for a particular performance. Once he had gone with her—the time she took that stupid Mrs Mostyn. She had been struck, when he sketched it, with the subject of his drama, and had spoken words that helped him to believe in it. As soon as he had rung down his curtain on the last act he rushed off to see her, but after that he kept the thing for repeated last touches. Finally, on Christmas day, by arrangement, she sat there and listened to it. It was in three acts and in prose, but rather of the romantic order, though dealing with contemporary English life, and he fondly believed that it showed the hand if not of the master, at least of the prize pupil.

Allan Wayworth had returned to England, at two-and-twenty, after a miscellaneous continental education; his father, the correspondent, for years, in several foreign countries successively, of a conspicuous London journal, had died just after this, leaving his mother and her two other children, portionless girls, to subsist on a very small income in a very dull German town. The young man's beginnings in London were difficult, and he had aggravated them by his dislike of journalism. His father's connection with it would have helped him, but he was (insanely, most of his friends judged— the great exception was always Mrs Alsager) *intraitable* on the question of form. Form—in his sense—was not demanded by English newspapers, and he couldn't give it to them in *their* sense. The demand for it was not great anywhere, and Wayworth spent costly weeks in polishing little compositions for magazines that didn't pay for style. The only person who paid for it was really Mrs Alsager: she had an infallible instinct for the perfect. She paid in her own way, and if Allan Wayworth had been a wage-earning person it would have made him feel that if he didn't receive his legal dues his palm was at least occasionally conscious of a gratuity. He had his limitations, his perversities, but the finest parts of him were the most alive, and he was restless and sincere. It is however the impression he produced on Mrs Alsager that most concerns us: she thought him not only remarkably good-looking but altogether original. There were some usual bad things he would never do—too many prohibitive puddles for him in the short cut to success.

For himself, he had never been so happy as since he had seen his way, as he fondly believed, to some sort of mastery of the scenic idea, which struck him as a very different matter now that he looked at it from within. He had had his early days of contempt for it, when it seemed to him a jewel, dim at the best, hidden in a dunghill, a taper burning low in an air thick with vulgarity. It was hedged about with sordid approaches, it was not worth sacrifice and suffering. The man of letters, in dealing with it, would have to put off all literature, which was like asking the bearer of a noble name to forego his immemorial heritage. Aspects change, however, with the point of view: Wayworth had waked up one morning in a different bed altogether. It is needless here to trace this accident to its source; it would have been much more interesting to a spectator of the young man's life to follow some of the consequences. He had been made (as he felt) the subject of a special revelation, and he wore his hat like a man in love. An angel had taken him by the hand and guided him to the shabby door which opens, it appears, into an interior both splendid and austere. The scenic idea was magnificent when once you had embraced it—the dramatic form had a purity which made some others look ingloriously rough. It had the high dignity of the exact sciences, it was mathematical and architectural. It was full of the refreshment of calculation and construction, the incorruptibility of line and law. It was bare, but it was erect, it was poor, but it was noble; it reminded him of some sovereign famed for justice who should have lived in a palace despoiled. There was a fearful amount of concession in it, but what you kept had a rare intensity. You were perpetually throwing over the cargo to save the ship, but what a motion you gave her when you made her ride the waves—a motion as rhythmic as the dance of a goddess! Wayworth took long London walks and thought of these things—London poured into his ears the mighty hum of its suggestion. His imagination glowed and melted down material, his intentions multiplied and made the air a golden haze. He saw not only the thing he should do, but the next and the next and the next; the future opened before him and he seemed to walk on marble slabs. The more he tried the dramatic form the more he loved it, the more he looked at it the more he perceived in it. What he perceived in it indeed he now perceived everywhere; if he stopped, in the London dusk, before some flaring shop-window, the place immediately constituted itself behind footlights, became a framed stage for his figures. He hammered at these figures in his lonely lodging, he shaped them and he shaped their tabernacle; he was like a goldsmith chiselling a casket, bent over with the passion for perfection. When he was neither roaming the streets with his vision nor worrying his problem at his table, he was exchanging ideas on the general question with Mrs Alsager, to whom he promised details that would amuse her in later and still happier hours. Her eyes were full of tears when he read her the last words of the finished work, and she murmured, divinely—

"And now—to get it done, to get it done!"

"Yes, indeed—to get it done!" Wayworth stared at the fire, slowly rolling up his type-copy. "But that's a totally different part of the business, and altogether secondary."

"But of course you want to be acted?"

"Of course I do—but it's a sudden descent. I want to intensely, but I'm sorry I want to."

"It's there indeed that the difficulties begin," said Mrs Alsager, a little off her guard.

"How can you say that? It's there that they end!"

"Ah, wait to see where they end!"

"I mean they'll now be of a totally different order," Wayworth explained. "It seems to me there can be nothing in the world more difficult than to write a play that will stand an all-round test, and that in comparison with them the complications that spring up at this point are of an altogether smaller kind."

"Yes, they're not inspiring," said Mrs Alsager; "they're discouraging, because they're vulgar. The other problem, the working out of the thing itself, is pure art."

"How well you understand everything!" The young man had got up, nervously, and was leaning against the chimney-piece with his back to the fire and his arms folded. The roll of his copy, in his fist, was squeezed into the hollow of one of them. He looked down at Mrs Alsager, smiling gratefully, and she answered him with a smile from eyes still charmed and suffused. "Yes, the vulgarity will begin now," he presently added.

"You'll suffer dreadfully."

"I shall suffer in a good cause."

"Yes, giving *that* to the world! You must leave it with me, I must read it over and over," Mrs Alsager pleaded, rising to come nearer and draw the copy, in its cover of greenish-grey paper, which had a generic identity now to him, out of his grasp. "Who in the world will do it?—who in the world *can?*" she went on, close to him, turning over the leaves. Before he could answer she had stopped at one of the pages; she turned the book round to him, pointing out a speech. "That's the most beautiful place—those lines are a perfection." He glanced at the spot she indicated, and she begged him to read them again—he had read them admirably before. He knew them by heart, and, closing the book while she held the other end of it, he murmured them over to her—they had indeed a cadence that pleased him—watching, with a facetious complacency which he hoped was pardonable, the applause in her face. "Ah, who can utter such lines as *that?*" Mrs Alsager broke out; "whom can you find to do *her?*"

"We'll find people to do them all!"

"But not people who are worthy."

"They'll be worthy enough if they're willing enough. I'll work with them—I'll grind it into them." He spoke as if he had produced twenty plays.

"Oh, it will be interesting!" she echoed.

"But I shall have to find my theatre first. I shall have to get a manager to believe in me."

"Yes—they're so stupid!"

"But fancy the patience I shall want, and how I shall have to watch and wait," said Allan Wayworth. "Do you see me hawking it about London?"

"Indeed I don't—it would be sickening."

"It's what I shall have to do. I shall be old before it's produced."

"I shall be old very soon if it isn't!" Mrs Alsager cried. "I know one or two of them," she mused.

"Do you mean you would speak to them?"

"The thing is to get them to read it. I could do that."

"That's the utmost I ask. But it's even for that I shall have to wait."

She looked at him with kind sisterly eyes. "You sha'n't wait."

"Ah, you dear lady!" Wayworth murmured.

"That is *you* may, but *I* won't! Will you leave me your copy?" she went on, turning the pages again.

"Certainly; I have another." Standing near him she read to herself a passage here and there; then, in her sweet voice, she read some of them out. "Oh, if *you* were only an actress!" the young man exclaimed.

"That's the last thing I am. There's no comedy in *me!*"

She had never appeared to Wayworth so much his good genius. "Is there any tragedy?" he asked, with the levity of complete confidence.

She turned away from him, at this, with a strange and charming laugh and a "Perhaps that will be for you to determine!" But before he could disclaim such a responsibility she had faced him again and was talking about Nona Vincent as if she had been the most interesting of their friends and her situation at that moment an irresistible appeal to their sympathy. Nona Vincent was the heroine of the play, and Mrs Alsager had taken a tremendous fancy to her. "I can't *tell* you how I like that woman!" she exclaimed in a pensive rapture of credulity which could only be balm to the artistic spirit.

"I'm awfully glad she lives a bit. What I feel about her is that she's a good deal like *you*," Wayworth observed.

Mrs Alsager stared an instant and turned faintly red. This was evidently a view that failed to strike her; she didn't, however, treat it as a joke. "I'm not impressed with the resemblance. I don't see myself doing what she does."

"It isn't so much what she *does*," the young man argued, drawing out his moustache.

"But what she does is the whole point. She simply tells her love—I should never do that."

"If you repudiate such a proceeding with such energy, why do you like her for it?"

"It isn't what I like her for."

"What else, then? That's intensely characteristic."

Mrs Alsager reflected, looking down at the fire; she had the air of having half-a-dozen reasons to choose from. But the one she produced was unexpectedly simple; it might even have been prompted by despair at not finding others. "I like her because *you* made her!" she exclaimed with a laugh, moving again away from her companion.

Wayworth laughed still louder. "You made her a little yourself. I've thought of her as looking like you."

8:L

"She ought to look much better," said Mrs Alsager. "No, certainly, I shouldn't do what *she* does."

"Not even in the same circumstances?"

"I should never find myself in such circumstances. They're exactly your play, and have nothing in common with such a life as mine. However," Mrs Alsager went on, "her behaviour was natural for *her*, and not only natural, but, it seems to me, thoroughly beautiful and noble. I can't sufficiently admire the talent and tact with which you make one accept it, and I tell you frankly that it's evident to me there must be a brilliant future before a young man who, at the start, has been capable of such a stroke as that. Thank heaven I can admire Nona Vincent as intensely as I feel that I don't resemble her!"

"Don't exaggerate that," said Allan Wayworth.

"My admiration?"

"Your dissimilarity. She has your face, your air, your voice, your motion; she has many elements of your being."

"Then she'll damn your play!" Mrs Alsager replied. They joked a little over this, though it was not in the tone of pleasantry that Wayworth's hostess soon remarked: "You've got your remedy, however: have her done by the right woman."

"Oh, have her 'done'—have her 'done'!" the young man gently wailed.

"I see what you mean, my poor friend. What a pity, when it's such a magnificent part—such a chance for a clever serious girl! Nona Vincent is practically your play—it will be open to her to carry it far or to drop it at the first corner."

"It's a charming prospect," said Allan Wayworth, with sudden scepticism. They looked at each other with eyes that, for a lurid moment, saw the worst of the worst; but before they parted they had exchanged vows and confidences that were dedicated wholly to the ideal. It is not to be supposed, however, that the knowledge that Mrs Alsager would help him made Wayworth less eager to help himself. He did what he could and felt that she, on her side, was doing no less; but at the end of a year he was obliged to recognise that their united effort had mainly produced the fine flower of discouragement. At the end of a year the lustre had, to his own eyes, quite faded from his unappreciated masterpiece, and he found himself writing for a biographical dictionary little lives of celebrities he had never heard of. To be printed, anywhere and anyhow, was a form of glory for a man so unable to be acted, and to be paid, even at encyclopædic rates, had the consequence of making one resigned and verbose. He couldn't smuggle style into a dictionary, but he could at least reflect that he had done his best to learn from the drama that it is a gross impertinence almost anywhere. He had knocked at the door of every theatre in London, and, at a ruinous expense, had multiplied type-copies of *Nona Vincent* to replace the neat transcripts that had descended into the managerial abyss. His play was not even declined—no such flattering intimation was given him that it had been read. What the managers would do for Mrs Alsager concerned him little today; the thing that was relevant was that they would do nothing for *him*. That charming woman felt humbled to the earth, so little response had she had from the powers on which she counted. The two never talked about the play now, but he tried to show her a still finer friendship, that she might not think he felt she had failed him. He still walked about London with his dreams, but as months succeeded months and he left the year behind him they were dreams not so much of success as of revenge. Success seemed a colourless name for the reward of his patience; something fiercely florid, something sanguinolent was more to the point. His best consolation however was still in the scenic idea; it was not till now that he discovered how incurably he was in love with it. By the time a vain second year had chafed itself away he cherished his fruitless faculty the more for the obloquy it seemed to suffer. He lived, in his best hours, in a world of subjects and situations; he wrote another play and made it as different from its predecessor as such a very good thing could be. It might be a very good thing, but when he had committed it to the theatrical limbo indiscriminating fate took no account of the difference. He was at last able to leave England for three or four months; he went to Germany to pay a visit long deferred to his mother and sisters.

Shortly before the time he had fixed for his return he received from Mrs Alsager a telegram consisting of the words: "Loder wishes see you—putting *Nona* instant rehearsal." He spent the few hours before his departure in kissing his mother and sisters, who knew enough about Mrs Alsager to judge it lucky this respectable married lady was not there—a relief, however, accompanied with speculative glances at London and the morrow. Loder, as our young man was aware, meant the new "Renaissance," but though he reached home in the evening it was not to this convenient modern theatre that Wayworth first proceeded. He spent a late hour with Mrs Alsager, an hour that throbbed with calculation. She told him that Mr Loder was charming, he had simply taken up the play in its turn; he had hopes of it, moreover, that on the part of a professional pessimist might almost be qualified as ecstatic. It had been cast, with a margin for objections, and Violet Grey was to do the heroine. She had been capable, while he was away, of a good piece of work at that foggy old playhouse the "Legitimate;" the piece was a clumsy *réchauffé*, but she at least had been fresh. Wayworth remembered Violet Grey—hadn't he, for two years, on a fond policy of "looking out," kept dipping into the London theatres to pick up prospective interpreters? He had not picked up many as yet, and this young lady at all events had never wriggled in his net. She was pretty and she was odd, but he had never prefigured her as Nona Vincent, nor indeed found himself attracted by what he already felt sufficiently launched in the profession to speak of as her artistic personality. Mrs Alsager was different—she declared that she had been struck not a little by some of her tones. The girl was interesting in the thing at the "Legitimate," and Mr Loder, who had his eye on her, described her as ambitious and intelligent. She wanted awfully to get on—and some of those ladies were so lazy! Wayworth was sceptical—he had seen Miss Violet Grey, who was terribly itinerant, in a dozen theatres but only in one aspect. Nona Vincent had a dozen aspects, but only one theatre; yet with what a feverish curiosity the young man promised himself to watch the actress on the morrow! Talking the matter over with Mrs Alsager now seemed the very stuff that rehearsal was made of. The near prospect of being acted laid a finger even on the lip of inquiry; he wanted to go on tiptoe till the first night, to make no condition but that they should speak his lines, and he felt that he wouldn't so much as raise an eyebrow at the scene-painter if he should give him an old oak chamber.

He became conscious, the next day, that his danger would be other than this, and yet he couldn't have expressed to himself what it would be. Danger was there, doubtless—danger was everywhere, in the world of art, and still more in the world of commerce; but what he really seemed to catch, for the hour, was the beating of the wings of victory. Nothing could undermine that, since it was victory simply to be acted. It would be victory even to be acted badly; a reflection that didn't prevent him, however, from banishing, in his politic optimism, the word "bad" from his vocabulary. It had no application, in the compromise of practice; it didn't apply even to his play, which he was conscious he had already outlived and as to which he foresaw that, in the coming weeks, frequent alarm would alternate, in his spirit, with frequent esteem. When he went down to the dusky daylit theatre (it arched over him like the temple of fame) Mr Loder, who was as charming as Mrs Alsager had announced, struck him as the genius of hospitality. The manager began to explain why, for so long, he had given no sign; but that was the last thing that interested Wayworth now, and he could never remember afterwards what reasons Mr Loder had enumerated. He liked, in the whole business of discussion and preparation, even the things he had thought he should probably dislike, and he revelled in those he had thought he should like. He watched Miss Violet Grey that evening with eyes that sought to penetrate her possibilities. She certainly had a few; they were qualities of voice and face, qualities perhaps even of intelligence; he sat there at any rate with a fostering, coaxing attention, repeating over to himself as convincingly as he could that she was not common—a circumstance all the more creditable as the part she was playing seemed to him desperately so. He perceived that this was why it pleased the audience; he divined that it was the part they enjoyed rather than the actress. He had a private panic, wondering how, if they liked *that* form, they could possibly like his. His form had now become quite an ultimate idea to him. By the time the evening was over some of Miss Violet Grey's features, several of the turns of her head, a certain vibration of her voice, had taken their place in the same category. She *was* interesting, she was distinguished; at any rate he had accepted her: it came to the same thing. But he left the theatre that night without speaking to her—moved (a little even to his own mystification) by an odd procrastinating impulse. On the morrow he was to read his three acts to the company, and then he should have a good deal to say; what he felt for the moment was a vague indisposition to commit himself. Moreover he found a slight confusion of annoyance in the fact that though he had been trying all the evening to look at Nona Vincent in Violet Grey's person, what subsisted in his vision was simply Violet Grey in Nona's. He didn't wish to see the actress so directly, or even so simply as that; and it had been very fatiguing, the effort to focus Nona both through the performer and through the "Legitimate." Before he went to bed that night he posted three words to Mrs Alsager—"She's not a bit like it, but I dare say I can make her do."

He was pleased with the way the actress listened, the next day, at the reading; he was pleased indeed with many things, at the reading, and most of all with the reading itself. The whole affair loomed large to him and he magnified it and mapped it out. He enjoyed his occupation of the big, dim, hollow theatre, full of the echoes of "effect" and of a queer smell of gas and success—it all seemed such a passive canvas for his picture. For the first time in his life he was in command of resources; he was acquainted with the phrase, but had never thought he should know the feeling. He was surprised at what Loder appeared ready to do, though he reminded himself that he must never show it. He foresaw that there would be two distinct concomitants to the artistic effort of producing a play, one consisting of a great deal of anguish and the other of a great deal of amusement. He looked back upon the reading, afterwards, as the best hour in the business, because it was then that the piece had most struck him as represented. What came later was the doing of others; but this, with its imperfections and failures, was all his own. The drama lived, at any rate, for that hour, with an intensity that it was promptly to lose in the poverty and patchiness of rehearsal; he could see its life reflected, in a way that was sweet to him, in the stillness of the little semi-circle of attentive and inscrutable, of water-proofed and muddy-booted, actors. Miss Violet Grey was the auditor he had most to say to, and he tried on the spot, across the shabby stage, to let her have the soul of her part. Her attitude was graceful, but though she appeared to listen with all her faculties her face remained perfectly blank; a fact, however, not discouraging to Wayworth, who liked her better for not being premature. Her companions gave discernible signs of recognising the passages of comedy; yet Wayworth forgave her even then for being inexpressive. She evidently wished before everything else to be simply sure of what it was all about.

He was more surprised even than at the revelation of the scale on which Mr Loder was ready to proceed by the discovery that some of the actors didn't like their parts, and his heart sank as he asked himself what he could possibly do with them if they were going to be so stupid. This was the first of his disappointments; somehow he had expected every individual to become instantly and gratefully conscious of a rare opportunity, and from the moment such a calculation failed he was at sea, or mindful at any rate that more disappointments would come. It was impossible to make out what the manager liked or disliked; no judgment, no comment escaped him; his acceptance of the play and his views about the way it should be mounted had apparently converted him into a veiled and shrouded figure. Wayworth was able to grasp the idea that they would all move now in a higher and sharper air than that of compliment and confidence. When he talked with Violet Grey after the reading he gathered that she was really rather crude: what better proof of it could there be than her failure to break out instantly with an expression of delight about her great chance? This reserve, however, had evidently nothing to do with high pretensions; she had no wish to make him feel that a person of her eminence was superior to easy raptures. He guessed, after a little, that she was puzzled and even somewhat frightened—to a certain extent she had not understood. Nothing could appeal to him more than the opportunity to clear up her difficulties, in the course of the examination of which he quickly discovered that, so far as she *had* understood, she had understood wrong. If she was crude it was only a reason the more for talking to her; he kept saying to her "Ask me—ask me: ask me everything you can think of."

She asked him, she was perpetually asking him, and at the first rehearsals, which were without form and void to a degree that made them strike him much more as the death of an experiment than as the dawn of a success, they threshed things out immensely in a corner of the stage, with the effect of his coming to feel that at any rate she was in earnest. He felt more and more that his heroine was the keystone of his arch, for which indeed the actress was very ready to take her. But when he reminded this young lady of the way the whole thing practically depended on her she was alarmed and even slightly scandalised: she spoke more than once as if that could scarcely be the right way to construct a play—make it stand or fall by one poor nervous girl. She was almost morbidly conscientious, and in theory he liked her for this, though he lost patience three or four times with the things she couldn't do and the things she could. At such times the tears came to her eyes; but they were produced by her own stupidity, she hastened to assure him, not by the way he spoke, which was awfully kind under the circumstances. Her sincerity made her beautiful, and he wished to heaven (and made a point of telling her so) that she could sprinkle a little of it over Nona. Once, however, she was so touched and troubled that the sight of it brought the tears for an instant to his own eyes; and it so happened that, turning at this moment, he found himself face to face with Mr Loder. The manager stared, glanced at the actress, who turned in the other direction, and then smiling at Wayworth, exclaimed, with the humour of a man who heard the gallery laugh every night:

"I say—I say!"

"What's the matter?" Wayworth asked.

"I'm glad to see Miss Grey is taking such pains with you."

"Oh, yes—she'll turn me out!" said the young man, gaily. He was quite aware that it was apparent he was not superficial about Nona, and abundantly determined, into the bargain, that the rehearsal of the piece should not sacrifice a shade of thoroughness to any extrinsic consideration.

Mrs Alsager, whom, late in the afternoon, he used often to

go and ask for a cup of tea, thanking her in advance for the rest she gave him and telling her how he found that rehearsal (as *they* were doing it—it was a caution!) took it out of one—Mrs Alsager, more and more his good genius and, as he repeatedly assured her, his ministering angel, confirmed him in this superior policy and urged him on to every form of artistic devotion. She had, naturally, never been more interested than now in his work; she wanted to hear everything about everything. She treated him as heroically fatigued, plied him with luxurious restoratives, made him stretch himself on cushions and rose-leaves. They gossipped more than ever, by her fire, about the artistic life; he confided to her, for instance, all his hopes and fears, all his experiments and anxieties, on the subject of the representative of Nona. She was immensely interested in this young lady and showed it by taking a box again and again (she had seen her half-a-dozen times already), to study her capacity through the veil of her present part. Like Allan Wayworth she found her encouraging only by fits, for she had fine flashes of badness. She was intelligent, but she cried aloud for training, and the training was so absent that the intelligence had only a fraction of its effect. She was like a knife without an edge—good steel that had never been sharpened; she hacked away at her hard dramatic loaf, she couldn't cut it smooth.

II

"CERTAINLY my leading lady won't make Nona much like *you!*" Wayworth one day gloomily remarked to Mrs Alsager. There were days when the prospect seemed to him awful.

"So much the better. There's no necessity for that."

"I wish you'd train her a little—you could so easily," the young man went on; in response to which Mrs Alsager requested him not to make such cruel fun of her. But she was curious about the girl, wanted to hear of her character, her private situation, how she lived and where, seemed indeed desirous to befriend her. Wayworth might not have known much about the private situation of Miss Violet Grey, but, as it happened, he was able, by the time his play had been three weeks in rehearsal, to supply information on such points. She was a charming, exemplary person, educated, cultivated, with highly modern tastes, an excellent musician. She had lost her parents and was very much alone in the world, her only two relations being a sister, who was married to a civil servant (in a highly responsible post) in India, and a dear little old-fashioned aunt (really a great-aunt) with whom she lived at Notting Hill, who wrote children's books and who, it appeared, had once written a Christmas pantomime. It was quite an artistic home—not on the scale of Mrs Alsager's (to compare the smallest things with the greatest!) but intensely refined and honourable. Wayworth went so far as to hint that it would be rather nice and human on Mrs Alsager's part to go there—they would take it so kindly if she should call on them. She had acted so often on his hints that he had formed a pleasant habit of expecting it: it made him feel so wisely responsible about giving them. But this one appeared to fall to the ground, so that he let the subject drop. Mrs Alsager, however, went yet once more to the "Legitimate," as he found by her saying to him abruptly, on the morrow: "Oh, she'll be very good—she'll be very good." When they said "she," in these days, they always meant Violet Grey, though they pretended, for the most part, that they meant Nona Vincent.

"Oh yes," Wayworth assented, "she wants so to!"

Mrs Alsager was silent a moment; then she asked, a little inconsequently, as if she had come back from a reverie: "Does she want to *very* much?"

"Tremendously—and it appears she has been fascinated by the part from the first."

"Why then didn't she say so?"

"Oh, because she's so funny."

"She *is* funny," said Mrs Alsager, musingly; and presently she added: "She's in love with you."

Wayworth stared, blushed very red, then laughed out. "What is there funny in that?" he demanded; but before his interlocutress could satisfy him on this point he inquired, further, how she knew anything about it. After a little graceful evasion she explained that the night before, at the "Legitimate," Mrs Beaumont, the wife of the actor-manager, had paid her a visit in her box; which had happened, in the course of their brief gossip, to lead to her remarking that she had never been "behind." Mrs Beaumont offered on the spot to take her round, and the fancy had seized her to accept the invitation. She had been amused for the moment, and in this way it befell that her conductress, at her request, had introduced her to Miss Violet Grey, who was waiting in the wing for one of her scenes. Mrs Beaumont had been called away for three minutes, and during this scrap of time, face to face with the actress, she had discovered the poor girl's secret. Wayworth qualified it as a senseless thing, but wished to know what had led to the discovery. She characterised this inquiry as superficial for a painter of the ways of women; and he doubtless didn't improve it by remarking profanely that a cat might look at a king and that such things were convenient to know. Even on this ground, however, he was threatened by Mrs Alsager, who contended that it might not be a joking matter to the poor girl. To this Wayworth, who now professed to hate talking about the passions he might have inspired, could only reply that he meant it couldn't make a difference to Mrs Alsager.

"How in the world do you know what makes a difference to *me?*" this lady asked, with incongruous coldness, with a haughtiness indeed remarkable in so gentle a spirit.

He saw Violet Grey that night at the theatre, and it was

she who spoke first of her having lately met a friend of his.

"She's in love with you," the actress said, after he had made a show of ignorance; "doesn't that tell you anything?"

He blushed redder still than Mrs Alsager had made him blush, but replied, quickly enough and very adequately, that hundreds of women were naturally dying for him.

"Oh, I don't care, for you're not in love with *her!*" the girl continued.

"Did she tell you that too?" Wayworth asked; but she had at that moment to go on.

Standing where he could see her he thought that on this occasion she threw into her scene, which was the best she had in the play, a brighter art than ever before, a talent that could play with its problem. She was perpetually doing things out of rehearsal (she did two or three to-night, in the other man's piece), that he as often wished to heaven Nona Vincent might have the benefit of. She appeared to be able to do them for every one but him—that is for every one but Nona. He was conscious, in these days, of an odd new feeling, which mixed (this was a part of its oddity) with a very natural and comparatively old one and which in its most definite form was a dull ache of regret that this young lady's unlucky star should have placed her on the stage. He wished in his worst uneasiness that, without going further, she would give it up; and yet it soothed that uneasiness to remind himself that he saw grounds to hope she would go far enough to make a marked success of Nona. There were strange and painful moments when, as the interpretress of Nona, he almost hated her; after which, however, he always assured himself that he exaggerated, inasmuch as what made this aversion seem great, when he was nervous, was simply its contrast with the growing sense that there *were* grounds—totally different—on which she pleased him. She pleased him as a charming creature—by her sincerities and her perversities, by the varieties and surprises of her character and by certain happy facts of her person. In private her eyes were sad to him and her voice was rare. He detested the idea that she should have a disappointment or an humiliation, and he wanted to rescue her altogether, to save and transplant her. One way to save her was to see to it, to the best of his ability, that the production of his play should be a triumph; and the other way—it was really too queer to express—was almost to wish that it shouldn't be. Then, for the future, there would be safety and peace, and not the peace of death—the peace of a different life. It is to be added that our young man clung to the former of these ways in proportion as the latter perversely tempted him. He was nervous at the best, increasingly and intolerably nervous; but the immediate remedy was to rehearse harder and harder, and above all to work it out with Violet Grey. Some of her comrades reproached him with working it out only with her, as if she were the whole affair; to which he replied that they could afford to be neglected, they were all so tremendously good. She was the only person concerned whom he didn't flatter.

The author and the actress stuck so to the business in hand that she had very little time to speak to him again of Mrs Alsager, of whom indeed her imagination appeared adequately to have disposed. Wayworth once remarked to her that Nona Vincent was supposed to be a good deal like his charming friend; but she gave a blank "Supposed by whom?" in consequence of which he never returned to the subject. He confided his nervousness as freely as usual to Mrs Alsager, who easily understood that he had a peculiar complication of anxieties. His suspense varied in degree from hour to hour, but any relief there might have been in this was made up for by its being of several different kinds. One afternoon, as the first performance drew near, Mrs Alsager said to him, in giving him his cup of tea and on his having mentioned that he had not closed his eyes the night before:

"You must indeed be in a dreadful state. Anxiety for another is still worse than anxiety for one's self."

"For another?" Wayworth repeated, looking at her over the rim of his cup.

"My poor friend, you're nervous about Nona Vincent, but you're infinitely more nervous about Violet Grey."

"She *is* Nona Vincent!"

"No, she isn't—not a bit!" said Mrs Alsager, abruptly.

"Do you really think so?" Wayworth cried, spilling his tea in his alarm.

"What I think doesn't signify—I mean what I think about that. What I meant to say was that great as is your suspense about your play, your suspense about your actress is greater still."

"I can only repeat that my actress *is* my play."

Mrs Alsager looked thoughtfully into the teapot.

"Your actress is your—"

"My what?" the young man asked, with a little tremor in his voice, as his hostess paused.

"Your very dear friend. You're in love with her—at present." And with a sharp click Mrs Alsager dropped the lid on the fragrant receptacle.

"Not yet—not yet!" laughed her visitor.

"You will be if she pulls you through."

"You declare that she *won't* pull me through."

Mrs Alsager was silent a moment, after which she softly murmured: "I'll pray for her."

"You're the most generous of women!" Wayworth cried; then coloured as if the words had not been happy. They would have done indeed little honour to a man of tact.

The next morning he received five hurried lines from Mrs Alsager. She had suddenly been called to Torquay, to see a relation who was seriously ill; she should be detained there several days, but she had an earnest hope of being able to return in time for his first night. In any event he had her unrestricted good wishes. He missed her extremely, for these last days were a great strain and there was little comfort to be derived from Violet Grey. She was even more nervous than himself, and so pale and altered that he was afraid she would be too ill to act. It was settled between them that they made each other worse and that he had now much better leave her alone. They had pulled Nona so to pieecs that nothing seemed left of her—she must at least have time to grow together again. He left Violet Grey alone, to the best of his ability, but she carried out imperfectly her own side of the bargain. She came to him with new questions—she waited for him with old doubts, and half an hour before the last dress-rehearsal, on the eve of production, she proposed to him a totally fresh rendering of his heroine. This incident gave him such a sense of insecurity that he turned his back on her without a word, bolted out of the theatre, dashed along the Strand and walked as far as the Bank. Then he jumped into a hansom and came westward, and when he reached the theatre again the business was nearly over. It appeared, almost to his disappointment, not bad enough to give him the consolation of the old playhouse adage that the worst dress-rehearsals make the best first nights.

The morrow, which was a Wednesday, was the dreadful day; the theatre had been closed on the Monday and the Tuesday. Every one, on the Wednesday, did his best to let every one else alone, and every one signally failed in the attempt. The day, till seven o'clock, was understood to be consecrated to rest, but every one except Violet Grey turned up at the theatre. Wayworth looked at Mr Loder, and Mr Loder looked in another direction, which was as near as they came to conversation. Wayworth was in a fidget, unable to eat or sleep or sit still, at times almost in terror. He kept quiet by keeping, as usual, in motion; he tried to walk away from his nervousness. He walked in the afternoon toward Notting Hill, but he succeeded in not breaking the vow he had taken not to meddle with his actress. She was like an acrobat poised on a slippery ball—if he should touch her she would topple over. He passed her door three times and he thought of her three hundred. This was the hour at which he most regretted that Mrs Alsager had not come back—for he had called at her house only to learn that she was still at Torquay. This was probably queer, and it was probably queerer still that she hadn't written to him; but even of these things he wasn't sure, for in losing, as he had now completely lost, his judgment of his play, he seemed to himself to have lost his judgment of everything. When he went home, however, he found a telegram from the lady of Grosvenor Place—"Shall be able to come— reach town by seven." At half-past eight o'clock, through a little aperture in the curtain of the "Renaissance," he saw her in her box with a cluster of friends—completely beautiful and beneficent. The house was magnificent—too good for his play, he felt; too good for any play. Everything now seemed too good—the scenery, the furniture, the dresses, the very programmes. He seized upon the idea that this was probably what was the matter with the representative of Nona—she was only too good. He had completely arranged with this young lady the plan of their relations during the evening; and though they had altered everything else that they had arranged they had promised each other not to alter this. It was wonderful the number of things they had promised each other. He would start her, he would see her off—then he would quit the theatre and stay away till just before the end. She besought him to stay away—it would make her infinitely easier. He saw that she was exquisitely dressed—she had made one or two changes for the better since the night before, and that seemed something definite to turn over and over in his mind as he rumbled foggily home in the four-wheeler in which, a few steps from the stage-door, he had taken refuge as soon as he knew that the curtain was up. He lived a couple of miles off, and he had chosen a four-wheeler to drag out the time.

8:M

When he got home his fire was out, his room was cold, and he lay down on his sofa in his overcoat. He had sent his land-lady to the dress-circle, on purpose; she would overflow with words and mistakes. The house seemed a black void, just as the streets had done—every one was, formidably, at his play. He was quieter at last than he had been for a fortnight, and he felt too weak even to wonder how the thing was going. He believed afterwards that he had slept an hour; but even if he had he felt it to be still too early to return to the theatre. He sat down by his lamp and tried to read—to read a little com-pendious life of a great English statesman, out of a "series." It struck him as brilliantly clever, and he asked himself whether that perhaps were not rather the sort of thing he ought to have taken up; not the statesmanship, but the art of brief biography. Suddenly he became aware that he must hurry if he was to reach the theatre at all—it was a quarter to eleven o'clock. He scrambled out and, this time, found a hansom—he had lately spent enough money in cabs to add to his hope that the profits of his new profession would be great. His anxiety, his suspense flamed up again, and as he rattled eastward—he went fast now—he was almost sick with alter-nations. As he passed into the theatre the first man—some underling—who met him, cried to him, breathlessly: "You're wanted, sir—you're wanted!" He thought his tone very ominous—he devoured the man's eyes with his own, for a betrayal: did he mean that he was wanted for execution? Some one else pressed him, almost pushed him, forward; he was already on the stage. Then he became conscious of a sound more or less continuous, but seemingly faint and far, which he took at first for the voice of the actors heard through their canvas walls, the beautiful built-in room of the last act. But the actors were in the wing, they surrounded him; the curtain was down and they were coming off from before it. They had been called, and *he* was called—they all greeted him with "Go on—go on!" He was terrified—he couldn't go on—he didn't believe in the applause, which seemed to him only audible enough to sound half-hearted.

"Has it gone?—*has* it gone?" he gasped to the people round him; and he heard them say "Rather—rather!" perfunctorily, mendaciously too, as it struck him, and even with mocking laughter, the laughter of defeat and despair. Suddenly, though all this must have taken but a moment, Loder burst upon him from somewhere with a "For God's sake don't keep them, or they'll *stop!*" "But I can't go on for *that!*" Wayworth cried, in anguish; the sound seemed to him already to have ceased. Loder had hold of him and was shoving him; he resisted and looked round frantically for Violet Grey, who perhaps would tell him the truth. There was by this time a crowd in the wing, all with strange grimacing painted faces, but Violet was not among them and her very absence frightened him. He uttered her name with an accent that he afterwards regretted—it gave them, as he thought, both away; and while Loder hustled him before the curtain he heard some one say "She took her call and disappeared." She had had a call, then—this was what was most present to the young man as he stood for an instant in the glare of the footlights, looking blindly at the great vaguely-peopled horseshoe and greeted with plaudits which now seemed to him at once louder than he deserved and feebler than he desired. They sank to rest quickly, but he felt it to be long before he could back away, before he could, in his turn, seize the manager by the arm and cry huskily—"Has it really gone—*really?*"

Mr Loder looked at him hard and replied after an instant: "The play's all right!"

Wayworth hung upon his lips. "Then what's all wrong?"

"We must do something to Miss Grey."

"What's the matter with her?"

"She isn't *in* it!"

"Do you mean she has failed?"

"Yes, damn it—she has failed."

Wayworth stared. "Then how can the play be all right?"

"Oh, we'll save it—we'll save it."

"Where's Miss Grey—where *is* she?" the young man asked.

Loder caught his arm as he was turning away again to look for his heroine. "Never mind her now—she knows it!"

Wayworth was approached at the same moment by a gentleman he knew as one of Mrs Alsager's friends—he had perceived him in that lady's box. Mrs Alsager was waiting there for the successful author; she desired very earnestly that he would come round and speak to her. Wayworth assured himself first that Violet had left the theatre—one of the actresses could tell him that she had seen her throw on a cloak, without changing her dress, and had learnt afterwards that she had, the next moment, flung herself, after flinging her aunt, into a cab. He had wished to invite half a dozen persons, of whom Miss Grey and her elderly relative were two, to come home to supper with him; but she had refused to make any engagement beforehand (it would be so dreadful to have to keep it if she shouldn't have made a hit), and this attitude had blighted the pleasant plan, which fell to the ground. He had called her morbid, but she was immovable. Mrs Alsager's messenger let him know that he was expected to supper in Grosvenor Place, and half an hour afterwards he was seated there among complimentary people and flowers and popping corks, eating the first orderly meal he had partaken of for a week. Mrs Alsager had carried him off in her brougham—the other people who were coming got into things of their own. He stopped her short as soon as she began to tell him how tremendously every one had been struck by the piece; he nailed her down to the question of Violet Grey. Had she spoilt the play, had she jeopardised or compromised it—had she been utterly bad, had she been good in any degree?

"Certainly the performance would have seemed better if *she* had been better," Mrs Alsager confessed.

"And the play would have seemed better if the performance had been better," Wayworth said, gloomily, from the corner of the brougham.

"She does what she can, and she has talent, and she looked lovely. But she doesn't *see* Nona Vincent. She doesn't see the type—she doesn't see the individual—she doesn't see the woman you meant. She's out of it—she gives you a different person."

"Oh, the woman I meant!" the young man exclaimed, looking at the London lamps as he rolled by them. "I wish to God she had known *you!*" he added, as the carriage stopped. After they had passed into the house he said to his companion: "You see she·won't pull me through."

"Forgive her—be kind to her!" Mrs Alsager pleaded.

"I shall only thank her. The play may go to the dogs."

"If it does—if it does," Mrs Alsager began, with her pure eyes on him.

"Well, what if it does?"

She couldn't tell him, for the rest of her guests came in together; she only had time to say: "It *sha'n't* go to the dogs!"

He came away before the others, restless with the desire to go to Notting Hill even that night, late as it was, haunted with the sense that Violet Grey had measured her fall. When he got into the street, however, he allowed second thoughts to counsel another course; the effect of knocking her up at two o'clock in the morning would hardly be to soothe her. He looked at six newspapers the next day and found in them never a good word for her. They were well enough about the piece, but they were unanimous as to the disappointment caused by the young actress whose former efforts had excited such hopes and on whom, on this occasion, such pressing responsibilities rested. They asked in chorus what was the matter with her, and they declared in chorus that the play, which was not without promise, was handicapped (they all used the same word) by the odd want of correspondence between the heroine and her interpreter. Wayworth drove early to Notting Hill, but he didn't take the newspapers with him; Violet Grey could be trusted to have sent out for them by the peep of dawn and to have fed her anguish full. She declined to see him—she only sent down word by her aunt that she was extremely unwell and should be unable to act that night unless she were suffered to spend the day unmolested and in bed. Wayworth sat for an hour with the old lady, who understood everything and to whom he could speak frankly. She gave him a touching picture of her niece's condition, which was all the more vivid for the simple words in which it was expressed: "She feels she isn't right, you know—she feels she isn't right!"

"Tell her it doesn't matter—it doesn't matter a straw!" said Wayworth.

"And she's so proud—you know how proud she is!" the old lady went on.

"Tell her I'm more than satisfied, that I accept her gratefully as she is."

"She says she injures your play, that she ruins it," said his interlocutress.

"She'll improve, immensely—she'll grow into the part," the young man continued.

"She'd improve if she knew how—but she says she doesn't. She has given all she has got, and she doesn't know what's wanted."

"What's wanted is simply that she should go straight on and trust me."

"How can she trust you when she feels she's losing you?"

"Losing me?" Wayworth cried.

"You'll never forgive her if your play is taken off!"

"It will run six months," said the author of the piece.

The old lady laid her hand on his arm. "What will you do for her if it does?"

He looked at Violet Grey's aunt a moment. "Do you say your niece is very proud?"

"Too proud for her dreadful profession."

"Then she wouldn't wish you to ask me that," Wayworth answered, getting up.

When he reached home he was very tired, and for a person to whom it was open to consider that he had scored a success he spent a remarkably dismal day. All his restlessness had gone, and fatigue and depression possessed him. He sank into his old chair by the fire and sat there for hours with his eyes closed. His landlady came in to bring his luncheon and mend the fire, but he feigned to be asleep, so as not to be spoken to. It is to be supposed that sleep at last overtook him, for about the hour that dusk began to gather he had an extraordinary impression, a visit that, it would seem, could have belonged to no waking consciousness. Nona Vincent, in face and form, the living heroine of his play, rose before him in his little silent room, sat down with him at his dingy fireside. She was not Violet Grey, she was not Mrs Alsager, she was not any woman he had seen upon earth, nor was it any masquerade of friendship or of penitence. Yet she was more familiar to him than the women he had known best, and she was ineffably beautiful and consoling. She filled the poor room with her presence, the effect of which was as soothing as some odour of incense. She was as quiet as an affectionate sister, and there was no surprise in her being there. Nothing more real had ever befallen him, and nothing, somehow, more reassuring. He felt her hand rest upon his own, and all his senses seemed to open to her message. She struck him, in the strangest way, both as his creation and as his inspirer, and she gave him the happiest consciousness of success. If she was so charming, in the red firelight, in her vague, clear-coloured garments, it was because he had made her so, and yet if the weight seemed lifted from his spirit it was because she drew it away. When she bent her deep eyes upon him they seemed to speak of safety and freedom and to make a green garden of the future. From time to time she smiled and said: "I live—I live —I live." How long she stayed he couldn't have told, but when his landlady blundered in with the lamp Nona Vincent was no longer there. He rubbed his eyes, but no dream had ever been so intense; and as he slowly got out of his chair it was with a deep still joy—the joy of the artist—in the thought of how right he had been, how exactly like herself he had made her. She had come to show him that. At the end of five minutes, however, he felt sufficiently mystified to call his landlady back—he wanted to ask her a question. When the good woman reappeared the question hung fire an instant; then it shaped itself as the inquiry: "Has any lady been here?"

"No, sir—no lady at all."

The woman seemed slightly scandalised.

"Not Miss Vincent?"

"Miss Vincent, sir?"

"The young lady of my play, don't you know?"

"Oh, sir, you mean Miss Violet Grey!"

"No I don't, at all. I think I mean Mrs Alsager."

"There has been no Mrs Alsager, sir."

"Nor anybody at all like her?"

The woman looked at him as if she wondered what had suddenly taken him. Then she asked in an injured tone: "Why shouldn't I have told you if you'd 'ad callers, sir?"

"I thought you might have thought I was asleep."

"Indeed you were, sir, when I came in with the lamp—and well you'd earned it, Mr Wayworth!"

The landlady came back an hour later to bring him a telegram; it was just as he had begun to dress to dine at his club and go down to the theatre.

"See me to-night in front, and don't come near me till it's over."

It was in these words that Violet communicated her wishes

for the evening. He obeyed them to the letter; he watched her from the depths of a box. He was in no position to say how she might have struck him the night before, but what he saw during these charmed hours filled him with admiration and gratitude. She *was* in it, this time; she had pulled herself together, she had taken possession, she was felicitous at every turn. Fresh from his revelation of Nona he was in a position to judge, and as he judged he exulted. He was thrilled and carried away, and he was moreover intensely curious to know what had happened to her, by what unfathomable art she had managed in a few hours to effect such a change of base. It was as if *she* had had a revelation of Nona, so convincing a clearness had been breathed upon the picture. He kept himself quiet in the *entr'actes*—he would speak to her only at the end; but before the play was half over the manager burst into his box.

"It's prodigious, what she's up to!" cried Mr Loder, almost more bewildered than gratified. "She has gone in for a new reading—a blessed somersault in the air!"

"Is it quite different?" Wayworth asked, sharing his mystification.

"Different? Hyperion to a satyr! It's devilish good, my boy!"

"It's devilish good," said Wayworth, "and it's in a different key altogether from the key of her rehearsal."

"I'll run you six months!" the manager declared; and he rushed round again to the actress, leaving Wayworth with a sense that she had already pulled him through. She had with the audience an immense personal success.

When he went behind, at the end, he had to wait for her; she only showed herself when she was ready to leave the theatre. Her aunt had been in her dressing-room with her, and the two ladies appeared together. The girl passed him quickly, motioning him to say nothing till they should have got out of the place. He saw that she was immensely excited, lifted altogether above her common artistic level. The old lady said to him: "You must come home to supper with us: it has been all arranged." They had a brougham, with a little third seat, and he got into it with them. It was a long time before the actress would speak. She leaned back in her corner, giving no sign but still heaving a little, like a subsiding sea, and with all her triumph in the eyes that shone through the darkness. The old lady was hushed to awe, or at least to discretion, and Wayworth was happy enough to wait. He had really to wait till they had alighted at Notting Hill, where the elder of his companions went to see that supper had been attended to.

"I was better—I was better," said Violet Grey, throwing off her cloak in the little drawing-room.

"You were perfection. You'll be like that every night, won't you?"

She smiled at him. "Every night? There can scarcely be a miracle every day."

"What do you mean by a miracle?"

"I've had a revelation."

Wayworth stared. "At what hour?"

"The right hour—this afternoon. Just in time to save me—and to save *you*."

"At five o'clock? Do you mean you had a visit?"

"She came to me—she stayed two hours."

"Two hours? Nona Vincent?"

"Mrs Alsager." Violet Grey smiled more deeply. "It's the same thing."

"And how did Mrs Alsager save you?"

"By letting me look at her. By letting me hear her speak. By letting me know her."

"And what did she say to you?"

"Kind things—encouraging, intelligent things."

"Ah, the dear woman!" Wayworth cried.

"You ought to like her—she likes *you*. She was just what I wanted," the actress added.

"Do you mean she talked to you about Nona?"

"She said you thought she was like her. She *is*—she's exquisite."

"She's exquisite," Wayworth repeated. "Do you mean she tried to coach you?"

"Oh, no—she only said she would be so glad if it would help me to see her. And I felt it did help me. I don't know what took place—she only sat there, and she held my hand and smiled at me, and she had tact and grace, and she had goodness and beauty, and she soothed my nerves and lighted up my imagination. Somehow she seemed to *give* it all to me. I took it—I took it. I kept her before me, I drank her in. For the first time, in the whole study of the part, I had my model —I could make my copy. All my courage came back to me, and other things came that I hadn't felt before. She was different—she was delightful; as I've said, she was a revelation. She kissed me when she went away—and you may guess if I kissed *her*. We were awfully affectionate, but it's *you* she likes!" said Violet Grey.

Wayworth had never been more interested in his life, and he had rarely been more mystified. "Did she wear vague, clear-coloured garments?" he asked, after a moment.

Violet Grey stared, laughed, then bade him go in to supper. " *You* know how she dresses!"

He was very well pleased at supper, but he was silent and a little solemn. He said he would go to see Mrs Alsager the next day. He did so, but he was told at her door that she had returned to Torquay. She remained there all winter, all spring, and the next time he saw her his play had run two hundred nights and he had married Violet Grey. His plays sometimes succeed, but his wife is not in them now, nor in any others. At these representations Mrs Alsager continues frequently to be present.

THE MIDDLE YEARS

I

THE April day was soft and bright, and poor Dencombe, happy in the conceit of reasserted strength, stood in the garden of the hotel, comparing, with a deliberation in which, however, there was still something of languor, the attractions of easy strolls. He liked the feeling of the south, so far as you could have it in the north, he liked the sandy cliffs and the clustered pines, he liked even the colourless sea. "Bournemouth as a health-resort" had sounded like a mere advertisement, but now he was reconciled to the prosaic. The sociable country postman, passing through the garden, had just given him a small parcel, which he took out with him, leaving the hotel to the right and creeping to a convenient bench that he knew of, a safe recess in the cliff. It looked to the south, to the tinted walls of the Island, and was protected behind by the sloping shoulder of the down. He was tired enough when he reached it, and for a moment he was disappointed; he was better, of course, but better, after all, than what? He should never again, as at one or two great moments of the past, be better than himself. The infinite of life had gone, and what was left of the dose was a small glass engraved like a thermometer by the apothecary. He sat and stared at the sea, which appeared all surface and twinkle, far shallower than the spirit of man. It was the abyss of human illusion that was the real, the tideless deep. He held his packet, which had come by book-post, unopened on his knee, liking, in the lapse of so many joys (his illness had made him feel his age), to know that it was there, but taking for granted there could be no complete renewal of the pleasure,

dear to young experience, of seeing one's self "just out."
Dencombe, who had a reputation, had come out too often
and knew too well in advance how he should look.

His postponement associated itself vaguely, after a little,
with a group of three persons, two ladies and a young man,
whom, beneath him, straggling and seemingly silent, he could
see move slowly together along the sands. The gentleman had
his head bent over a book and was occasionally brought to a
stop by the charm of this volume, which, as Dencombe could
perceive even at a distance, had a cover alluringly red. Then
his companions, going a little further, waited for him to come
up, poking their parasols into the beach, looking around them
at the sea and sky and clearly sensible of the beauty of the day.
To these things the young man with the book was still more
clearly indifferent; lingering, credulous, absorbed, he was an
object of envy to an observer from whose connection with
literature all such artlessness had faded. One of the ladies was
large and mature; the other had the spareness of comparative
youth and of a social situation possibly inferior. The large
lady carried back Dencombe's imagination to the age of
crinoline; she wore a hat of the shape of a mushroom, decorated
with a blue veil, and had the air, in her aggressive amplitude, of
clinging to a vanished fashion or even a lost cause. Presently
her companion produced from under the folds of a mantle a
limp, portable chair which she stiffened out and of which the
large lady took possession. This act, and something in the
movement of either party, instantly characterised the performers—they performed for Dencombe's recreation—as opulent
matron and humble dependant. What, moreover, was the use
of being an approved novelist if one couldn't establish a
relation between such figures; the clever theory, for instance,
that the young man was the son of the opulent matron, and
that the humble dependant, the daughter of a clergyman or an
officer, nourished a secret passion for him? Was that not visible
from the way she stole behind her protectress to look back at

him?—back to where he had let himself come to a full stop when his mother sat down to rest. His book was a novel; it had the catchpenny cover, and while the romance of life stood neglected at his side he lost himself in that of the circulating library. He moved mechanically to where the sand was softer, and ended by plumping down in it to finish his chapter at his ease. The humble dependant, discouraged by his remoteness, wandered, with a martyred droop of the head, in another direction, and the exorbitant lady, watching the waves, offered a confused resemblance to a flying-machine that had broken down.

When his drama began to fail Dencombe remembered that he had, after all, another pastime. Though such promptitude on the part of the publisher was rare, he was already able to draw from its wrapper his "latest," perhaps his last. The cover of "The Middle Years" was duly meretricious, the smell of the fresh pages the very odour of sanctity; but for the moment he went no further—he had become conscious of a strange alienation. He had forgotten what his book was about. Had the assault of his old ailment, which he had so fallaciously come to Bournemouth to ward off, interposed utter blankness as to what had preceded it? He had finished the revision of proof before quitting London, but his subsequent fortnight in bed had passed the sponge over colour. He couldn't have chanted to himself a single sentence, couldn't have turned with curiosity or confidence to any particular page. His subject had already gone from him, leaving scarcely a superstition behind. He uttered a low moan as he breathed the chill of this dark void, so desperately it seemed to represent the completion of a sinister process. The tears filled his mild eyes; something precious had passed away. This was the pang that had been sharpest during the last few years—the sense of ebbing time, of shrinking opportunity; and now he felt not so much that his last chance was going as that it was gone indeed. He had done all that he should ever do, and yet he had not done what he wanted. This was the laceration—that practically his career was over: it was as violent as a rough hand at his throat. He rose from his seat nervously, like a creature hunted by a dread; then he fell back in his weakness and nervously opened his book. It was a single volume; he preferred single volumes and aimed at a rare compression. He began to read, and little by little, in this occupation, he was pacified and reassured. Everything came back to him, but came back with a wonder, came back, above all, with a high and magnificent beauty. He read his own prose, he turned his own leaves, and had, as he sat there with the spring sunshine on the page, an emotion peculiar and intense. His career was over, no doubt, but it was over, after all, with *that*.

He had forgotten during his illness the work of the previous year; but what he had chiefly forgotten was that it was extraordinarily good. He dived once more into his story and was drawn down, as by a siren's hand, to where, in the dim underworld of fiction, the great glazed tank of art, strange silent subjects float. He recognised his motive and surrendered to his talent. Never, probably, had that talent, such as it was, been so fine. His difficulties were still there, but what was also there, to his perception, though probably, alas! to nobody's else, was the art that in most cases had surmounted them. In his surprised enjoyment of this ability he had a glimpse of a possible reprieve. Surely its force was not spent—there was life and service in it yet. It had not come to him easily, it had been backward and roundabout. It was the child of time, the nursling of delay; he had struggled and suffered for it, making sacrifices not to be counted, and now that it was really mature was it to cease to yield, to confess itself brutally beaten? There was an infinite charm for Dencombe in feeling as he had never felt before that diligence *vincit omnia*. The result produced in his little book was somehow a result beyond his conscious intention: it was as if he had planted his genius, had trusted his method, and they had grown up and flowered with this sweetness. If the achievement had been real, however, the process had been painful enough. What he saw so intensely to-day, what he felt as a nail driven in, was that only now, at the very last, had he come into possession. His development had been abnormally slow, almost grotesquely gradual. He had been hindered and retarded by experience, and for long periods had only groped his way. It had taken too much of his life to produce too little of his art. The art had come, but it had come after everything else. At such a rate a first existence was too short—long enough only to collect material; so that to fructify, to use the material, one must have a second age, an extension. This extension was what poor Dencombe sighed for. As he turned the last leaves of his volume he murmured: "Ah for another go!—ah for a better chance!"

The three persons he had observed on the sands had vanished and then reappeared; they had now wandered up a path, an artificial and easy ascent, which led to the top of the cliff. Dencombe's bench was half-way down, on a sheltered ledge, and the large lady, a massive, heterogeneous person, with bold black eyes and kind red cheeks, now took a few moments to rest. She wore dirty gauntlets and immense diamond ear-rings; at first she looked vulgar, but she contradicted this announcement in an agreeable off-hand tone. While her companions stood waiting for her she spread her skirts on the end of Dencombe's seat. The young man had gold spectacles, through which, with his finger still in his red-covered book, he glanced at the volume, bound in the same shade of the same colour, lying on the lap of the original occupant of the bench. After an instant, Dencombe understood that he was struck with a resemblance, had recognised the gilt stamp on the crimson cloth, was reading "The Middle Years," and now perceived that somebody else had kept pace with him. The stranger was startled, possibly even a little ruffled, to find that he was not the only person who had been favoured with an early copy. The eyes of the two proprietors met for a moment, and Dencombe borrowed amusement from the expression of those of his competitor, those, it might even be inferred, of his admirer. They confessed to some resentment— they seemed to say: "Hang it, has he got it *already?*—Of course he's a brute of a reviewer!" Dencombe shuffled his copy out of sight while the opulent matron, rising from her repose, broke out: "I feel already the good of this air!"

"I can't say I do," said the angular lady. "I find myself quite let down."

"I find myself horribly hungry. At what time did you order lunch?" her protectress pursued.

The young person put the question by. "Doctor Hugh always orders it."

"I ordered nothing to-day—I'm going to make you diet," said their comrade.

"Then I shall go home and sleep. *Qui dort dine!*"

"Can I trust you to Miss Vernham?" asked Doctor Hugh of his elder companion.

"Don't I trust *you?*" she archly inquired.

"Not too much!" Miss Vernham, with her eyes on the ground, permitted herself to declare. "You must come with us at least to the house," she went on, while the personage on whom they appeared to be in attendance began to mount higher. She had got a little out of ear-shot; nevertheless Miss Vernham became, so far as Dencombe was concerned, less distinctly audible to murmur to the young man: "I don't think you realise all you owe the Countess!"

Absently, a moment, Doctor Hugh caused his gold-rimmed spectacles to shine at her.

"Is that the way I strike you? I see—I see!"

"She's awfully good to us," continued Miss Vernham, com- pelled by her interlocutor's immovability to stand there in spite of his discussion of private matters. Of what use would it have been that Dencombe should be sensitive to shades had he not detected in that immovability a strange influence from the quiet old convalescent in the great tweed cape? Miss Vernham appeared suddenly to become aware of some such connection, for she added in a moment: "If you want to sun yourself here you can come back after you've seen us home."

Doctor Hugh, at this, hesitated, and Dencombe, in spite of a desire to pass for unconscious, risked a covert glance at him. What his eyes met this time, as it happened, was on the part of the young lady a queer stare, naturally vitreous, which made her aspect remind him of some figure (he couldn't name it) in a play or a novel, some sinister governess or tragic old maid. She seemed to scrutinise him, to challenge him, to say, from general spite: "What have you got to do with us?" At the same instant the rich humour of the Countess reached them from above: "Come, come, my little lambs, you should follow your old *bergère!*" Miss Vernham turned away at this, pursuing the ascent, and Doctor Hugh, after another mute appeal to Dencombe and a moment's evident demur, deposited his book on the bench, as if to keep his place or even as a sign that he would return, and bounded without difficulty up the rougher part of the cliff.

Equally innocent and infinite are the pleasures of observation and the resources engendered by the habit of analysing life. It amused poor Dencombe, as he dawdled in his tepid air-bath, to think that he was waiting for a revelation of something at the back of a fine young mind. He looked hard at the book on the end of the bench, but he wouldn't have touched it for the world. It served his purpose to have a theory which should not be exposed to refutation. He already felt better of his melancholy; he had, according to his old formula, put his head at the window. A passing Countess could draw off the fancy when, like the elder of the ladies who had just retreated, she was as obvious as the giantess of a caravan. It was indeed general views that were terrible; short ones, contrary to an opinion sometimes expressed, were the refuge, were the remedy. Doctor Hugh couldn't possibly be anything but a reviewer who had understandings for early copies with publishers or with newspapers. He reappeared in a quarter of an hour, with visible relief at finding Dencombe on the spot, and the gleam of white teeth in an embarrassed but generous smile. He was perceptibly disappointed at the eclipse of the other copy of the book; it was a pretext the less for speaking to the stranger. But he spoke notwithstanding; he held up his own copy and broke out pleadingly:

"*Do* say, if you have occasion to speak of it, that it's the best thing he has done yet!"

Dencombe responded with a laugh: "Done yet" was so amusing to him, made such a grand avenue of the future. Better still, the young man took *him* for a reviewer. He pulled out "The Middle Years" from under his cape, but instinctively concealed any tell-tale look of fatherhood. This was partly because a person was always a fool for calling attention to his work. "Is that what you're going to say yourself?" he inquired of his visitor.

"I'm not quite sure I shall write anything. I don't, as a regular thing—I enjoy in peace. But it's awfully fine."

Dencombe debated a moment. If his interlocutor had begun to abuse him he would have confessed on the spot to his identity, but there was no harm in drawing him on a little to praise. He drew him on with such success that in a few moments his new acquaintance, seated by his side, was confessing candidly that Dencombe's novels were the only ones he could read a second time. He had come the day before from London, where a friend of his, a journalist, had lent him his copy of the last—the copy sent to the office of the journal and already the subject of a "notice" which, as was pretended there (but one had to allow for "swagger") it had taken a full quarter of an hour to prepare. He intimated that he was ashamed for his friend, and in the case of a work demanding and repaying study, of such inferior manners; and, with his fresh appreciation and inexplicable wish to express it, he speedily became for poor Dencombe a remarkable, a delightful apparition. Chance had brought the weary man of letters face to face with the greatest admirer in the new generation whom it was supposable he possessed. The admirer, in truth, was mystifying, so rare a case was it to find a bristling young doctor—he looked like a German physiologist—enamoured of literary form. It was an accident, but happier than most accidents, so that Dencombe, exhilarated as well as confounded, spent half an hour in making his visitor talk while he kept himself quiet. He explained his premature possession of "The Middle Years" by an allusion to the friendship of the publisher, who, knowing he was at Bournemouth for his health, had paid him this graceful attention. He admitted that he had been ill, for Doctor Hugh would infallibly have guessed it; he even went so far as to wonder whether he mightn't look for some hyginic "tip" from a personage combining so bright an enthusiasm with a presumable knowledge of the remedies now in vogue. It would shake his faith a little perhaps to have to take a doctor seriously who could take *him* so seriously, but he enjoyed this gushing modern youth and he felt with an acute pang that there would still be work to do in a world in which such odd combinations were presented. It was not true, what he had tried for renunciation's sake to believe, that all the combinations were exhausted. They were not, they were not—they were infinite: the exhaustion was in the miserable artist.

Doctor Hugh was an ardent physiologist, saturated with the spirit of the age—in other words he had just taken his degree; but he was independent and various, he talked like a man who would have preferred to love literature best. He would fain have made fine phrases, but nature had denied him the trick. Some of the finest in "The Middle Years" had struck him inordinately, and he took the liberty of reading them to Dencombe in support of his plea. He grew vivid, in the balmy air, to his companion, for whose deep refreshment he seemed to have been sent; and was particularly ingenuous in describing how recently he had become acquainted, and how instantly infatuated, with the only man who had put flesh between the ribs of an art that was starving on superstitions. He had not yet written to him—he was deterred by a sentiment of respect. Dencombe at this moment felicitated himself more than ever on having never answered the photographers. His visitor's attitude promised him a luxury of intercourse, but he surmised that a certain security in it, for Doctor Hugh, would depend not a little on the Countess. He learned without delay with what variety of Countess they were concerned, as well as the nature of the tie that united the curious trio. The large lady, an Englishwoman by birth and the daughter of a celebrated baritone, whose taste, without his talent, she had inherited, was the widow of a French nobleman and mistress of all that remained of the handsome fortune, the fruit of her father's earnings, that had constituted her dower. Miss Vernham, an odd creature but an accomplished pianist, was attached to her person at a salary. The Countess was generous, independent, eccentric; she travelled with her minstrel and her medical man. Ignorant and passionate, she had nevertheless moments in which she was almost irresistible. Dencombe saw her sit for her portrait in Doctor Hugh's free sketch, and felt the picture of his young friend's relation to her frame itself in his mind. This young friend, for a representative of the new psychology, was himself easily hypnotised, and if he became abnormally communicative it was only a sign of his real subjection. Dencombe did accordingly what he wanted with him, even without being known as Dencombe.

Taken ill on a journey in Switzerland the Countess had picked him up at an hotel, and the accident of his happening to please her had made her offer him, with her imperious liberality, terms that couldn't fail to dazzle a practitioner without patients and whose resources had been drained dry by his studies. It was not the way he would have elected to spend his time, but it was time that would pass quickly, and meanwhile she was wonderfully kind. She exacted perpetual attention, but it was impossible not to like her. He gave details about his queer patient, a "type" if there ever was one, who had in connection with her flushed obesity and in addition to the morbid strain of a violent and aimless will a grave organic disorder; but he came back to his loved novelist, whom he was so good as to pronounce more essentially a poet than many of those who went in for verse, with a zeal excited, as all his indiscretion had been excited, by the happy chance of Dencombe's sympathy and the coincidence of their occupation. Dencombe had confessed to a slight personal acquaintance with the author of "The Middle Years," but had not felt himself as ready as he could have wished when his companion, who had never yet encountered a being so privileged, began to be eager for particulars. He even thought that Doctor Hugh's eye at that moment emitted a glimmer of suspicion. But the young man was too inflamed to be shrewd and repeatedly caught up the book to exclaim: "Did you notice this?" or "Weren't you immensely struck with that?" "There's a beautiful passage toward the end," he broke out; and again he laid his hand upon the volume. As he turned the pages he came upon something else, while Dencombe saw him suddenly change colour. He had taken up, as it lay on the bench, Dencombe's copy instead of his own, and his neighbour immediately guessed the reason of his start. Doctor Hugh looked grave an instant; then he said: "I see you've been altering the text!" Dencombe was a passionate corrector, a fingerer of style; the last thing he ever arrived at was a form final for himself. His ideal would have been to publish secretly, and then, on the published text, treat himself to the terrified revise, sacrificing always a first edition and beginning for posterity and even for the collectors, poor dears, with a second. This morning, in "The Middle Years," his pencil had pricked a dozen lights. He was amused at the effect of the young man's reproach; for an instant it made him change colour. He stammered, at any rate, ambiguously; then, through a blur of ebbing consciousness, saw Doctor Hugh's mystified eyes. He only had time to feel he was about to be ill again—that emotion, excitement, fatigue, the heat of the sun, the solicitation of the air, had combined to play him a trick, before, stretching out a hand to his visitor with a plaintive cry, he lost his senses altogether.

Later he knew that he had fainted and that Doctor Hugh had got him home in a bath-chair, the conductor of which, prowling within hail for custom, had happened to remember seeing him in the garden of the hotel. He had recovered his perception in the transit, and had, in bed, that afternoon, a vague recollection of Doctor Hugh's young face, as they went together, bent over him in a comforting laugh and expressive of something more than a suspicion of his identity. That identity was ineffaceable now, and all the more that he was disappointed, disgusted. He had been rash, been stupid, had gone out too soon, stayed out too long. He oughtn't to have exposed himself to strangers, he ought to have taken his servant. He felt as if he had fallen into a hole too deep to descry any little patch of heaven. He was confused about the time that had elapsed—he pieced the fragments together. He had seen his doctor, the real one, the one who had treated him from the first and who had again been very kind. His servant was in and out on tiptoe, looking very wise after the fact. He said more than once something about the sharp young gentleman. The rest was vagueness, in so far as it wasn't despair. The vagueness, however, justified itself by dreams, dozing anxieties from which he finally emerged to the consciousness of a dark room and a shaded candle.

"You'll be all right again—I know all about you now," said a voice near him that he knew to be young. Then his meeting with Doctor Hugh came back. He was too discouraged to joke about it yet, but he was able to perceive, after a little, that the interest of it was intense for his visitor. "Of course I can't attend you professionally—you've got your own man, with whom I've talked and who's excellent," Doctor Hugh went on. "But you must let me come to see you as a good friend. I've just looked in before going to bed. You're doing beautifully, but it's a good job I was with you on the cliff. I shall come in early to-morrow. I want to do something for you. I want to do everything. You've done a tremendous lot for me." The young man held his hand, hanging over him, and poor Dencombe, weakly aware of this living pressure, simply lay there and accepted his devotion. He couldn't do anything less—he needed help too much.

The idea of the help he needed was very present to him that night, which he spent in a lucid stillness, an intensity of thought that constituted a reaction from his hours of stupor. He was lost, he was lost—he was lost if he couldn't be saved. He was not afraid of suffering, of death; he was not even in love with life; but he had had a deep demonstration of desire. It came over him in the long, quiet hours that only with "The Middle Years" had he taken his flight; only on that day, visited by soundless processions, had he recognised his kingdom. He had had a revelation of his range. What he dreaded was the idea that his reputation should stand on the unfinished. It was not with his past but with his future that it should properly be concerned. Illness and age rose before him like spectres with pitiless eyes: how was he to bribe such fates to give him the second chance? He had had the one chance that all men have—he had had the chance of life. He went to sleep again very late, and when he awoke Doctor Hugh was sitting by his head. There was already, by this time, something beautifully familiar in him.

"Don't think I've turned out your physician," he said; "I'm acting with his consent. He has been here and seen you. Somehow he seems to trust me. I told him how we happened to come together yesterday, and he recognises that I've a peculiar right."

Dencombe looked at him with a calculating earnestness. "How have you squared the Countess?"

The young man blushed a little, but he laughed. "Oh, never mind the Countess!"

"You told me she was very exacting."

Doctor Hugh was silent a moment. "So she is."

"And Miss Vernham's an *intrigante*."

"How do you know that?"

"I know everything. One *has* to, to write decently!"

"I think she's mad," said limpid Doctor Hugh.

"Well, don't quarrel with the Countess—she's a present help to you."

"I don't quarrel," Doctor Hugh replied. "But I don't get on with silly women." Presently he added: "You seem very much alone."

"That often happens at my age. I've outlived, I've lost by the way."

Doctor Hugh hesitated; then surmounting a soft scruple: "Whom have you lost?"

"Every one."

"Ah, no," the young man murmured, laying a hand on his arm.

"I once had a wife—I once had a son. My wife died when my child was born, and my boy, at school, was carried off by typhoid."

"I wish I'd been there!" said Doctor Hugh simply.

"Well—if you're here!" Dencombe answered, with a smile that, in spite of dimness, showed how much he liked to be sure of his companion's whereabouts.

"You talk strangely of your age. You're not old."

"Hypocrite—so early!"

"I speak physiologically."

"That's the way I've been speaking for the last five years, and it's exactly what I've been saying to myself. It isn't till we *are* old that we begin to tell ourselves we're not!"

"Yet I know I myself am young," Doctor Hugh declared.

"Not so well as I!" laughed his patient, whose visitor indeed

would have established the truth in question by the honesty
with which he changed the point of view, remarking that it
must be one of the charms of age—at any rate in the case of
high distinction—to feel that one has laboured and achieved.
Doctor Hugh employed the common phrase about earning
one's rest, and it made poor Dencombe, for an instant, almost
angry. He recovered himself, however, to explain, lucidly
enough, that if he, ungraciously, knew nothing of such a balm,
it was doubtless because he had wasted inestimable years. He
had followed literature from the first, but he had taken a lifetime to get alongside of her. Only to-day, at last, had he begun
to *see*, so that what he had hitherto done was a movement
without a direction. He had ripened too late and was so
clumsily constituted that he had had to teach himself by mistakes.

"I prefer your flowers, then, to other people's fruit, and
your mistakes to other people's successes," said gallant Doctor
Hugh. "It's for your mistakes I admire you."

"You're happy—you don't know," Dencombe answered.

Looking at his watch the young man had got up; he named
the hour of the afternoon at which he would return. Dencombe warned him against committing himself too deeply,
and expressed again all his dread of making him neglect the
Countess—perhaps incur her displeasure.

"I want to be like you—I want to learn by mistakes!"
Doctor Hugh laughed.

"Take care you don't make too grave a one! But do
come back," Dencombe added, with the glimmer of a new
idea.

"You should have had more vanity!" Doctor Hugh spoke
as if he knew the exact amount required to make a man of
letters normal.

"No, no—I only should have had more time. I want
another go."

"Another go?"

"I want an extension."

"An extension?" Again Doctor Hugh repeated Dencombe's words, with which he seemed to have been struck.

"Don't you know?—I want to what they call 'live.'"

The young man, for good-bye, had taken his hand, which closed with a certain force. They looked at each other hard a moment. "You *will* live," said Doctor Hugh.

"Don't be superficial. It's too serious!"

"You *shall* live!" Dencombe's visitor declared, turning pale.

"Ah, that's better!" And as he retired the invalid, with a troubled laugh, sank gratefully back.

All that day and all the following night he wondered if it mightn't be arranged. His doctor came again, his servant was attentive, but it was to his confident young friend that he found himself mentally appealing. His collapse on the cliff was plausibly explained, and his liberation, on a better basis, promised for the morrow; meanwhile, however, the intensity of his meditations kept him tranquil and made him indifferent. The idea that occupied him was none the less absorbing because it was a morbid fancy. Here was a clever son of the age, ingenious and ardent, who happened to have set him up for connoisseurs to worship. This servant of his altar had all the new learning in science and all the old reverence in faith; wouldn't he therefore put his knowledge at the disposal of his sympathy, his craft at the disposal of his love? Couldn't he be trusted to invent a remedy for a poor artist to whose art he had paid a tribute? If he couldn't, the alternative was hard: Dencombe would have to surrender to silence, unvindicated and undivined. The rest of the day and all the next he toyed in secret with this sweet futility. Who would work the miracle for him but the young man who could combine such lucidity with such passion? He thought of the fairy-tales of science and charmed himself into forgetting that he looked for a magic that was not of this world. Doctor Hugh was an apparition, and that placed him above the law. He came and went while his patient, who sat up, followed him with supplicating eyes. The interest of knowing the great author had made the young man begin "The Middle Years" afresh, and would help him to find a deeper meaning in its pages. Dencombe had told him what he "tried for;" with all his intelligence, on a first perusal, Doctor Hugh had failed to guess it. The baffled celebrity wondered then who in the world *would* guess it: he was amused once more at the fine, full way with which an intention could be missed. Yet he wouldn't rail at the general mind to-day—consoling as that ever had been: the revelation of his own slowness had seemed to make all stupidity sacred.

Doctor Hugh, after a little, was visibly worried, confessing, on inquiry, to a source of embarrassment at home. "Stick to the Countess—don't mind me," Dencombe said, repeatedly; for his companion was frank enough about the large lady's attitude. She was so jealous that she had fallen ill—she resented such a breach of allegiance. She paid so much for his fidelity that she must have it all: she refused him the right to other sympathies, charged him with scheming to make her die alone, for it was needless to point out how little Miss Vernham was a resource in trouble. When Doctor Hugh mentioned that the Countess would already have left Bournemouth if he hadn't kept her in bed, poor Dencombe held his arm tighter and said with decision: "Take her straight away." They had gone out together, walking back to the sheltered nook in which, the other day, they had met. The young man, who had given his companion a personal support, declared with emphasis that his conscience was clear—he could ride two horses at once. Didn't he dream, for his future, of a time when he should have to ride five hundred? Longing equally for virtue, Dencombe replied that in that golden age no patient would pretend to have contracted with him for his whole attention. On the part of the Countess was not such an avidity lawful? Doctor Hugh denied it, said there was no contract but only a free understanding, and that a sordid servitude was impossible to a generous spirit; he liked moreover to talk about art, and that was the subject on which, this time, as they sat together on the sunny bench, he tried most to engage the author of "The Middle Years." Dencombe, soaring again a little on the weak wings of convalescence and still haunted by that happy notion of an organised rescue, found another strain of eloquence to plead the cause of a certain splendid "last manner," the very citadel, as it would prove, of his reputation, the stronghold into which his real treasure would be gathered. While his listener gave up the morning and the great still sea appeared to wait, he had a wonderful explanatory hour. Even for himself he was inspired as he told of what his treasure would consist— the precious metals he would dig from the mine, the jewels rare, strings of pearls, he would hang between the columns of his temple. He was wonderful for himself, so thick his convictions crowded; but he was still more wonderful for Doctor Hugh, who assured him, none the less, that the very pages he had just published were already encrusted with gems. The young man, however, panted for the combinations to come, and, before the face of the beautiful day, renewed to Dencombe his guarantee that his profession would hold itself responsible for such a life. Then he suddenly clapped his hand upon his watch-pocket and asked leave to absent himself for half an hour. Dencombe waited there for his return, but was at last recalled to the actual by the fall of a shadow across the ground. The shadow darkened into that of Miss Vernham, the young lady in attendance on the Countess; whom Dencombe, recognising her, perceived so clearly to have come to speak to him that he rose from his bench to acknowledge the civility. Miss Vernham indeed proved not particularly civil; she looked strangely agitated, and her type was now unmistakable.

"Excuse me if I inquire," she said, "whether it's too much to hope that you may be induced to leave Doctor Hugh alone." Then, before Dencombe, greatly disconcerted, could protest:

"You ought to be informed that you stand in his light; that you may do him a terrible injury."

"Do you mean by causing the Countess to dispense with his services?"

"By causing her to disinherit him." Dencombe stared at this, and Miss Vernham pursued, in the gratification of seeing she could produce an impression: "It has depended on himself to come into something very handsome. He has had a magnificent prospect, but I think you've succeeded in spoiling it."

"Not intentionally, I assure you. Is there no hope the accident may be repaired?" Dencombe asked.

"She was ready to do anything for him. She takes great fancies, she lets herself go—it's her way. She has no relations, she's free to dispose of her money, and she's very ill."

"I'm very sorry to hear it," Dencombe stammered.

"Wouldn't it be possible for you to leave Bournemouth? That's what I've come to ask of you."

Poor Dencombe sank down on his bench. "I'm very ill myself, but I'll try!"

Miss Vernham still stood there with her colourless eyes and the brutality of her good conscience. "Before it's too late, please!" she said; and with this she turned her back, in order, quickly, as if it had been a business to which she could spare but a precious moment, to pass out of his sight.

Oh, yes, after this Dencombe was certainly very ill. Miss Vernham had upset him with her rough, fierce news; it was the sharpest shock to him to discover what was at stake for a penniless young man of fine parts. He sat trembling on his bench, staring at the waste of waters, feeling sick with the directness of the blow. He was indeed too weak, too unsteady, too alarmed; but he would make the effort to get away, for he couldn't accept the guilt of interference, and his honour was really involved. He would hobble home, at any rate, and then he would think what was to be done. He made his way back to the hotel and, as he went, had a characteristic vision of Miss

Vernham's great motive. The Countess hated women, of course; Dencombe was lucid about that; so the hungry pianist had no personal hopes and could only console herself with the bold conception of helping Doctor Hugh in order either to marry him after he should get his money or to induce him to recognise her title to compensation and buy her off. If she had befriended him at a fruitful crisis he would really, as a man of delicacy, and she knew what to think of that point, have to reckon with her.

At the hotel Dencombe's servant insisted on his going back to bed. The invalid had talked about catching a train and had begun with orders to pack; after which his humming nerves had yielded to a sense of sickness. He consented to see his physician, who immediately was sent for, but he wished it to be understood that his door was irrevocably closed to Doctor Hugh. He had his plan, which was so fine that he rejoiced in it after getting back to bed. Doctor Hugh, suddenly finding himself snubbed without mercy, would, in natural disgust and to the joy of Miss Vernham, renew his allegiance to the Countess. When his physician arrived Dencombe learned that he was feverish and that this was very wrong: he was to cultivate calmness and try, if possible, not to think. For the rest of the day he wooed stupidity; but there was an ache that kept him sentient, the probable sacrifice of his "extension," the limit of his course. His medical adviser was anything but pleased; his successive relapses were ominous. He charged this personage to put out a strong hand and take Doctor Hugh off his mind— it would contribute so much to his being quiet. The agitating name, in his room, was not mentioned again, but his security was a smothered fear, and it was not confirmed by the receipt, at ten o'clock that evening, of a telegram which his servant opened and read for him and to which, with an address in London, the signature of Miss Vernham was attached. "Beseech you to use all influence to make our friend join us here in the morning. Countess much the worse for dreadful journey, but everything may still be saved." The two ladies had gathered themselves up and had been capable in the afternoon of a spiteful revolution. They had started for the capital, and if the elder one, as Miss Vernham had announced, was very ill, she had wished to make it clear that she was proportionately reckless. Poor Dencombe, who was not reckless and who only desired that everything should indeed be "saved," sent this missive straight off to the young man's lodging and had on the morrow the pleasure of knowing that he had quitted Bournemouth by an early train.

Two days later he pressed in with a copy of a literary journal in his hand. He had returned because he was anxious and for the pleasure of flourishing the great review of "The Middle Years." Here at least was something adequate—it rose to the occasion; it was an acclamation, a reparation, a critical attempt to place the author in the niche he had fairly won. Dencombe accepted and submitted; he made neither objection nor inquiry, for old complications had returned and he had had two atrocious days. He was convinced not only that he should never again leave his bed, so that his young friend might pardonably remain, but that the demand he should make on the patience of beholders would be very moderate indeed. Doctor Hugh had been to town, and he tried to find in his eyes some confession that the Countess was pacified and his legacy clinched; but all he could see there was the light of his juvenile joy in two or three of the phrases of the newspaper. Dencombe couldn't read them, but when his visitor had insisted on repeating them more than once he was able to shake an unintoxicated head. "Ah, no; but they would have been true of what I *could* have done!"

"What people 'could have done' is mainly what they've in fact done," Doctor Hugh contended.

"Mainly, yes; but I've been an idiot!" said Dencombe.

Doctor Hugh did remain; the end was coming fast. Two days later Dencombe observed to him, by way of the feeblest of jokes, that there would now be no question whatever of a second chance. At this the young man stared; then he exclaimed: "Why, it has come to pass—it has come to pass! The second chance has been the public's—the chance to find the point of view, to pick up the pearl!"

"Oh, the pearl!" poor Dencombe uneasily sighed. A smile as cold as a winter sunset flickered on his drawn lips as he added: "The pearl is the unwritten—the pearl is the unalloyed, the *rest*, the lost!"

From that moment he was less and less present, heedless to all appearance of what went on around him. His disease was definitely mortal, of an action as relentless, after the short arrest that had enabled him to fall in with Doctor Hugh, as a leak in a great ship. Sinking steadily, though this visitor, a man of rare resources, now cordially approved by his physician, showed endless art in guarding him from pain, poor Dencombe kept no reckoning of favour or neglect, betrayed no symptom of regret or speculation. Yet toward the last he gave a sign of having noticed that for two days Doctor Hugh had not been in his room, a sign that consisted of his suddenly opening his eyes to ask of him if he had spent the interval with the Countess.

"The Countess is dead," said Doctor Hugh. "I knew that in a particular contingency she wouldn't resist. I went to her grave."

Dencombe's eyes opened wider. "She left you 'something handsome'?"

The young man gave a laugh almost too light for a chamber of woe. "Never a penny. She roundly cursed me."

"Cursed you?" Dencombe murmured.

"For giving her up. I gave her up for *you*. I had to choose," his companion explained.

"You chose to let a fortune go?"

"I chose to accept, whatever they might be, the consequences of my infatuation," smiled Doctor Hugh. Then, as a larger pleasantry: "A fortune be hanged! It's your own fault if I can't get your things out of my head."

The immediate tribute to his humour was a long, bewildered moan; after which, for many hours, many days, Dencombe lay motionless and absent. A response so absolute, such a glimpse of a definite result and such a sense of credit worked together in his mind and, producing a strange commotion, slowly altered and transfigured his despair. The sense of cold submersion left him—he seemed to float without an effort. The incident was extraordinary as evidence, and it shed an intenser light. At the last he signed to Doctor Hugh to listen, and, when he was down on his knees by the pillow, brought him very near.

"You've made me think it all a delusion."

"Not your glory, my dear friend," stammered the young man.

"Not my glory—what there is of it! It *is* glory—to have been tested, to have had our little quality and cast our little spell. The thing is to have made somebody care. You happen to be crazy, of course, but that doesn't affect the law."

"You're a great success!" said Doctor Hugh, putting into his young voice the ring of a marriage-bell.

Dencombe lay taking this in; then he gathered strength to speak once more. "A second chance—*that's* the delusion. There never was to be but one. We work in the dark—we do what we can—we give what we have. Our doubt is our passion and our passion is our task. The rest is the madness of art."

"If you've doubted, if you've despaired, you've always 'done' it," his visitor subtly argued.

"We've done something or other," Dencombe conceded.

"Something or other is everything. It's the feasible. It's *you!*"

"Comforter!" poor Dencombe ironically sighed.

"But it's true," insisted his friend.

"It's true. It's frustration that doesn't count."

"Frustration's only life," said Doctor Hugh.

"Yes, it's what passes." Poor Dencombe was barely audible, but he had marked with the words the virtual end of his first and only chance.

THE DEATH OF THE LION

I

I HAD simply, I suppose, a change of heart, and it must have begun when I received my manuscript back from Mr Pinhorn. Mr Pinhorn was my "chief," as he was called in the office: he had accepted the high mission of bringing the paper up. This was a weekly periodical, and had been supposed to be almost past redemption when he took hold of it. It was Mr Deedy who had let it down so dreadfully: he was never mentioned in the office now save in connection with that misdemeanour. Young as I was I had been in a manner taken over from Mr Deedy, who had been owner as well as editor; forming part of a promiscuous lot, mainly plant and office-furniture, which poor Mrs Deedy, in her bereavement and depression, parted with at a rough valuation. I could account for my continuity only on the supposition that I had been cheap. I rather resented the practice of fathering all flatness on my late protector, who was in his unhonoured grave; but as I had my way to make I found matter enough for complacency in being on a "staff." At the same time I was aware that I was exposed to suspicion as a product of the old lowering system. This made me feel that I was doubly bound to have ideas, and had doubtless been at the bottom of my proposing to Mr Pinhorn that I should lay my lean hands on Neil Paraday. I remember that he looked at me first as if he had never heard of this celebrity, who indeed at that moment was by no means in the centre of the heavens; and even when I had knowingly explained he expressed but little confidence in the demand for any such matter. When I had reminded him that the great

127

principle on which we were supposed to work was just to create the demand we required, he considered a moment and then rejoined: "I see; you want to write him up."

"Call it that if you like."

"And what's your inducement?"

"Bless my soul—my admiration!"

Mr Pinhorn pursed up his mouth. "Is there much to be done with him?"

"Whatever there is, we should have it all to ourselves, for he hasn't been touched."

This argument was effective, and Mr Pinhorn responded: "Very well, touch him." Then he added: "But where can you do it?"

"Under the fifth rib!"

Mr Pinhorn stared. "Where's that?"

"You want me to go down and see him?" I inquired when I had enjoyed his visible search for this obscure suburb.

"I don't 'want' anything—the proposal's your own. But you must remember that that's the way we do things *now*," said Mr Pinhorn, with another dig at Mr Deedy.

Unregenerate as I was, I could read the queer implications of this speech. The present owner's superior virtue as well as his deeper craft spoke in his reference to the late editor as one of that baser sort who deal in false representations. Mr Deedy would as soon have sent me to call on Neil Paraday as he would have published a "holiday-number;" but such scruples presented themselves as mere ignoble thrift to his successor, whose own sincerity took the form of ringing door-bells and whose definition of genius was the art of finding people at home. It was as if Mr Deedy had published reports without his young men's having, as Pinhorn would have said, really been there. I was unregenerate, as I have hinted, and I was not concerned to straighten out the journalistic morals of my chief, feeling them indeed to be an abyss over the edge of which it was better not to peer. Really to be there this time moreover was a vision that made the idea of writing something subtle about Neil Paraday only the more inspiring. I would be as considerate as even Mr Deedy could have wished, and yet I should be as present as only Mr Pinhorn could conceive. My allusion to the sequestered manner in which Mr Paraday lived (which had formed part of my explanation, though I knew of it only by hearsay) was, I could divine, very much what had made Mr Pinhorn nibble. It struck him as inconsistent with the success of his paper that any one should be so sequestered as that. And then was not an immediate exposure of everything just what the public wanted? Mr Pinhorn effectually called me to order by reminding me of the promptness with which I had met Miss Braby at Liverpool on her return from her fiasco in the States. Hadn't we published, while its freshness and flavour were unimpaired, Miss Braby's own version of that great international episode? I felt somewhat uneasy at this lumping of the actress and the author, and I confess that after having enlisted Mr Pinhorn's sympathies I procrastinated a little. I had succeeded better than I wished, and I had, as it happened, work nearer at hand. A few days later I called on Lord Crouchley and carried off in triumph the most unintelligible statement that had yet appeared of his lordship's reasons for his change of front. I thus set in motion in the daily papers columns of virtuous verbiage. The following week I ran down to Brighton for a chat, as Mr Pinhorn called it, with Mrs Bounder, who gave me, on the subject of her divorce, many curious particulars that had not been articulated in court. If ever an article flowed from the primal fount it was that article on Mrs Bounder. By this time, however, I became aware that Neil Paraday's new book was on the point of appearing and that its approach had been the ground of my original appeal to Mr Pinhorn, who was now annoyed with me for having lost so many days. He bundled me off—we would at least not lose another. I have always thought his sudden alertness a remarkable example of the journalistic instinct. Nothing had occurred, since I first

spoke to him, to create a visible urgency, and no enlighten-
ment could possibly have reached him. It was a pure case of
professional *flair*—he had smelt the coming glory as an animal
smells its distant prey.

II

I MAY as well say at once that this little record pretends in no
degree to be a picture either of my introduction to Mr Paraday
or of certain proximate steps and stages. The scheme of my
narrative allows no space for these things, and in any case a
prohibitory sentiment would be attached to my recollection of
so rare an hour. These meagre notes are essentially private, so
that if they see the light the insidious forces that, as my story
itself shows, make at present for publicity will simply have
overmastered my precautions. The curtain fell lately enough
on the lamentable drama. My memory of the day I alighted at
Mr Paraday's door is a fresh memory of kindness, hospitality,
compassion, and of the wonderful illuminating talk in which
the welcome was conveyed. Some voice of the air had taught
me the right moment, the moment of his life at which an act
of unexpected young allegiance might most come home. He
had recently recovered from a long, grave illness. I had gone
to the neighbouring inn for the night, but I spent the evening
in his company, and he insisted the next day on my sleeping
under his roof. I had not an indefinite leave: Mr Pinhorn supposed us to put our victims through on the gallop. It was later,
in the office, that the dance was set to music. I fortified myself,
however, as my training had taught me to do, by the conviction that nothing could be more advantageous for my
article than to be written in the very atmosphere. I said nothing to Mr Paraday about it, but in the morning, after my
removal from the inn, while he was occupied in his study, as

he had notified me that he should need to be, I committed to paper the quintessence of my impressions. Then thinking to commend myself to Mr Pinhorn by my celerity, I walked out and posted my little packet before luncheon. Once my paper was written I was free to stay on, and if it was designed to divert attention from my frivolity in so doing I could reflect with satisfaction that I had never been so clever. I don't mean to deny of course that I was aware it was much too good for Mr Pinhorn; but I was equally conscious that Mr Pinhorn had the supreme shrewdness of recognising from time to time the cases in which an article was not too bad only because it was too good. There was nothing he loved so much as to print on the right occasion a thing he hated. I had begun my visit to Mr Paraday on a Monday, and on the Wednesday his book came out. A copy of it arrived by the first post, and he let me go out into the garden with it immediately after breakfast. I read it from beginning to end that day, and in the evening he asked me to remain with him the rest of the week and over the Sunday.

That night my manuscript came back from Mr Pinhorn, accompanied with a letter, of which the gist was the desire to know what I meant by sending him such stuff. That was the meaning of the question, if not exactly its form, and it made my mistake immense to me. Such as this mistake was I could now only look it in the face and accept it. I knew where I had failed, but it was exactly where I couldn't have succeeded. I had been sent down there to be personal, and in point of fact I hadn't been personal at all: what I had sent up to London was just a little finicking, feverish study of my author's talent. Anything less relevant to Mr Pinhorn's purpose couldn't well be imagined, and he was visibly angry at my having (at his expense, with a second-class ticket) approached the object of our arrangement only to be so deucedly distant. For myself, I knew but too well what had happened, and how a miracle—as pretty as some old miracle of legend—had been wrought on the spot to save me. There had been a big brush of wings, the flash of an opaline robe, and then, with a great cool stir of the air, the sense of an angel's having swooped down and caught me to his bosom. He held me only till the danger was over, and it all took place in a minute. With my manuscript back on my hands I understood the phenomenon better, and the reflections I made on it are what I meant, at the beginning of this anecdote, by my change of heart. Mr Pinhorn's note was not only a rebuke decidedly stern, but an invitation immediately to send him (it was the case to say so) the genuine article, the revealing and reverberating sketch to the promise of which—and of which alone—I owed my squandered privilege. A week or two later I recast my peccant paper, and giving it a particular application to Mr Paraday's new book, obtained for it the hospitality of another journal, where, I must admit, Mr Pinhorn was so far justified that it attracted not the least attention.

III

I WAS frankly, at the end of three days, a very prejudiced critic, so that one morning when, in the garden, Neil Paraday had offered to read me something I quite held my breath as I listened. It was the written scheme of another book—something he had put aside long ago, before his illness, and lately taken out again to reconsider. He had been turning it round when I came down upon him, and it had grown magnificently under this second hand. Loose, liberal, confident, it might have passed for a great gossiping, eloquent letter—the overflow into talk of an artist's amorous plan. The subject I thought singularly rich, quite the strongest he had yet treated; and this familiar statement of it, full too of fine maturities, was really, in summarised splendour, a mine of gold, a precious, independent work. I remember rather profanely wondering whether the ultimate production could possibly be so happy. His reading of the epistle, at any rate, made me feel as if I were, for the advantage of posterity, in close correspondence with him—were the distinguished person to whom it had been affectionately addressed. It was high distinction simply to be told such things. The idea he now communicated had all the freshness, the flushed fairness of the conception untouched and untried: it was Venus rising from the sea, before the airs had blown upon her. I had never been so throbbingly present at such an unveiling. But when he had tossed the last bright word after the others, as I had seen cashiers in banks, weighing mounds of coin, drop a final sovereign into the tray, I became conscious of a sudden prudent alarm.

"My dear master, how, after all, are you going to do it?" I asked. "It's infinitely noble, but what time it will take, what patience and independence, what assured, what perfect conditions it will demand! Oh for a lone isle in a tepid sea!"

"Isn't this practically a lone isle, and aren't you, as an encircling medium, tepid enough?" he replied, alluding with a laugh to the wonder of my young admiration and the narrow limits of his little provincial home. "Time isn't what I've lacked hitherto: the question hasn't been to find it, but to use it. Of course my illness made a great hole, but I daresay there would have been a hole at any rate. The earth we tread has more pockets than a billiard-table. The great thing is now to keep on my feet."

"That's exactly what I mean."

Neil Paraday looked at me with eyes—such pleasant eyes as he had—in which, as I now recall their expression, I seem to have seen a dim imagination of his fate. He was fifty years old, and his illness had been cruel, his convalescence slow. "It isn't as if I weren't all right."

"Oh, if you weren't all right I wouldn't look at you!" I tenderly said.

We had both got up, quickened by the full sound of it all,

and he had lighted a cigarette. I had taken a fresh one, and, with an intenser smile, by way of answer to my exclamation, he touched it with the flame of his match. "If I weren't better I shouldn't have thought of *that!*" He flourished his epistle in his hand.

"I don't want to be discouraging, but that's not true," I returned. "I'm sure that during the months you lay here in pain you had visitations sublime. You thought of a thousand things. You think of more and more all the while. That's what makes you, if you will pardon my familiarity, so respectable. At a time when so many people are spent you come into your second wind. But, thank God, all the same, you're better! Thank God, too, you're not, as you were telling me yesterday, 'successful.' If *you* weren't a failure, what would be the use of trying? That's my one reserve on the subject of your recovery —that it makes you 'score,' as the newspapers say. It looks well in the newspapers, and almost anything that does that is horrible. 'We are happy to announce that Mr Paraday, the celebrated author, is again in the enjoyment of excellent health.' Somehow I shouldn't like to see it."

"You won't see it; I'm not in the least celebrated—my obscurity protects me. But couldn't you bear even to see I was dying or dead?" my companion asked.

"Dead—*passe encore;* there's nothing so safe. One never knows what a living artist may do—one has mourned so many. However, one must make the worst of it; you must be as dead as you can."

"Don't I meet that condition in having just published a book?"

"Adequately, let us hope; for the book is verily a master-piece."

At this moment the parlour-maid appeared in the door that opened into the garden: Paraday lived at no great cost, and the frisk of petticoats, with a timorous "Sherry, sir?" was about his modest mahogany. He allowed half his income to his wife, from whom he had succeeded in separating without redundancy of legend. I had a general faith in his having behaved well, and I had once, in London, taken Mrs Paraday down to dinner. He now turned to speak to the maid, who offered him, on a tray, some card or note, while agitated, excited, I wandered to the end of the garden. The idea of his security became supremely dear to me, and I asked myself if I were the same young man who had come down a few days before to scatter him to the four winds. When I retraced my steps he had gone into the house, and the woman (the second London post had come in) had placed my letters and a newspaper on a bench. I sat down there to the letters, which were a brief business, and then, without heeding the address, took the paper from its envelope. It was the journal of highest renown, *The Empire* of that morning. It regularly came to Paraday, but I remembered that neither of us had yet looked at the copy already delivered. This one had a great mark on the "editorial" page, and, uncrumpling the wrapper, I saw it to be directed to my host and stamped with the name of his publishers. I instantly divined that *The Empire* had spoken of him, and I have not forgotten the odd little shock of the circumstance. It checked all eagerness and made me drop the paper a moment. As I sat there conscious of a palpitation I think I had a vision of what was to be. I had also a vision of the letter I would presently address to Mr Pinhorn, breaking as it were with Mr Pinhorn. Of course, however, the next minute the voice of *The Empire* was in my ears.

The article was not, I thanked heaven, a review; it was a "leader," the last of three, presenting Neil Paraday to the human race. His new book, the fifth from his hand, had been but a day or two out, and *The Empire*, already aware of it, fired, as if on the birth of a prince, a salute of a whole column. The guns had been booming these three hours in the house without our suspecting them. The big blundering newspaper had discovered him, and now he was proclaimed and anointed and crowned. His place was assigned him as publicly as if a fat usher with a wand had pointed to the topmost chair; he was to pass up and still up, higher and higher, between the watching faces and the envious sounds—away up to the daïs and the throne. The article was a date; he had taken rank at a bound—waked up a national glory. A national glory was needed, and it was an immense convenience he was there. What all this meant rolled over me, and I fear I grew a little faint—it meant so much more than I could say "yea" to on the spot. In a flash, somehow, all was different; the tremendous wave I speak of had swept something away. It had knocked down, I suppose, my little customary altar, my twinkling tapers and my flowers, and had reared itself into the likeness of a temple vast and bare. When Neil Paraday should come out of the house he would come out a contemporary. That was what had happened: the poor man was to be squeezed into his horrible age. I felt as if he had been overtaken on the crest of the hill and brought back to the city. A little more and he would have dipped down the short cut to posterity and escaped.

IV

WHEN he came out it was exactly as if he had been in custody, for beside him walked a stout man with a big black beard, who, save that he wore spectacles, might have been a policeman, and in whom at a second glance I recognised the highest contemporary enterprise.

"This is Mr Morrow," said Paraday, looking, I thought, rather white: "he wants to publish heaven knows what about me."

I winced as I remembered that this was exactly what I myself had wanted. "Already?" I exclaimed, with a sort of sense that my friend had fled to me for protection.

Mr Morrow glared, agreeably, through his glasses: they

suggested the electric headlights of some monstrous modern ship, and I felt as if Paraday and I were tossing terrified under his bows. I saw that his momentum was irresistible. "I was confident that I should be the first in the field," he declared. "A great interest is naturally felt in Mr Paraday's surroundings."

"I hadn't the least idea of it," said Paraday, as if he had been told he had been snoring.

"I find he has not read the article in *The Empire*," Mr Morrow remarked to me. "That's so very interesting—it's something to start with," he smiled. He had begun to pull off his gloves, which were violently new, and to look encouragingly round the little garden. As a "surrounding" I felt that I myself had already been taken in; I was a little fish in the stomach of a bigger one. "I represent," our visitor continued, "a syndicate of influential journals, no less than thirty-seven, whose public—whose publics, I may say—are in peculiar sympathy with Mr Paraday's line of thought. They would greatly appreciate any expression of his views on the subject of the art he so brilliantly practises. Besides my connection with the syndicate just mentioned, I hold a particular commission from *The Tatler*, whose most prominent department, 'Smatter and Chatter'—I daresay you've often enjoyed it—attracts such attention. I was honoured only last week, as a representative of *The Tatler*, with the confidence of Guy Walsingham, the author of 'Obsessions.' She expressed herself thoroughly pleased with my sketch of her method; she went so far as to say that I had made her genius more comprehensible even to herself."

Neil Paraday had dropped upon the garden-bench and sat there at once detached and confused; he looked hard at a bare spot in the lawn, as if with an anxiety that had suddenly made him grave. His movement had been interpreted by his visitor as an invitation to sink sympathetically into a wicker chair that stood hard by, and as Mr Morrow so settled himself I felt that he had taken official possession and that there was no undoing it. One had heard of unfortunate people's having "a man in the house," and this was just what we had. There was a silence of a moment, during which we seemed to acknowledge in the only way that was possible the presence of universal fate; the sunny stillness took no pity, and my thought, as I was sure Paraday's was doing, performed within the minute a great distant revolution. I saw just how emphatic I should make my rejoinder to Mr Pinhorn, and that having come, like Mr Morrow, to betray, I must remain as long as possible to save. Not because I had brought my mind back, but because our visitor's last words were in my ear, I presently inquired with gloomy irrelevance if Guy Walsingham were a woman.

"Oh yes, a mere pseudonym; but convenient, you know, for a lady who goes in for the larger latitude. 'Obsessions, by Miss So-and-so,' would look a little odd, but men are more naturally indelicate. Have you peeped into 'Obsessions'?" Mr Morrow continued sociably to our companion.

Paraday, still absent, remote, made no answer, as if he had not heard the question: a manifestation that appeared to suit the cheerful Mr Morrow as well as any other. Imperturbably bland, he was a man of resources—he only needed to be on the spot. He had pocketed the whole poor place while Paraday and I were woolgathering, and I could imagine that he had already got his "heads." His system, at any rate, was justified by the inevitability with which I replied, to save my friend the trouble: "Dear, no; he hasn't read it. He doesn't read such things!" I unwarily added.

"Things that are *too* far over the fence, eh?" I was indeed a godsend to Mr Morrow. It was the psychological moment; it determined the appearance of his notebook, which, however, he at first kept slightly behind him, even as the dentist, approaching his victim, keeps the horrible forceps. "Mr Paraday holds with the good old proprieties—I see!" And thinking of the thirty-seven influential journals, I found myself, as I found poor Paraday, helplessly gazing at the promulgation of this ineptitude. "There's no point on which distinguished views are so acceptable as on this question—raised perhaps more strikingly than ever by Guy Walsingham—of the permissibility of the larger latitude. I have an appointment, precisely in connection with it, next week, with Dora Forbes, the author of 'The Other Way Round,' which everybody is talking about. Has Mr Paraday glanced at 'The Other Way Round'?" Mr Morrow now frankly appealed to me. I took upon myself to repudiate the supposition, while our companion, still silent, got up nervously and walked away. His visitor paid no heed to his withdrawal; he only opened out the notebook with a more motherly pat. "Dora Forbes, I gather, takes the ground, the same as Guy Walsingham's, that the larger latitude has simply got to come. He holds that it has got to be squarely faced. Of course his sex makes him a less prejudiced witness. But an authoritative word from Mr Paraday— from the point of view of *his* sex, you know—would go right round the globe. He takes the line that we *haven't* got to face it?"

I was bewildered: it sounded somehow as if there were three sexes. My interlocutor's pencil was poised, my private responsibility great. I simply sat staring, however, and only found presence of mind to say: "Is this Miss Forbes a gentleman?"

Mr Morrow hesitated an instant, smiling. "It wouldn't be 'Miss'—there's a wife!"

"I mean is she a man?"

"The wife?"—Mr Morrow, for a moment, was as confused as myself. But when I explained that I alluded to Dora Forbes in person he informed me, with visible amusement at my being so out of it, that this was the "pen-name" of an indubitable male—he had a big red moustache. "He only assumes a feminine personality because the ladies are such popular favourites. A great deal of interest is felt in this assumption, and there's every prospect of its being widely imitated." Our host at this moment joined us again, and Mr Morrow remarked invitingly that he should be happy to make a note of any observation the movement in question, the bid for success under a lady's name, might suggest to Mr Paraday. But the poor man, without catching the allusion, excused himself, pleading that, though he was greatly honoured by his visitor's interest, he suddenly felt unwell and should have to take leave of him—have to go and lie down and keep quiet. His young friend might be trusted to answer for him, but he hoped Mr Morrow didn't expect great things even of his young friend. His young friend, at this moment, looked at Neil Paraday with an anxious eye, greatly wondering if he were doomed to be ill again; but Paraday's own kind face met his question re-assuringly, seemed to say in a glance intelligible enough: "Oh, I'm not ill, but I'm scared: get him out of the house as quietly as possible." Getting newspaper-men out of the house was odd business for an emissary of Mr Pinhorn, and I was so exhilarated by the idea of it that I called after him as he left us:

"Read the article in *The Empire*, and you'll soon be all right!"

V

"DELICIOUS my having come down to tell him of it!" Mr Morrow ejaculated. "My cab was at the door twenty minutes after *The Empire* had been laid upon my breakfast-table. Now what have you got for me?" he continued, dropping again into his chair, from which, however, the next moment he quickly rose. "I was shown into the drawing-room, but there must be more to see—his study, his literary sanctum, the little things he has about, or other domestic objects or features. He wouldn't be lying down on his study-table? There's a great interest always felt in the scene of an author's labours. Sometimes we're favoured with very delightful peeps. Dora Forbes showed me all his table-drawers, and almost jammed my hand into one into which I made a dash! I don't ask that of you, but if we could talk things over right there where he sits I feel as if I should get the keynote."

I had no wish whatever to be rude to Mr Morrow, I was much too initiated not to prefer the safety of other ways; but I had a quick inspiration and I entertained an insurmountable, an almost superstitious objection to his crossing the threshold of my friend's little lonely, shabby, consecrated workshop. "No, no—we sha'n't get at his life that way," I said. "The way to get at his life is to—But wait a moment!" I broke off and went quickly into the house; then, in three minutes, I re-appeared before Mr Morrow with the two volumes of Para-day's new book. "His life's here," I went on, "and I'm so full of this admirable thing that I can't talk of anything else. The artist's life's his work, and this is the place to observe him. What he has to tell us he tells us with *this* perfection. My dear sir, the best interviewer's the best reader."

Mr Morrow good-humouredly protested. "Do you mean to say that no other source of information should be open to us?"

"None other till this particular one—by far the most copious—has been quite exhausted. Have you exhausted it, my dear sir? Had you exhausted it when you came down here? It seems to me in our time almost wholly neglected, and some-thing should surely be done to restore its ruined credit. It's the course to which the artist himself at every step, and with such pathetic confidence, refers us. This last book of Mr Paraday's is full of revelations."

"Revelations?" panted Mr Morrow, whom I had forced again into his chair.

"The only kind that count. It tells you with a perfection that seems to me quite final all the author thinks, for instance, about the advent of the 'larger latitude.'"

"Where does it do that?" asked Mr Morrow, who had picked up the second volume and was insincerely thumbing it.

"Everywhere—in the whole treatment of his case. Extract the opinion, disengage the answer—those are the real acts of homage."

Mr Morrow, after a minute, tossed the book away. "Ah, but you mustn't take me for a reviewer."

"Heaven forbid I should take you for anything so dreadful! You came down to perform a little act of sympathy, and so, I may confide to you, did I. Let us perform our little act together. These pages overflow with the testimony we want: let us read them and taste them and interpret them. You will of course have perceived for yourself that one scarcely does read Neil Paraday till one reads him aloud; he gives out to the ear an extraordinary quality, and it's only when you expose it confidently to that test that you really get near his style. Take up your book again and let me listen, while you pay it out, to that wonderful fifteenth chapter. If you feel that you can't do it justice, compose yourself to attention while I produce for you—I think I can!—this scarcely less admirable ninth."

Mr Morrow gave me a straight glance which was as hard as a blow between the eyes; he had turned rather red, and a question had formed itself in his mind which reached my sense as distinctly as if he had uttered it: "What sort of a damned fool are *you*?" Then he got up, gathering together his hat and gloves, buttoning his coat, projecting hungrily all over the place the big transparency of his mask. It seemed to flare over Fleet Street and somehow made the actual spot distressingly humble: there was so little for it to feed on unless he counted the blisters of our stucco or saw his way to do something with the roses. Even the poor roses were common kinds. Presently his eyes fell upon the manuscript from which Paraday had been reading to me and which still lay on the bench. As my own followed them I saw that it looked promising, looked pregnant, as if it gently throbbed with the life the reader had given it. Mr Morrow indulged in a nod toward it and a vague thrust of his umbrella. "What's that?"

"Oh, it's a plan—a secret."

"A secret!" There was an instant's silence, and then Mr Morrow made another movement. I may have been mistaken, but it affected me as the translated impulse of the desire to lay hands on the manuscript, and this led me to indulge in a quick anticipatory grab which may very well have seemed ungraceful, or even impertinent, and which at any rate left Mr Paraday's two admirers very erect, glaring at each other while one of them held a bundle of papers well behind him. An instant later Mr Morrow quitted me abruptly, as if he had really carried something off with him. To reassure myself, watching his broad back recede, I only grasped my manuscript the tighter. He went to the back-door of the house, the one he had come out from, but on trying the handle he appeared to find it fastened. So he passed round into the front garden, and by listening intently enough I could presently hear the outer gate close behind him with a bang. I thought again of the thirty-seven influential journals and wondered what would be his revenge. I hasten to add that he was magnanimous: which was just the most dreadful thing he could have been. *The Tatler* published a charming, chatty, familiar account of Mr Paraday's "Home-life," and on the wings of the thirty-seven influential journals it went, to use Mr Morrow's own expression, right round the globe.

VI

A WEEK later, early in May, my glorified friend came up to town, where, it may be veraciously recorded, he was the king of the beasts of the year. No advancement was ever more rapid, no exaltation more complete, no bewilderment more teachable. His book sold but moderately, though the article in *The Empire* had done unwonted wonders for it; but he circulated in person in a manner that the libraries might well have envied. His formula had been found—he was a "revelation." His momentary terror had been real, just as mine had been—the overclouding of his passionate desire to be left to finish his work. He was far from unsociable, but he had the finest conception of being let alone that I have ever met. For the time, however, he took his profit where it seemed most to crowd upon him, having in his pocket the portable sophistries about the nature of the artist's task. Observation too was a kind of work and experience a kind of success; London dinners were all material and London ladies were fruitful toil. "No one has the faintest conception of what I'm trying for," he said to me, "and not many have read three pages that I've written; but I must dine with them first—they'll find out why when they've time." It was rather rude justice, perhaps; but the fatigue had the merit of being a new sort, and the phantasmagoric town was probably after all less of a battlefield than the haunted study. He once told me that he had had no personal life to speak of since his fortieth year, but had had more than was good for him before. London closed the parenthesis and exhibited him in relations; one of the most inevitable of these being that in which he found himself to Mrs Weeks Wimbush, wife of the boundless brewer and proprietress of the universal menagerie. In this establishment, as everybody knows, on occasions when the crush is great, the animals rub shoulders freely with the spectators and the lions sit down for whole evenings with the lambs.

It had been ominously clear to me from the first that in Neil Paraday this lady, who, as all the world agreed, was tremendous fun, considered that she had secured a prime attraction, a creature of almost heraldic oddity. Nothing could exceed her enthusiasm over her capture, and nothing could exceed the confused apprehensions it excited in me. I had an instinctive fear of her which I tried without effect to conceal from her victim, but which I let her perceive with perfect impunity. Paraday heeded it, but she never did, for her conscience was that of a romping child. She was a blind, violent force, to which I could attach no more idea of responsibility than to the creaking of a sign in the wind. It was difficult to say what she conduced to but to circulation. She was constructed of steel and leather, and all I asked of her for our tractable friend was not to do him to death. He had consented for a time to be of india-rubber, but my thoughts were fixed on the day he should resume his shape or at least get back into his box. It was evidently all right, but I should be glad when it was well over. I had a special fear—the impression was ineffaceable of the hour when, after Mr Morrow's departure, I had found him on the sofa in his study. That pretext of indisposition had not in the least been meant as a snub to the envoy of *The Tatler*—he had gone to lie down in very truth. He had felt a pang of his old pain, the result of the agitation wrought in him by this forcing open of a new period. His old programme, his old ideal even had to be changed. Say what one would, success was a complication and recognition had to be reciprocal. The monastic life, the pious illumination of the missal in the convent cell were things of the gathered past. It didn't engender despair, but it at least required adjustment. Before I left him on that occasion we had passed a bargain, my part of which was that I should make it my business to take care of him. Let whoever would represent the interest in his presence (I had a mystical prevision of Mrs Weeks Wimbush) I should represent the interest in his work—in other words in his absence. These two interests were in their essence opposed; and I doubt, as youth is fleeting, if I shall ever again know the intensity of joy with which I felt that in so good a cause I was willing to make myself odious.

One day, in Sloane Street, I found myself questioning Paraday's landlord, who had come to the door in answer to my

knock. Two vehicles, a barouche and a smart hansom, were
drawn up before the house.

"In the drawing-room, sir? Mrs Weeks Wimbush."

"And in the dining-room?"

"A young lady, sir—waiting: I think a foreigner."

It was three o'clock, and on days when Paraday didn't lunch
out he attached a value to these subjugated hours. On which
days, however, didn't the dear man lunch out? Mrs Wimbush,
at such a crisis, would have rushed round immediately after
her own repast. I went into the dining-room first, postponing
the pleasure of seeing how, upstairs, the lady of the barouche
would, on my arrival, point the moral of my sweet solicitude.
No one took such an interest as herself in his doing only what
was good for him, and she was always on the spot to see that
he did it. She made appointments with him to discuss the best
means of economising his time and protecting his privacy. She
further made his health her special business, and had so much
sympathy with my own zeal for it that she was the author of
pleasing fictions on the subject of what my devotion had led
me to give up. I gave up nothing (I don't count Mr Pinhorn)
because I had nothing, and all I had as yet achieved was to find
myself also in the menagerie. I had dashed in to save my
friend, but I had only got domesticated and wedged; so that I
could do nothing for him but exchange with him over people's
heads looks of intense but futile intelligence.

VII

THE young lady in the dining-room had a brave face, black
hair, blue eyes, and in her lap a big volume. "I've come for his
autograph," she said when I had explained to her that I was
under bonds to see people for him when he was occupied.
"I've been waiting half an hour, but I'm prepared to wait

all day." I don't know whether it was this that told me she was American, for the propensity to wait all day is not in general characteristic of her race. I was enlightened probably not so much by the spirit of the utterance as by some quality of its sound. At any rate I saw she had an individual patience and a lovely frock, together with an expression that played among her pretty features like a breeze among flowers. Putting her book upon the table, she showed me a massive album, showily bound and full of autographs of price. The collection of faded notes, of still more faded "thoughts," of quotations, platitudes, signatures, represented a formidable purpose.

"Most people apply to Mr Paraday by letter, you know," I said.

"Yes, but he doesn't answer. I've written three times."

"Very true," I reflected; "the sort of letter you mean goes straight into the fire."

"How do you know the sort I mean?" My interlocutress had blushed and smiled, and in a moment she added: "I don't believe he gets many like them!"

"I'm sure they're beautiful, but he burns without reading." I didn't add that I had told him he ought to.

"Isn't he then in danger of burning things of importance?"

"He would be, if distinguished men hadn't an infallible nose for nonsense."

She looked at me a moment—her face was sweet and gay. "Do *you* burn without reading, too?" she asked; in answer to which I assured her that if she would trust me with her repository I would see that Mr Paraday should write his name in it.

She considered a little. "That's very well, but it wouldn't make me see him."

"Do you want very much to see him?" It seemed ungracious to catechise so charming a creature, but somehow I had never yet taken my duty to the great author so seriously.

"Enough to have come from America for the purpose."

9:G

I stared. "All alone?"

"I don't see that that's exactly your business; but if it will make me more appealing I'll confess that I'm quite by myself. I had to come alone or not come at all."

She was interesting; I could imagine that she had lost parents, natural protectors—could conceive even that she had inherited money. I was in a phase of my own fortune when keeping hansoms at doors seemed to me pure swagger. As a trick of this bold and sensitive girl, however, it became romantic—a part of the general romance of her freedom, her errand, her innocence. The confidence of young Americans was notorious, and I speedily arrived at a conviction that no impulse could have been more generous than the impulse that had operated here. I foresaw at that moment that it would make her my peculiar charge, just as circumstances had made Neil Paraday. She would be another person to look after, and one's honour would be concerned in guiding her straight. These things became clearer to me later; at the instant I had scepticism enough to observe to her, as I turned the pages of her volume, that her net had, all the same, caught many a big fish. She appeared to have had fruitful access to the great ones of the earth; there were people moreover whose signatures she had presumably secured without a personal interview. She couldn't have worried George Washington and Friedrich Schiller and Hannah More. She met this argument, to my surprise, by throwing up the album without a pang. It wasn't even her own; she was responsible for none of its treasures. It belonged to a girl-friend in America, a young lady in a western city. This young lady had insisted on her bringing it, to pick up more autographs: she thought they might like to see, in Europe, in what company they would be. The "girl-friend," the western city, the immortal names, the curious errand, the idyllic faith, all made a story as strange to me, and as beguiling, as some tale in the Arabian Nights. Thus it was that my informant had encumbered herself with the ponderous tome; but she hastened to assure me that this was the first time she had brought it out. For her visit to Mr Paraday it had simply been a pretext. She didn't really care a straw that he should write his name; what she did want was to look straight into his face.

I demurred a little. "And why do you require to do that?"

"Because I just love him!" Before I could recover from the agitating effect of this crystal ring my companion had continued: "Hasn't there ever been any face that you've wanted to look into?"

How could I tell her so soon how much I appreciated the opportunity of looking into hers? I could only assent in general to the proposition that there were certainly for every one such hankerings, and even such faces; and I felt that the crisis demanded all my lucidity, all my wisdom. "Oh, yes, I'm a student of physiognomy. Do you mean," I pursued, "that you've a passion for Mr Paraday's books?"

"They've been everything to me and a little more beside— I know them by heart. They've completely taken hold of me. There's no author about whom I feel as I do about Neil Paraday."

"Permit me to remark then," I presently rejoined, "that you're one of the right sort."

"One of the enthusiasts? Of course I am!"

"Oh, there are enthusiasts who are quite of the wrong. I mean you're one of those to whom an appeal can be made."

"An appeal?" Her face lighted as if with the chance of some great sacrifice.

If she was ready for one it was only waiting for her, and in a moment I mentioned it. "Give up this crude purpose of seeing him. Go away without it. That will be far better."

She looked mystified; then she turned visibly pale. "Why, hasn't he any personal charm?" The girl was terrible and laughable in her bright directness.

"Ah, that dreadful word 'personal!'" I exclaimed; "we're dying of it, and you women bring it out with murderous effect.

When you encounter a genius as fine as this idol of ours, let him off the dreary duty of being a personality as well. Know him only by what's best in him, and spare him for the same sweet sake."

My young lady continued to look at me in confusion and mistrust, and the result of her reflection on what I had just said was to make her suddenly break out: "Look here, sir—what's the matter with him?"

"The matter with him is that, if he doesn't look out, people will eat a great hole in his life."

She considered a moment. "He hasn't any disfigurement?"

"Nothing to speak of!"

"Do you mean that social engagements interfere with his occupations?"

"That but feebly expresses it."

"So that he can't give himself up to his beautiful imagination?"

"He's badgered, bothered, overwhelmed, on the pretext of being applauded. People expect him to give them his time, his golden time, who wouldn't themselves give five shillings for one of his books."

"Five? I'd give five thousand!"

"Give your sympathy—give your forbearance. Two-thirds of those who approach him only do it to advertise themselves."

"Why, it's too bad!" the girl exclaimed with the face of an angel. "It's the first time I was ever called crude!" she laughed.

I followed up my advantage. "There's a lady with him now who's a terrible complication, and who yet hasn't read, I am sure, ten pages that he ever wrote."

My visitor's wide eyes grew tenderer. "Then how does she talk——?"

"Without ceasing. I only mention her as a single case. Do you want to know how to show a superlative consideration? Simply avoid him."

"Avoid him?" she softly wailed.

"Don't force him to have to take account of you; admire him in silence, cultivate him at a distance and secretly appropriate his message. Do you want to know," I continued, warming to my idea, "how to perform an act of homage really sublime?" Then as she hung on my words: "Succeed in never seeing him at all!"

"Never at all?" she pathetically gasped.

"The more you get into his writings the less you'll want to; and you'll be immensely sustained by the thought of the good you're doing him."

She looked at me without resentment or spite, and at the truth I had put before her with candour, credulity, pity. I was afterwards happy to remember that she must have recognised in my face the liveliness of my interest in herself. "I think I see what you mean."

"Oh, I express it badly; but I should be delighted if you would let me come to see you—to explain it better."

She made no response to this, and her thoughtful eyes fell on the big album, on which she presently laid her hands as if to take it away. "I did use to say out West that they might write a little less for autographs (to all the great poets, you know) and study the thoughts and style a little more."

"What do they care for the thoughts and style? They didn't even understand you. I'm not sure," I added, "that I do myself, and I daresay that you by no means make me out." She had got up to go, and though I wanted her to succeed in not seeing Neil Paraday I wanted her also, inconsequently, to remain in the house. I was at any rate far from desiring to hustle her off. As Mrs Weeks Wimbush, upstairs, was still saving our friend in her own way, I asked my young lady to let me briefly relate, in illustration of my point, the little incident of my having gone down into the country for a profane purpose and been converted on the spot to holiness. Sinking again into her chair to listen, she showed a deep interest in the anecdote. Then thinking it over gravely, she exclaimed with her odd intonation:

"Yes, but you do see him!" I had to admit that this was the case; and I was not so prepared with an effective attenuation as I could have wished. She eased the situation off, however, by the charming quaintness with which she finally said: "Well, I wouldn't want him to be lonely!" This time she rose in earnest, but I persuaded her to let me keep the album to show to Mr Paraday. I assured her I would bring it back to her myself. "Well, you'll find my address somewhere in it, on a paper!" she sighed resignedly, at the door.

VIII

I BLUSH to confess it, but I invited Mr Paraday that very day to transcribe into the album one of his most characteristic passages. I told him how I had got rid of the strange girl who had brought it—her ominous name was Miss Hurter, and she lived at an hotel; quite agreeing with him moreover as to the wisdom of getting rid with equal promptitude of the book itself. This was why I carried it to Albemarle Street no later than on the morrow. I failed to find her at home, but she wrote to me and I went again: she wanted so much to hear more about Neil Paraday. I returned repeatedly, I may briefly declare, to supply her with this information. She had been immensely taken, the more she thought of it, with that idea of mine about the act of homage: it had ended by filling her with a generous rapture. She positively desired to do something sublime for him, though indeed I could see that, as this particular flight was difficult, she appreciated the fact that my visits kept her up. I had it on my conscience to keep her up; I neglected nothing that would contribute to it, and her conception of our cherished author's independence became at last

as fine as his own conception. "Read him, read him," I constantly repeated; while, seeking him in his works, she represented herself as convinced that, according to my assurance,
this was the system that had, as she expressed it, weaned her.
We read him together when I could find time, and the generous
creature's sacrifice was fed by our conversation. There were
twenty selfish women, about whom I told her, who stirred her
with a beautiful rage. Immediately after my first visit her sister,
Mrs Milsom, came over from Paris, and the two ladies began to
present, as they called it, their letters. I thanked our stars that
none had been presented to Mr Paraday. They received invitations and dined out, and some of these occasions enabled
Fanny Hurter to perform, for consistency's sake, touching
feats of submission. Nothing indeed would now have induced
her even to look at the object of her admiration. Once, hearing
his name announced at a party, she instantly left the room by
another door and then straightway quitted the house. At
another time, when I was at the opera with them (Mrs Milsom
had invited me to their box) I attempted to point Mr Paraday
out to her in the stalls. On this she asked her sister to change
places with her, and while that lady devoured the great man
through a powerful glass, presented, all the rest of the
evening, her inspired back to the house. To torment her tenderly I pressed the glass upon her, telling her how wonderfully
near it brought our friend's handsome head. By way of answer
she simply looked at me in charged silence, letting me see that
tears had gathered in her eyes. These tears, I may remark, produced an effect on me of which the end is not yet. There was a
moment when I felt it my duty to mention them to Neil Paraday; but I was deterred by the reflection that there were questions more relevant to his happiness.

These questions indeed, by the end of the season, were
reduced to a single one—the question of reconstituting, so far
as might be possible, the conditions under which he had produced his best work. Such conditions could never all come

back, for there was a new one that took up too much place; but some perhaps were not beyond recall. I wanted above all things to see him sit down to the subject of which, on my making his acquaintance, he had read me that admirable sketch. Something told me there was no security but in his doing so before the new factor, as we used to say at Mr Pinhorn's, should render the problem incalculable. It only half reassured me that the sketch itself was so copious and so eloquent that even at the worst there would be the making of a small but complete book, a tiny volume which, for the faithful, might well become an object of adoration. There would even not be wanting critics to declare, I foresaw, that the plan was a thing to be more thankful for than the structure to have been reared on it. My impatience for the structure, none the less, grew and grew with the interruptions. He had, on coming up to town, begun to sit for his portrait to a young painter, Mr Rumble, whose little game, as we also used to say at Mr Pinhorn's, was to be the first to perch on the shoulders of renown. Mr Rumble's studio was a circus in which the man of the hour, and still more the woman, leaped through the hoops of his showy frames almost as electrically as they burst into telegrams and "specials." He pranced into the exhibitions on their back; he was the reporter on canvas, the Vandyke up to date, and there was one roaring year in which Mrs Bounder and Miss Braby, Guy Walsingham and Dora Forbes proclaimed in chorus from the same pictured walls that no one had yet got ahead of him.

Paraday had been promptly caught and saddled, accepting with characteristic good-humour his confidential hint that to figure in his show was not so much a consequence as a cause of immortality. From Mrs Wimbush to the last "representative" who called to ascertain his twelve favourite dishes, it was the same ingenuous assumption that he would rejoice in the reper- cussion. There were moments when I fancied I might have had more patience with them if they had not been so fatally benevolent. I hated, at all events, Mr Rumble's picture, and had my bottled resentment ready when, later on, I found my distracted friend had been stuffed by Mrs Wimbush into the mouth of another cannon. A young artist in whom she was intensely interested, and who had no connection with Mr Rumble, was to show how far he could make him go. Poor Paraday, in return, was naturally to write something somewhere about the young artist. She played her victims against each other with admirable ingenuity, and her establishment was a huge machine in which the tiniest and the biggest wheels went round to the same treadle. I had a scene with her in which I tried to express that the function of such a man was to exercise his genius—not to serve as a hoarding for pictorial posters. The people I was perhaps angriest with were the editors of magazines who had introduced what they called new features, so aware were they that the newest feature of all would be to make him grind their axes by contributing his views on vital topics and taking part in the periodical prattle about the future of fiction. I made sure that before I should have done with him there would scarcely be a current form of words left me to be sick of; but meanwhile I could make surer still of my animosity to bustling ladies for whom he drew the water that irrigated their social flower-beds.

I had a battle with Mrs Wimbush over the artist she protected, and another over the question of a certain week, at the end of July, that Mr Paraday appeared to have contracted to spend with her in the country. I protested against this visit; I intimated that he was too unwell for hospitality without a *nuance*, for caresses without imagination; I begged he might rather take the time in some restorative way. A sultry air of promises, of ponderous parties, hung over his August, and he would greatly profit by the interval of rest. He had not told me he was ill again—that he had had a warning; but I had not needed this, and I found his reticence his worst symptom. The only thing he said to me was that he believed a comfortable attack of something or other would set him up; it would put out of the question everything but the exemptions he prized. I am afraid I shall have presented him as a martyr in a very small cause if I fail to explain that he surrendered himself much more liberally than I surrendered him. He filled his lungs, for the most part, with the comedy of his queer fate: the tragedy was in the spectacles through which I chose to look. He was conscious of inconvenience, and above all of a great renouncement; but how could he have heard a mere dirge in the bells of his accession? The sagacity and the jealousy were mine, and his the impressions and the anecdotes. Of course, as regards Mrs Wimbush, I was worsted in my encounters, for was not the state of his health the very reason for his coming to her at Prestidge? Wasn't it precisely at Prestidge that he was to be coddled, and wasn't the dear Princess coming to help her to coddle him? The dear Princess, now on a visit to England, was of a famous foreign house, and, in her gilded cage, with her retinue of keepers and feeders, was the most expensive specimen in the good lady's collection. I don't think her august presence had had to do with Paraday's consenting to go, but it is not impossible that he had operated as a bait to the illustrious stranger. The party had been made up for him, Mrs Wimbush averred, and every one was counting on it, the dear Princess most of all. If he was well enough he was to read them something absolutely fresh, and it was on that particular prospect the Princess had set her heart. She was so fond of genius, in *any* walk of life, and she was so used to it, and understood it so well; she was the greatest of Mr Paraday's admirers, she devoured everything he wrote. And then he read like an angel. Mrs Wimbush reminded me that he had again and again given her, Mrs Wimbush, the privilege of listening to him.

I looked at her a moment. "What has he read to you?" I crudely inquired.

For a moment too she met my eyes, and for the fraction of a moment she hesitated and coloured. "Oh, all sorts of things!"

I wondered whether this were an imperfect recollection or

only a perfect fib, and she quite understood my unuttered comment on her perception of such things. But if she could forget
Neil Paraday's beauties she could of course forget my rude-
ness, and three days later she invited me, by telegraph, to join
the party at Prestidge. This time she might indeed have had a
story about what I had given up to be near the master. I
addressed from that fine residence several communications to
a young lady in London, a young lady whom, I confess, I
quitted with reluctance and whom the reminder of what she
herself could give up was required to make me quit at all. It
adds to the gratitude I owe her on other grounds that she
kindly allows me to transcribe from my letters a few of the
passages in which that hateful sojourn is candidly commemorated.

IX

"I suppose I ought to enjoy the joke of what's going on
here," I wrote, "but somehow it doesn't amuse me. Pessimism
on the contrary possesses me and cynicism solicits. I positively
feel my own flesh sore from the brass nails in Neil Paraday's
social harness. The house is full of people who like him, as
they mention, awfully, and with whom his talent for talking
nonsense has prodigious success. I delight in his nonsense
myself; why is it therefore that I grudge these happy folk their
artless satisfaction? Mystery of the human heart—abyss of the
critical spirit! Mrs Wimbush thinks she can answer that question, and as my want of gaiety has at last worn out her patience
she has given me a glimpse of her shrewd guess. I am made
restless by the selfishness of the insincere friend—I want to
monopolise Paraday in order that he may push me on. To be
intimate with him is a feather in my cap; it gives me an importance that I couldn't naturally pretend to, and I seek to deprive

him of social refreshment because I fear that meeting more
disinterested people may enlighten him as to my real motive.
All the disinterested people here are his particular admirers
and have been carefully selected as such. There is supposed to
be a copy of his last book in the house, and in the hall I come
upon ladies, in attitudes, bending gracefully over the first
volume. I discreetly avert my eyes, and when I next look
round the precarious joy has been superseded by the book of
life. There is a sociable circle or a confidential couple, and the
relinquished volume lies open on its face, as if it had been
dropped under extreme coercion. Somebody else presently
finds it and transfers it, with its air of momentary desolation,
to another piece of furniture. Every one is asking every one
about it all day, and every one is telling every one where they
put it last. I'm sure it's rather smudgy about the twentieth
page. I have a strong impression too that the second volume is
lost—has been packed in the bag of some departing guest; and
yet everybody has the impression that somebody else has read
to the end. You see therefore that the beautiful book plays a
great part in our conversation. Why should I take the
occasion of such distinguished honours to say that I begin to
see deeper into Gustave Flaubert's doleful refrain about the
hatred of literature? I refer you again to the perverse constitution of man.

"The Princess is a massive lady with the organisation of an
athlete and the confusion of tongues of a *valet de place*. She
contrives to commit herself extraordinarily little in a great
many languages, and is entertained and conversed with in
detachments and relays, like an institution which goes on from
generation to generation or a big building contracted for under
a forfeit. She can't have a personal taste any more than, when
her husband succeeds, she can have a personal crown, and her
opinion on any matter is rusty and heavy and plain—made, in
the night of ages, to last and be transmitted. I feel as if I ought
to pay some one a fee for my glimpse of it. She has been told

everything in the world and has never perceived anything, and the echoes of her education respond awfully to the rash foot-fall—I mean the casual remark—in the cold Valhalla of her memory. Mrs Wimbush delights in her wit and says there is nothing so charming as to hear Mr Paraday draw it out. He is perpetually detailed for this job, and he tells me it has a peculiarly exhausting effect. Every one is beginning—at the end of two days—to sidle obsequiously away from her, and Mrs Wimbush pushes him again and again into the breach. None of the uses I have yet seen him put to irritate me quite so much. He looks very fagged, and has at last confessed to me that his condition makes him uneasy—has even promised me that he will go straight home instead of returning to his final engagements in town. Last night I had some talk with him about going to-day, cutting his visit short; so sure am I that he will be better as soon as he is shut up in his lighthouse. He told me that this is what he would like to do; reminding me, how-ever, that the first lesson of his greatness has been precisely that he can't do what he likes. Mrs Wimbush would never for-give him if he should leave her before the Princess has received the last hand. When I say that a violent rupture with our hostess would be the best thing in the world for him he gives me to understand that if his reason assents to the proposition his courage hangs wofully back. He makes no secret of being mortally afraid of her, and when I ask what harm she can do him that she hasn't already done he simply repeats: 'I'm afraid, I'm afraid! Don't inquire too closely,' he said last night; 'only believe that I feel a sort of terror. It's strange, when she's so kind! At any rate, I would as soon overturn that piece of priceless Sèvres as tell her that I must go before my date.' It sounds dreadfully weak, but he has some reason, and he pays for his imagination, which puts him (I should hate it) in the place of others and makes him feel, even against himself, their feelings, their appetites, their motives. It's indeed inveterately against himself that he makes his imagination

act. What a pity he has such a lot of it! He's too beastly
intelligent. Besides, the famous reading is still to come off,
and it has been postponed a day, to allow Guy Walsingham to
arrive. It appears that this eminent lady is staying at a house
a few miles off, which means of course that Mrs Wimbush has
forcibly annexed her. She's to come over in a day or two—
Mrs Wimbush wants her to hear Mr Paraday.

"To-day's wet and cold, and several of the company, at the
invitation of the Duke, have driven over to luncheon at Bigwood. I saw poor Paraday wedge himself, by command, into
the little supplementary seat of a brougham in which the
Princess and our hostess were already ensconced. If the front
glass isn't open on his dear old back perhaps he'll survive.
Bigwood, I believe, is very grand and frigid, all marble and
precedence, and I wish him well out of the adventure. I can't
tell you how much more and more *your* attitude to him, in the
midst of all this, shines out by contrast. I never willingly talk
to these people about him, but see what a comfort I find it to
scribble to you! I appreciate it—it keeps me warm; there are
no fires in the house. Mrs Wimbush goes by the calendar, the
temperature goes by the weather, the weather goes by God
knows what, and the Princess is easily heated. I have nothing
but my acrimony to warm me, and have been out under an
umbrella to restore my circulation. Coming in an hour ago, I
found Lady Augusta Minch rummaging about the hall. When
I asked her what she was looking for she said she had mislaid
something that Mr Paraday had lent her. I ascertained in a
moment that the article in question is a manuscript, and I have
a foreboding that it's the noble morsel he read me six weeks
ago. When I expressed my surprise that he should have ban-
died about anything so precious (I happen to know it's his
only copy—in the most beautiful hand in all the world) Lady
Augusta confessed to me that she had not had it from himself,
but from Mrs Wimbush, who had wished to give her a glimpse
of it as a salve for her not being able to stay and hear it read.

" 'Is that the piece he's to read,' I asked, 'when Guy Walsingham arrives?'

" 'It's not for Guy Walsingham they're waiting now, it's for Dora Forbes,' Lady Augusta said. 'She's coming, I believe, early to-morrow. Meanwhile Mrs Wimbush has found out about *him*, and is actively wiring to him. She says he also must hear him.'

" 'You bewilder me a little,' I replied; 'in the age we live in one gets lost among the genders and the pronouns. The clear thing is that Mrs Wimbush doesn't guard such a treasure as jealously as she might.'

" 'Poor dear, she has the Princess to guard! Mr Paraday lent her the manuscript to look over.'

" 'Did she speak as if it were the morning paper?'

"Lady Augusta stared—my irony was lost upon her. 'She didn't have time, so she gave me a chance first; because unfortunately I go to-morrow to Bigwood.'

" 'And your chance has only proved a chance to lose it?'

" 'I haven't lost it. I remember now—it was very stupid of me to have forgotten. I told my maid to give it to Lord Dorimont—or at least to his man.'

" 'And Lord Dorimont went away directly after luncheon.'

" 'Of course he gave it back to my maid—or else his man did,' said Lady Augusta. 'I daresay it's all right.'

"The conscience of these people is like a summer sea. They haven't time to 'look over' a priceless composition; they've only time to kick it about the house. I suggested that the 'man,' fired with a noble emulation, had perhaps kept the work for his own perusal; and her ladyship wanted to know whether, if the thing didn't turn up again in time for the session appointed by our hostess, the author wouldn't have something else to read that would do just as well. Their questions are too delightful! I declared to Lady Augusta briefly that nothing in the world can ever do so well as the thing that does best; and at this she looked a little confused and scared.

But I added that if the manuscript had gone astray our little circle would have the less of an effort of attention to make. The piece in question was very long—it would keep them three hours.

" 'Three hours! Oh, the Princess will get up!' said Lady Augusta.

" 'I thought she was Mr Paraday's greatest admirer.'

" 'I daresay she is—she's so awfully clever. But what's the use of being a Princess——'

" 'If you can't dissemble your love?' I asked, as Lady Augusta was vague. She said, at any rate, that she would question her maid; and I am hoping that when I go down to dinner I shall find the manuscript has been recovered."

X

"It has not been recovered," I wrote early the next day, "and I am moreover much troubled about our friend. He came back from Bigwood with a chill and, being allowed to have a fire in his room, lay down awhile before dinner. I tried to send him to bed, and indeed thought I had put him in the way of it; but after I had gone to dress Mrs Wimbush came up to see him, with the inevitable result that when I returned I found him under arms and flushed and feverish, though decorated with the rare flower she had brought him for his button-hole. He came down to dinner, but Lady Augusta Minch was very shy of him. To-day he's in great pain, and the advent of *ces dames* —I mean of Guy Walsingham and Dora Forbes—doesn't at all console me. It does Mrs Wimbush however, for she has consented to his remaining in bed, so that he may be all right to-morrow for the listening circle. Guy Walsingham is already on the scene, and the doctor, for Paraday, also arrived early. I haven't yet seen the author of 'Obsessions,' but of course I've had a moment by myself with the doctor. I tried to get him to say that our invalid must go straight home—I mean to-morrow or next day; but he quite refuses to talk about the future. Absolute quiet and warmth and the regular administration of an important remedy are the points he mainly insists on. He returns this afternoon, and I'm to go back to see the patient at one o'clock, when he next takes his medicine. It consoles me a little that he certainly won't be able to read—an exertion he was already more than unfit for. Lady Augusta went off after breakfast, assuring me that her first care would be to follow up the lost manuscript. I can see she thinks me a shocking busybody and doesn't understand my alarm, but she will do what she can, for she's a good-natured woman. 'So are they all honourable men.' That was precisely what made her give the thing to Lord Dorimont and made Lord Dorimont bag it. What use *he* has for it God only knows. I have the worst forebodings, but somehow I'm strangely without passion—desperately calm. As I consider the unconscious, the well-meaning ravages of our appreciative circle I bow my head in submission to some great natural, some universal accident; I'm rendered almost indifferent, in fact quite gay (ha-ha!) by the sense of immitigable fate. Lady Augusta promises me to trace the precious object and let me have it, through the post, by the time Paraday is well enough to play his part with it. The last evidence is that her maid did give it to his lordship's valet. One would think it was some thrilling number of *The Family Budget*. Mrs Wimbush, who is aware of the accident, is much less agitated by it than she would doubtless be were she not for the hour inevitably engrossed with Guy Walsingham."

Later in the day I informed my correspondent, for whom indeed I kept a sort of diary of the situation, that I had made the acquaintance of this celebrity and that she was a pretty little girl who wore her hair in what used to be called a crop. She looked so juvenile and so innocent that if, as Mr Morrow had announced, she was resigned to the larger latitude, her superiority to prejudice must have come to her early. I spent most of the day hovering about Neil Paraday's room, but it was communicated to me from below that Guy Walsingham, at Prestidge, was a success. Towards evening I became conscious somehow that her superiority was contagious, and by the time the company separated for the night I was sure that the larger latitude had been generally accepted. I thought of Dora Forbes and felt that he had no time to lose. Before dinner I received a telegram from Lady Augusta Minch. "Lord Dorimont thinks he must have left bundle in train—inquire." How could I inquire—if I was to take the word as command? I was too worried and now too alarmed about Neil Paraday. The doctor came back, and it was an immense satisfaction to me to feel that he was wise and interested. He was proud of being called to so distinguished a patient, but he admitted to me that night that my friend was gravely ill. It was really a relapse, a recrudescence of his old malady. There could be no question of moving him: we must at any rate see first, on the spot, what turn his condition would take. Meanwhile, on the morrow, he was to have a nurse. On the morrow the dear man was easier, and my spirits rose to such cheerfulness that I could almost laugh over Lady Augusta's second telegram: "Lord Dorimont's servant been to station—nothing found. Push inquiries." I did laugh, I am sure, as I remembered this to be the mystic scroll I had scarcely allowed poor Mr Morrow to point his umbrella at. Fool that I had been: the thirty-seven influential journals wouldn't have destroyed it, they would only have printed it. Of course I said nothing to Paraday.

When the nurse arrived she turned me out of the room, on which I went downstairs. I should premise that at breakfast the news that our brilliant friend was doing well excited universal complacency, and the Princess graciously remarked that he was only to be commiserated for missing the society of

Miss Collop. Mrs Wimbush, whose social gift never shone brighter than in the dry decorum with which she accepted this fizzle in her fireworks, mentioned to me that Guy Walsingham had made a very favourable impression on her Imperial Highness. Indeed I think every one did so, and that, like the money-market or the national honour, her Imperial Highness was constitutionally sensitive. There was a certain gladness, a perceptible bustle in the air, however, which I thought slightly anomalous in a house where a great author lay critically ill. "*Le roy est mort—vive le roy:*" I was reminded that another great author had already stepped into his shoes. When I came down again after the nurse had taken possession I found a strange gentleman hanging about the hall and pacing to and fro by the closed door of the drawing-room. This personage was florid and bald; he had a big red moustache and wore showy knickerbockers—characteristics all that fitted into my conception of the identity of Dora Forbes. In a moment I saw what had happened: the author of "The Other Way Round" had just alighted at the portals of Prestidge, but had suffered a scruple to restrain him from penetrating further. I recognised his scruple when, pausing to listen at his gesture of caution, I heard a shrill voice lifted in a sort of rhythmic, uncanny chant. The famous reading had begun, only it was the author of "Obsessions" who now furnished the sacrifice. The new visitor whispered to me that he judged something was going on that he oughtn't to interrupt.

"Miss Collop arrived last night," I smiled, "and the Princess has a thirst for the *inédit.*"

Dora Forbes lifted his bushy brows. "Miss Collop?"

"Guy Walsingham, your distinguished *confrère*—or shall I say your formidable rival?"

"Oh!" growled Dora Forbes. Then he added: "Shall I spoil it if I go in?"

"I should think nothing could spoil it!" I ambiguously laughed.

Dora Forbes evidently felt the dilemma; he gave an irritated crook to his moustache. "*Shall* I go in?" he presently asked.

We looked at each other hard a moment; then I expressed something bitter that was in me, expressed it in an infernal "Do!" After this I got out into the air, but not so fast as not to hear, when the door of the drawing-room opened, the disconcerted drop of Miss Collop's public manner: she must have been in the midst of the larger latitude. Producing with extreme rapidity, Guy Walsingham has just published a work in which amiable people who are not initiated have been pained to see the genius of a sister-novelist held up to unmistakable ridicule; so fresh an exhibition does it seem to them of the dreadful way men have always treated women. Dora Forbes, it is true, at the present hour, is immensely pushed by Mrs Wimbush, and has sat for his portrait to the young artists she protects, sat for it not only in oils but in monumental alabaster.

What happened at Prestidge later in the day is of course contemporary history. If the interruption I had whimsically sanctioned was almost a scandal, what is to be said of that general dispersal of the company which, under the doctor's rule, began to take place in the evening? His rule was soothing to behold, small comfort as I was to have at the end. He decreed in the interest of his patient an absolutely soundless house and a consequent break-up of the party. Little country practitioner as he was, he literally packed off the Princess. She departed as promptly as if a revolution had broken out, and Guy Walsingham emigrated with her. I was kindly permitted to remain, and this was not denied even to Mrs Wimbush. The privilege was withheld indeed from Dora Forbes; so Mrs Wimbush kept her latest capture temporarily concealed. This was so little, however, her usual way of dealing with her eminent friends that a couple of days of it exhausted her patience, and she went up to town with him in great publicity. The sudden turn for the worse her afflicted guest had, after a brief improvement, taken on the third night raised an obstacle to her seeing him before her retreat; a fortunate circumstance doubtless, for she was fundamentally disappointed in him. This was not the kind of performance for which she had invited him to Prestidge, or invited the Princess. Let me hasten to add that none of the generous acts which have characterised her patronage of intellectual and other merit have done so much for her reputation as her lending Neil Paraday the most beautiful of her numerous homes to die in. He took advantage to the utmost of the singular favour. Day by day I saw him sink, and I roamed alone about the empty terraces and gardens. His wife never came near him, but I scarcely noticed it: as I paced there with rage in my heart I was too full of another wrong. In the event of his death it would fall to me perhaps to bring out in some charming form, with notes, with the tenderest editorial care, that precious heritage of his written project. But where *was* that precious heritage, and were both the author and the book to have been snatched from us? Lady Augusta wrote me that she had done all she could and that poor Lord Dorimont, who had really been worried to death, was extremely sorry. I couldn't have the matter out with Mrs Wimbush, for I didn't want to be taunted by her with desiring to aggrandise myself by a public connection with Mr Paraday's sweepings. She had signified her willingness to meet the expense of all advertising, as indeed she was always ready to do. The last night of the horrible series, the night before he died, I put my ear closer to his pillow.

"That thing I read you that morning, you know."

"In your garden that dreadful day? Yes!"

"Won't it do as it is?"

"It would have been a glorious book."

"It *is* a glorious book," Neil Paraday murmured. "Print it as it stands—beautifully."

"Beautifully!" I passionately promised.

It may be imagined whether, now that he is gone, the promise seems to me less sacred. I am convinced that if such pages had appeared in his lifetime the Abbey would hold him to-day. I have kept the advertising in my own hands, but the manuscript has not been recovered. It's impossible, and at any rate intolerable, to suppose it can have been wantonly destroyed. Perhaps some hazard of a blind hand, some brutal ignorance has lighted kitchen-fires with it. Every stupid and hideous accident haunts my meditations. My undiscourageable search for the lost treasure would make a long chapter. Fortunately I have a devoted associate in the person of a young lady who has every day a fresh indignation and a fresh idea, and who maintains with intensity that the prize will still turn up. Sometimes I believe her, but I have quite ceased to believe myself. The only thing for us, at all events, is to go on seeking and hoping together; and we should be closely united by this firm tie even were we not at present by another.

THE COXON FUND

I

"THEY'VE got him for life!" I said to myself that evening on my way back to the station; but later, alone in the compartment (from Wimbledon to Waterloo, before the glory of the District Railway) I amended this declaration in the light of the sense that my friends would probably after all not enjoy a monopoly of Mr Saltram. I won't pretend to have taken his vast measure on that first occasion, but I think I had achieved a glimpse of what the privilege of his acquaintance might mean for many persons in the way of charges accepted. He had been a great experience, and it was this perhaps that had put me into the frame of foreseeing how we should all, sooner or later, have the honour of dealing with him as a whole. Whatever impression I then received of the amount of this total, I had a full enough vision of the patience of the Mulvilles. He was staying with them all the winter: Adelaide dropped it in a tone which drew the sting from the temporary. These excellent people might indeed have been content to give the circle of hospitality a diameter of six months; but if they didn't say that he was staying for the summer as well it was only because this was more than they ventured to hope. I remember that at dinner that evening he wore slippers, new and predominantly purple, of some queer carpet-stuff; but the Mulvilles were still in the stage of supposing that he might be snatched from them by higher bidders. At a later time they grew, poor dears, to fear no snatching; but theirs was a fidelity which needed no help from competition to make them proud. Wonderful indeed as, when all was said, you inevitably pronounced Frank

Saltram, it was not to be overlooked that the Kent Mulvilles were in their way still more extraordinary: as striking an instance as could easily be encountered of the familiar truth that remarkable men find remarkable conveniences.

They had sent for me from Wimbledon to come out and dine, and there had been an implication in Adelaide's note (judged by her notes alone she might have been thought silly) that it was a case in which something momentous was to be determined or done. I had never known them not be in a "state" about somebody, and I daresay I tried to be droll on this point in accepting their invitation. On finding myself in the presence of their latest revelation I had not at first felt irreverence droop—and, thank heaven, I have never been absolutely deprived of that alternative in Mr Saltram's company. I saw, however (I hasten to declare it), that compared to this specimen their other phœnixes had been birds of inconsiderable feather, and I afterwards took credit to myself for not having even in primal bewilderments made a mistake about the essence of the man. He had an incomparable gift; I never was blind to it—it dazzles me at present. It dazzles me perhaps even more in remembrance than in fact, for I'm not unaware that for a subject so magnificent the imagination goes to some expense, inserting a jewel here and there or giving a twist to a plume. How the art of portraiture would rejoice in this figure if the art of portraiture had only the canvas! Nature, in truth, had largely rounded it, and if memory, hovering about it, sometimes holds her breath, this is because the voice that comes back was really golden.

Though the great man was an inmate and didn't dress, he kept dinner on this occasion waiting, and the first words he uttered on coming into the room were a triumphant announcement to Mulville that he had found out something. Not catching the allusion and gaping doubtless a little at his face, I privately asked Adelaide what he had found out. I shall never forget the look she gave me as she replied: "Everything!"

She really believed it. At that moment, at any rate, he had found out that the mercy of the Mulvilles was infinite. He had previously of course discovered, as I had myself for that matter, that their dinners were *soignés*. Let me not indeed, in saying this, neglect to declare that I shall falsify my counterfeit if I seem to hint that there was in his nature any ounce of calculation. He took whatever came, but he never plotted for it, and no man who was so much of an absorbent can ever have been so little of a parasite. He had a system of the universe, but he had no system of sponging—that was quite hand-to-mouth. He had fine, gross, easy senses, but it was not his good-natured appetite that wrought confusion. If he had loved us for our dinners we could have paid with our dinners, and it would have been a great economy of finer matter. I make free in these connections with the plural possessive because if I was never able to do what the Mulvilles did, and people with still bigger houses and simpler charities, I met, first and last, every demand of reflection, of emotion—particularly perhaps those of gratitude and of resentment. No one, I think, paid the tribute of giving him up so often, and if it's rendering honour to borrow wisdom I have a right to talk of my sacrifices. He yielded lessons as the sea yields fish—I lived for a while on this diet. Sometimes it almost appeared to me that his massive, monstrous failure—if failure after all it was—had been intended for my private recreation. He fairly pampered my curiosity; but the history of that experience would take me too far. This is not the large canvas I just now spoke of, and I would not have approached him with my present hand had it been a question of all the features. Frank Saltram's features, for artistic purposes, are verily the anecdotes that are to be gathered. Their name is legion, and this is only one, of which the interest is that it concerns even more closely several other persons. Such episodes, as one looks back, are the little dramas that made up the innumerable facets of the big drama—which is yet to be reported.

II

IT is furthermore remarkable that though the two stories are distinct—my own, as it were, and this other—they equally began, in a manner, the first night of my acquaintance with Frank Saltram, the night I came back from Wimbledon so agitated with a new sense of life that, in London, for the very thrill of it, I could only walk home. Walking and swinging my stick, I overtook, at Buckingham Gate, George Gravener, and George Gravener's story may be said to have begun with my making him, as our paths lay together, come home with me for a talk. I duly remember, let me parenthesise, that it was still more that of another person, and also that several years were to elapse before it was to extend to a second chapter. I had much to say to him, none the less, about my visit to the Mulvilles, whom he more indifferently knew, and I was at any rate so amusing that for long afterwards he never encountered me without asking for news of the old man of the sea. I hadn't said Mr Saltram was old, and it was to be seen that he was of an age to outweather George Gravener. I had at that time a lodging in Ebury Street, and Gravener was staying at his brother's empty house in Eaton Square. At Cambridge, five years before, even in our devastating set, his intellectual power had seemed to me almost awful. Some one had once asked me privately, with blanched cheeks, what it was then that after all such a mind as that left standing. "It leaves itself!" I could recollect devoutly replying. I could smile at present at this reminiscence, for even before we got to Ebury Street I was struck with the fact that, save in the sense of being well set up on his legs, George Gravener had actually ceased to tower. The universe he laid low had somehow bloomed again—the usual eminences were visible. I wondered whether he had lost his humour, or only, dreadful thought, had never had any—not even when I had fancied him most Aristophanesque. What was the need of appealing to laughter, however, I could enviously inquire, where you might appeal so confidently to measurement? Mr Saltram's queer figure, his thick nose and hanging lip, were fresh to me: in the light of my old friend's fine cold symmetry they presented mere success in amusing as the refuge of conscious ugliness. Already, at hungry twenty-six, Gravener looked as blank and parliamentary as if he were fifty and popular. In my scrap of a residence (he had a worldling's eye for its futile conveniences, but never a comrade's joke) I sounded Frank Saltram in his ears; a circumstance I mention in order to note that even then I was surprised at his impatience of my enlivenment. As he had never before heard of the personage, it took indeed the form of impatience of the preposterous Mulvilles, his relation to whom, like mine, had had its origin in an early, a childish intimacy with the young Adelaide, the fruit of multiplied ties in the previous generation. When she married Kent Mulville, who was older than Gravener and I and much more amiable, I gained a friend, but Gravener practically lost one. We were affected in different ways by the form taken by what he called their deplorable social action—the form (the term was also his) of nasty second-rate gush. I may have held in my *for intérieur* that the good people at Wimbledon were beautiful fools, but when he sniffed at them I couldn't help taking the opposite line, for I already felt that even should we happen to agree it would always be for reasons that differed. It came home to me that he was admirably British as, without so much as a sociable sneer at my bookbinder, he turned away from the serried rows of my little French library.

"Of course I've never seen the fellow, but it's clear enough he's a humbug."

"Clear 'enough' is just what it isn't," I replied; "if it only were!" That ejaculation on my part must have been the beginning of what was to be later a long ache for final frivolous rest. Gravener was profound enough to remark after a moment that in the first place he couldn't be anything but a Dissenter, and when I answered that the very note of his fascination was his extraordinary speculative breadth, my friend retorted that there was no cad like your cultivated cad and that I might depend upon discovering (since I had had the levity not already to have inquired) that my shining light proceeded, a generation back, from a Methodist cheesemonger. I confess I was struck with his insistence, and I said, after reflection: "It may be—I admit it may be; but why on earth are you so sure?"—asking the question mainly to lay him the trap of saying that it was because the poor man didn't dress for dinner. He took an instant to circumvent my trap and come blandly out the other side.

"Because the Kent Mulvilles have invented him. They've an infallible hand for frauds. All their geese are swans. They were born to be duped, they like it, they cry for it, they don't know anything from anything, and they disgust one (luckily perhaps!) with Christian charity." His vehemence was doubtless an accident, but it might have been a strange foreknowledge. I forget what protest I dropped; it was at any rate something which led him to go on after a moment: "I only ask one thing—it's perfectly simple. Is a man, in a given case, a real gentleman?"

"A real gentleman, my dear fellow—that's so soon said!"

"Not so soon when he isn't! If they've got hold of one this time he must be a great rascal!"

"I might feel injured," I answered, "if I didn't reflect that they don't rave about *me*."

"Don't be too sure! I'll grant that he's a gentleman," Gravener presently added, "if you'll admit that he's a scamp."

"I don't know which to admire most, your logic or your benevolence."

My friend coloured at this, but he didn't change the subject. "Where did they pick him up?"

"I think they were struck with something he had published."

"I can fancy the dreary thing!"

"I believe they found out he had all sorts of worries and difficulties."

"That, of course, was not to be endured, and they jumped at the privilege of paying his debts!" I replied that I knew nothing about his debts, and I reminded my visitor that though the dear Mulvilles were angels they were neither idiots nor millionaires. What they mainly aimed at was re-uniting Mr Saltram to his wife. "I was expecting to hear that he has basely abandoned her," Gravener went on, at this, "and I'm too glad you don't disappoint me."

I tried to recall exactly what Mrs Mulville had told me. "He didn't leave her—no. It's she who has left him."

"Left him to *us?*" Gravener asked. "The monster—many thanks! I decline to take him."

"You'll hear more about him in spite of yourself. I can't, no, I really can't resist the impression that he's a big man." I was already learning—to my shame perhaps be it said—just the tone that my old friend least liked.

"It's doubtless only a trifle," he returned, "but you haven't happened to mention what his reputation's to rest on."

"Why, on what I began by boring you with—his extraordinary mind."

"As exhibited in his writings?"

"Possibly in his writings, but certainly in his talk, which is far and away the richest I ever listened to."

"And what is it all about?"

"My dear fellow, don't ask me! About everything!" I pursued, reminding myself of poor Adelaide. "About his ideas of things," I then more charitably added. "You must have heard him to know what I mean—it's unlike anything that ever *was* heard." I coloured, I admit, I overcharged a little, for such a picture was an anticipation of Saltram's later development and still more of my fuller acquaintance with him. However, I really expressed, a little lyrically perhaps, my actual imagination of him when I proceeded to declare that, in a cloud of tradition, of legend, he might very well go down to posterity as the greatest of all great talkers. Before we parted George Gravener demanded why such a row should be made about a chatterbox the more and why he should be pampered and pensioned. The greater the wind-bag the greater the calamity. Out of proportion to everything else on earth had come to be this wagging of the tongue. We were drenched with talk—our wretched age was dying of it. I differed from him here sincerely, only going so far as to concede, and gladly, that we were drenched with sound. It was not however the mere speakers who were killing us—it was the mere stammerers. Fine talk was as rare as it was refreshing—the gift of the gods themselves, the one starry spangle on the ragged cloak of humanity. How many men were there who rose to this privilege, of how many masters of conversation could he boast the acquaintance? Dying of talk?—why, we were dying of the lack of it! Bad writing wasn't talk, as many people seemed to think, and even good wasn't always to be compared to it. From the best talk indeed the best writing had something to learn. I fancifully added that we too should peradventure be gilded by the legend, should be pointed at for having listened, for having actually heard. Gravener, who had glanced at his watch and discovered it was midnight, found to all this a response beautifully characteristic of him.

"There is one little fact to be borne in mind in the presence equally of the best talk and of the worst." He looked, in saying this, as if he meant so much that I thought he could only mean once more that neither of them mattered if a man wasn't a real gentleman. Perhaps it was what he did mean; he deprived me however of the exultation of being right by putting the truth in a slightly different way. "The only thing that really counts for one's estimate of a person is his conduct." He had his watch still in his hand, and I reproached him with unfair play in having ascertained beforehand that it was now the hour at which I always gave in. My pleasantry so far failed to mollify him that he promptly added that to the rule he had just enunciated there was absolutely no exception.

"None whatever?"

"None whatever."

"Trust me then to try to be good at any price!" I laughed as I went with him to the door. "I declare I will be, if I have to be horrible!"

III

IF that first night was one of the liveliest, or at any rate was the freshest, of my exaltations, there was another, four years later, that was one of my great discomposures. Repetition, I well knew by this time, was the secret of Saltram's power to alienate, and of course one would never have seen him at his finest if one hadn't seen him in his remorses. They set in mainly at this season and were magnificent, orchestral. I was perfectly aware that something of the sort was now due; but none the less, in our arduous attempt to set him on his feet as a lecturer, it was impossible not to feel that two failures were a large order, as we said, for a short course of five. This was the second time, and it was past nine o'clock; the audience, a muster unprecedented and really encouraging, had fortunately the attitude of blandness that might have been looked for in persons whom the promise (if I am not mistaken) of an Analysis of Primary Ideas had drawn to the neighbourhood of Upper Baker Street. There was in those days in that region a petty lecture-hall to be secured on terms as moderate as the funds

left at our disposal by the irrepressible question of the maintenance of five small Saltrams (I include the mother) and one
large one. By the time the Saltrams, of different sizes, were all
maintained, we had pretty well poured out the oil that might
have lubricated the machinery for enabling the most original
of men to appear to maintain them.

It was I, the other time, who had been forced into the breach,
standing up there for an odious lamplit moment to explain to
half a dozen thin benches, where the earnest brows were vir-
tuously void of anything so cynical as a suspicion, that we
couldn't put so much as a finger on Mr Saltram. There was
nothing to plead but that our scouts had been out from the
early hours and that we were afraid that on one of his walks
abroad—he took one, for meditation, whenever he was to
address such a company—some accident had disabled or
delayed him. The meditative walks were a fiction, for he never,
that any one could discover, prepared anything but a magnificent prospectus; so that his circulars and programmes, of
which I possess an almost complete collection, are the solemn
ghosts of generations never born. I put the case, as it seemed
to me, at the best; but I admit I had been angry, and Kent Mulville was shocked at my want of public optimism. This time
therefore I left the excuses to his more practised patience, only
relieving myself in response to a direct appeal from a young
lady next whom, in the hall, I found myself sitting. My
position was an accident, but if it had been calculated the
reason would scarcely have eluded an observer of the fact that
no one else in the room had an approach to an appearance.
Our philosopher's "tail" was deplorably limp. This visitor
was the only person who looked at her ease, who had come a
little in the spirit of adventure. She seemed to carry amusement in her handsome young head, and her presence quite
gave me the sense of a sudden extension of Saltram's sphere of
influence. He was doing better than we hoped, and he had
chosen such an occasion, of all occasions, to succumb to

heaven knew which of his infirmities. The young lady produced an impression of auburn hair and black velvet, and had
on her other hand a companion of obscurer type, presumably
a waiting-maid. She herself might perhaps have been a foreign
countess, and before she spoke to me I had beguiled our sorry
interval by thinking that she brought vaguely back the first
page of some novel of Madame Sand. It didn't make her more
fathomable to perceive in a few minutes that she could only be
an American; it simply engendered depressing reflections as to
the possible check to contributions from Boston. She asked me
if, as a person apparently more initiated, I would recommend
further waiting, and I replied that if she considered I was on
my honour I would privately deprecate it. Perhaps she didn't;
at any rate something passed between us that led us to talk until
she became aware that we were almost the only people left. I
presently discovered that she knew Mrs Saltram, and this
explained in a manner the miracle. The brotherhood of the
friends of the husband was as nothing to the brotherhood, or
perhaps I should say the sisterhood, of the friends of the wife.
Like the Kent Mulvilles I belonged to both fraternities, and
even better than they I think I had sounded the abyss of Mrs
Saltram's wrongs. She bored me to extinction, and I knew but
too well how she had bored her husband; but she had those who
stood by her, the most efficient of whom were indeed the handful
of poor Saltram's backers. They did her liberal justice, whereas
her mere patrons and partisans had nothing but hatred for our
philosopher. I am bound to say it was we, however—we of
both camps, as it were—who had always done most for her.

I thought my young lady looked rich—I scarcely knew
why; and I hoped she had put her hand in her pocket. But I
soon discovered that she was not a fine fanatic—she was only
a generous, irresponsible inquirer. She had come to England
to see her aunt, and it was at her aunt's she had met the dreary
lady we had all so much on our mind. I saw she would help to
pass the time when she observed that it was a pity this lady

wasn't intrinsically more interesting. That was refreshing, for it was an article of faith in Mrs Saltram's circle—at least among those who scorned to know her horrid husband—that she was attractive on her merits. She was really a very common person, as Saltram himself would have been if he hadn't been a prodigy. The question of vulgarity had no application to him, but it was a measure that his wife kept challenging you to apply. I hasten to add that the consequences of your doing so were no sufficient reason for his having left her to starve. "He doesn't seem to have much force of character," said my young lady; at which I laughed out so loud that my departing friends looked back at me over their shoulders as if I were making a joke of their discomfiture. My joke probably cost Saltram a subscription or two, but it helped me on with my interlocutress. "She says he drinks like a fish," she sociably continued, "and yet she admits that his mind is wonderfully clear." It was amusing to converse with a pretty girl who could talk of the clearness of Saltram's mind. I expected her next to say that she had been assured he was awfully clever. I tried to tell her—I had it almost on my conscience—what was the proper way to regard him; an effort attended perhaps more than ever on this occasion with the usual effect of my feeling that I wasn't after all very sure of it. She had come to-night out of high curiosity—she had wanted to find out this proper way for herself. She had read some of his papers and hadn't understood them; but it was at home, at her aunt's, that her curiosity had been kindled—kindled mainly by his wife's remarkable stories of his want of virtue. "I suppose they ought to have kept me away," my companion dropped, "and I suppose they would have done so if I hadn't somehow got an idea that he's fascinating. In fact Mrs Saltram herself says he is."

"So you came to see where the fascination resides? Well, you've seen!"

My young lady raised her fine eyebrows. "Do you mean in his bad faith?"

"In the extraordinary effects of it; his possession, that is, of some quality or other that condemns us in advance to forgive him the humiliation, as I may call it, to which he has subjected us."

"The humiliation?"

"Why mine, for instance, as one of his guarantors, before you as the purchaser of a ticket."

"You don't look humiliated a bit, and if you did I should let you off, disappointed as I am; for the mysterious quality you speak of is just the quality I came to see."

"Oh, you can't 'see' it!" I exclaimed.

"How then do you get at it?"

"You don't! You mustn't suppose he's good-looking," I added.

"Why, his wife says he's lovely!"

My hilarity may have struck my interlocutress as excessive, but I confess it broke out afresh. Had she acted only in obedience to this singular plea, so characteristic, on Mrs Saltram's part, of what was irritating in the narrowness of that lady's point of view? "Mrs Saltram," I explained, "undervalues him where he is strongest, so that, to make up for it perhaps, she overpraises him where he's weak. He's not, assuredly, superficially attractive; he's middle-aged, fat, featureless save for his great eyes."

"Yes, his great eyes," said my young lady attentively. She had evidently heard all about his great eyes—the *beaux yeux* for which alone we had really done it all.

"They're tragic and splendid—lights on a dangerous coast. But he moves badly and dresses worse, and altogether he's anything but smart."

My companion appeared to reflect on this, and after a moment she inquired: "Do you call him a real gentleman?"

I started slightly at the question, for I had a sense of recognising it: George Gravener, years before, that first flushed night, had put me face to face with it. It had embarrassed me then, but it didn't embarrass me now, for I had lived with it and overcome it and disposed of it. "A real gentleman? Emphatically not!"

My promptitude surprised her a little, but I quickly felt that it was not to Gravener I was now talking. "Do you say that because he's—what do you call it in England?—of humble extraction?"

"Not a bit. His father was a country schoolmaster and his mother the widow of a sexton, but that has nothing to do with it. I say it simply because I know him well."

"But isn't it an awful drawback?"

"Awful—quite awful."

"I mean isn't it positively fatal?"

"Fatal to what? Not to his magnificent vitality."

Again there was a meditative moment. "And is his magnificent vitality the cause of his vices?"

"Your questions are formidable, but I'm glad you put them. I was thinking of his noble intellect. His vices, as you say, have been much exaggerated: they consist mainly after all in one comprehensive defect."

"A want of will?"

"A want of dignity."

"He doesn't recognise his obligations?"

"On the contrary, he recognises them with effusion, especially in public: he smiles and bows and beckons across the street to them. But when they pass over he turns away, and he speedily loses them in the crowd. The recognition is purely spiritual—it isn't in the least social. So he leaves all his belongings to other people to take care of. He accepts favours, loans, sacrifices, with nothing more deterrent than an agony of shame. Fortunately we're a little faithful band, and we do what we can." I held my tongue about the natural children, engendered, to the number of three, in the wantonness of his youth. I only remarked that he did make efforts—often tremendous ones. "But the efforts," I said, "never come to much: the only things that come to much are the abandonments, the surrenders."

"And how much do they come to?"

"You're right to put it as if we had a big bill to pay, but, as I've told you before, your questions are rather terrible. They come, these mere exercises of genius, to a great sum total of poetry, of philosophy, a mighty mass of speculation, of notation. The genius is there, you see, to meet the surrender; but there's no genius to support the defence."

"But what is there, after all, at his age, to show?"

"In the way of achievement recognised and reputation established?" I interrupted. "To 'show' if you will, there isn't much, for his writing, mostly, isn't as fine, isn't certainly as showy, as his talk. Moreover two-thirds of his work are merely colossal projects and announcements. 'Showing' Frank Saltram is often a poor business: we endeavoured, you will have observed, to show him to-night! However, if he *had* lectured, he would have lectured divinely. It would just have been his talk."

"And what would his talk just have been?"

I was conscious of some ineffectiveness as well perhaps as of a little impatience as I replied: "The exhibition of a splendid intellect." My young lady looked not quite satisfied at this, but as I was not prepared for another question I hastily pursued: "The sight of a great suspended, swinging crystal, huge, lucid, lustrous, a block of light, flashing back every impression of life and every possibility of thought!" This gave her something to think about till we had passed out to the dusky porch of the hall, in front of which the lamps of a quiet brougham were almost the only thing Saltram's treachery hadn't extinguished. I went with her to the door of her carriage, out of which she leaned a moment after she had thanked me and taken her seat. Her smile even in the darkness was pretty. "I do want to see that crystal!"

"You've only to come to the next lecture."

"I go abroad in a day or two with my aunt."

"Wait over till next week," I suggested. "It's quite worth it."

She became grave. "Not unless he really comes!" At which the brougham started off, carrying her away too fast, fortunately for my manners, to allow me to exclaim "Ingratitude!"

IV

MRS SALTRAM made a great affair of her right to be informed where her husband had been the second evening he failed to meet his audience. She came to me to ascertain, but I couldn't satisfy her, for in spite of my ingenuity I remained in ignorance. It was not till much later that I found this had not been the case with Kent Mulville, whose hope for the best never twirled his thumbs more placidly than when he happened to know the worst. He had known it on the occasion I speak of —that is immediately after. He was impenetrable then, but he ultimately confessed. What he confessed was more than I shall venture to confess to-day. It was of course familiar to me that Saltram was incapable of keeping the engagements which, after their separation, he had entered into with regard to his wife, a deeply wronged, justly resentful, quite irreproachable and insufferable person. She often appeared at my chambers to talk over his lapses, for if, as she declared, she had washed her hands of him, she had carefully preserved the water of this ablution and she handed it about for inspection. She had arts of her own of exciting one's impatience, the most infallible of which was perhaps her assumption that we were kind to her because we liked her. In reality her personal fall had been a sort of social rise, for there had been a moment when, in our little conscientious circle, her desolation almost made her the fashion. Her voice was grating and her children ugly; moreover she hated the good Mulvilles, whom I more and more loved. They were the people who by doing most for her husband had in the long run done most for herself; and the warm confidence with which he had laid his length upon them was a pressure gentle compared with her stiffer persuadability. I am bound to say he didn't criticise his benefactors, though practically he got tired of them; she, however, had the highest standards about eleemosynary forms. She offered the odd spectacle of a spirit puffed up by dependence, and indeed it had introduced her to some excellent society. She pitied me for not knowing certain people who aided her and whom she doubtless patronised in turn for their luck in not knowing me. I daresay I should have got on with her better if she had had a ray of imagination—if it had occasionally seemed to occur to her to regard Saltram's manifestations in any other manner than as separate subjects of woe. They were all flowers of his nature, pearls strung on an endless thread; but she had a stubborn little way of challenging them one after the other, as if she never suspected that he *had* a nature, such as it was, or that deficiencies might be organic; the irritating effect of a mind incapable of a generalisation. One might doubtless have overdone the idea that there was a general exemption for such a man; but if this had happened it would have been through one's feeling that there could be none for such a woman.

I recognised her superiority when I asked her about the aunt of the disappointed young lady: it sounded like a sentence from a phrase-book. She triumphed in what she told me and she may have triumphed still more in what she withheld. My friend of the other evening, Miss Anvoy, had but lately come to England; Lady Coxon, the aunt, had been established here for years in consequence of her marriage with the late Sir Gregory of that ilk. She had a house in the Regent's Park, a Bath-chair and a fernery; and above all she had sympathy. Mrs Saltram had made her acquaintance through mutual friends. This vagueness caused me to feel how much I was out of it and how large an independent circle Mrs Saltram had at her command. I should have been glad to know more about the disappointed young lady, but I felt that I should know most by not depriving her of her advantage, as she might have mysterious means of depriving me of my knowledge. For the present, moreover, this experience was arrested, Lady Coxon having in fact gone abroad, accompanied by her niece. The niece, besides being immensely clever, was an heiress, Mrs Saltram said; the only daughter and the light of the eyes of some great American merchant, a man, over there, of endless indulgences and dollars. She had pretty clothes and pretty manners, and she had, what was prettier still, the great thing of all. The great thing of all for Mrs Saltram was always sympathy, and she spoke as if during the absence of these ladies she might not know where to turn for it. A few months later indeed, when they had come back, her tone perceptibly changed: she alluded to them, on my leading her up to it, rather as to persons in her debt for favours received. What had happened I didn't know, but I saw it would take only a little more or a little less to make her speak of them as thankless subjects of social countenance —people for whom she had vainly tried to do something. I confess I saw that it would not be in a mere week or two that I should rid myself of the image of Ruth Anvoy, in whose very name, when I learnt it, I found something secretly to like. I should probably neither see her nor hear of her again: the knight's widow (he had been mayor of Clockborough) would pass away and the heiress would return to her inheritance. I gathered with surprise that she had not communicated to his wife the story of her attempt to hear Mr Saltram, and I founded this reticence on the easy supposition that Mrs Saltram had fatigued by over-pressure the spring of the sympathy of which she boasted. The girl at any rate would forget the small adventure, be distracted, take a husband; besides which she would lack opportunity to repeat her experiment.

We clung to the idea of the brilliant course, delivered with-

out an accident, that, as a lecturer, would still make the paying
public aware of our great mind; but the fact remained that in
the case of an inspiration so unequal there was treachery, there
was fallacy at least, in the very conception of a series. In our
scrutiny of ways and means we were inevitably subject to the
old convention of the synopsis, the syllabus, partly of course
not to lose the advantage of his grand free hand in drawing up
such things; but for myself I laughed at our play-bills even
while I stickled for them. It was indeed amusing work to be
scrupulous for Frank Saltram, who also at moments laughed
about it, so far as the comfort of a sigh so unstudied as to be
cheerful might pass for such a sound. He admitted with a candour all his own that he was in truth only to be depended on in
the Mulvilles' drawing-room. "Yes," he suggestively conceded, "it's there, I think, that I am at my best; quite late,
when it gets toward eleven—and if I've not been too much
worried." We all knew what too much worry meant; it meant
too enslaved for the hour to the superstition of sobriety. On
the Saturdays I used to bring my portmanteau, so as not to
have to think of eleven o'clock trains. I had a bold theory that
as regards this temple of talk and its altars of cushioned chintz,
its pictures and its flowers, its large fireside and clear lamp-
light, we might really arrive at something if the Mulvilles
would only charge for admission. But here it was that the Mulvilles shamelessly broke down; as there is a flaw in every
perfection, this was the inexpugnable refuge of their egotism.
They declined to make their saloon a market, so that Saltram's
golden words continued to be the only coin that rang there. It
can have happened to no man, however, to be paid a greater
price than such an enchanted hush as surrounded him on his
greatest nights. The most profane, on these occasions, felt a
presence; all minor eloquence grew dumb. Adelaide Mulville,
for the pride of her hospitality, anxiously watched the door or
stealthily poked the fire. I used to call it the music-room, for
we had anticipated Bayreuth. The very gates of the kingdom

of light seemed to open and the horizon of thought to flash
with the beauty of a sunrise at sea.

In the consideration of ways and means, the sittings of our
little board, we were always conscious of the creak of Mrs
Saltram's shoes. She hovered, she interrupted, she almost presided, the state of affairs being mostly such as to supply her
with every incentive for inquiring what was to be done next.
It was the pressing pursuit of this knowledge that, in con-
catenations of omnibuses and usually in very wet weather, led
her so often to my door. She thought us spiritless creatures
with editors and publishers; but she carried matters to no great
effect when she personally pushed into back-shops. She wanted
all moneys to be paid to herself: they were otherwise liable to
such strange adventures. They trickled away into the desert,
and they were mainly at best, alas, but a slender stream. The
editors and the publishers were the last people to take this
remarkable thinker at the valuation that has now pretty well
come to be established. The former were half distraught
between the desire to "cut" him and the difficulty of finding a
crevice for their shears; and when a volume on this or that
portentous subject was proposed to the latter they suggested
alternative titles which, as reported to our friend, brought into
his face the noble blank melancholy that sometimes made it
handsome. The title of an unwritten book didn't after all much
matter, but some masterpiece of Saltram's may have died in his
bosom of the shudder with which it was then convulsed. The
ideal solution, failing the fee at Kent Mulville's door, would
have been some system of subscription to projected treatises
with their non-appearance provided for—provided for, I mean,
by the indulgence of subscribers. The author's real misfortune
was that subscribers were so wretchedly literal. When they
tastelessly inquired why publication had not ensued I was
tempted to ask who in the world had ever been so published.
Nature herself had brought him out in voluminous form, and
the money was simply a deposit on borrowing the work.

V

I WAS doubtless often a nuisance to my friends in those years; but there were sacrifices I declined to make, and I never passed the hat to George Gravener. I never forgot our little discussion in Ebury Street, and I think it stuck in my throat to have to make to him the admission I had made so easily to Miss Anvoy. It had cost me nothing to confide to this charming girl, but it would have cost me much to confide to the friend of my youth, that the character of the "real gentleman" was not an attribute of the man I took such pains for. Was this because I had already generalised to the point of perceiving that women are really the unfastidious sex? I knew at any rate that Gravener, already quite in view but still hungry and frugal, had naturally enough more ambition than charity. He had sharp aims for stray sovereigns, being in view most from the tall steeple of Clockborough. His immediate ambition was to wholly occupy the field of vision of that smokily-seeing city, and all his move- ments and postures were calculated for this angle. The move- ment of the hand to the pocket had thus to alternate gracefully with the posture of the hand on the heart. He talked to Clock- borough in short only less beguilingly than Frank Saltram talked to his electors; with the difference in our favour, how- ever, that we had already voted and that our candidate had no antagonist but himself. He had more than once been at Wimbledon—it was Mrs Mulville's work, not mine—and, by the time the claret was served, had seen the god descend. He took more pains to swing his censer than I had expected, but on our way back to town he forestalled any little triumph I might have been so artless as to express by the observation that such a man was—a hundred times!—a man to use and never a man to be used by. I remember that this neat remark humiliated me almost as much as if virtually, in the fever of broken slumbers, I hadn't often made it myself. The difference was that on Gravener's part a force attached to it that could never attach to it on mine. He was able to use people—he had the machinery; and the irony of Saltram's being made showy at Clockborough came out to me when he said, as if he had no memory of our original talk and the idea were quite fresh to him: "I hate his type, you know, but I'll be hanged if I don't put some of those things in. I can find a place for them: we might even find a place for the fellow himself." I myself should have had some fear, not, I need scarcely say, for the "things" themselves, but for some other things very near them—in fine for the rest of my eloquence.

Later on I could see that the oracle of Wimbledon was not in this case so appropriate as he would have been had the politics of the gods only coincided more exactly with those of the party. There was a distinct moment when, without saying anything more definite to me, Gravener entertained the idea of annexing Mr Saltram. Such a project was delusive, for the discovery of analogies between his body of doctrine and that pressed from headquarters upon Clockborough—the bottling, in a word, of the air of those lungs for convenient public uncorking in corn-exchanges—was an experiment for which no one had the leisure. The only thing would have been to carry him massively about, paid, caged, clipped; to turn him on for a particular occasion in a particular channel. Frank Saltram's channel, however, was essentially not calculable, and there was no knowing what disastrous floods might have ensued. For what there would have been to do *The Empire*, the great newspaper, was there to look to; but it was no new misfortune that there were delicate situations in which *The Empire* broke down. In fine there was an instinctive apprehension that a clever young journalist commissioned to report upon Mr Saltram might never come back from the errand. No one knew better than George Gravener that that was a time when prompt returns counted double. If he therefore found our friend an exasperating waste of orthodoxy it was because he was, as he said, up in the clouds, not because he was down in the dust. He would have been a real enough gentleman if he could have helped to put in a real gentleman. Gravener's great objection to the actual member was that he was not one.

Lady Coxon had a fine old house, a house with "grounds," at Clockborough, which she had let; but after she returned from abroad I learned from Mrs Saltram that the lease had fallen in and that she had gone down to resume possession. I could see the faded red livery, the big square shoulders, the high-walled garden of this decent abode. As the rumble of dissolution grew louder the suitor would have pressed his suit, and I found myself hoping that the politics of the late Mayor's widow would not be such as to enjoin upon her to ask him to dinner; perhaps indeed I went so far as to hope that they would be such as to put all countenance out of the question. I tried to focus the page, in the daily airing, as he perhaps even pushed the Bath-chair over somebody's toes. I was destined to hear, however, through Mrs Saltram (who, I afterwards learned, was in correspondence with Lady Coxon's housekeeper) that Gravener was known to have spoken of the habitation I had in my eye as the pleasantest thing at Clockborough. On his part, I was sure, this was the voice not of envy but of experience. The vivid scene was now peopled, and I could see him in the old-time garden with Miss Anvoy, who would be certain, and very justly, to think him good-looking. It would be too much to say that I was troubled by this evocation; but I seem to remember the relief, singular enough, of feeling it suddenly brushed away by an annoyance really much greater; an annoyance the result of its happening to come over me about that time with a rush that I was simply ashamed of Frank Saltram. There were limits after all, and my mark at last had been reached.

I had had my disgusts, if I may allow myself to-day such an

expression; but this was a supreme revolt. Certain things cleared up in my mind, certain values stood out. It was all very well to have an unfortunate temperament; there was nothing so unfortunate as to have, for practical purposes, nothing else. I avoided George Gravener at this moment and reflected that at such a time I should do so most effectually by leaving England. I wanted to forget Frank Saltram—that was all. I didn't want to do anything in the world to him but that. Indignation had withered on the stalk, and I felt that one could pity him as much as one ought only by never thinking of him again. It wasn't for anything he had done to me; it was for something he had done to the Mulvilles. Adelaide cried about it for a week, and her husband, profiting by the example so signally given him of the fatal effect of a want of character, left the letter unanswered. The letter, an incredible one, addressed by Saltram to Wimbledon during a stay with the Pudneys at Ramsgate, was the central feature of the incident, which, however, had many features, each more painful than whichever other we compared it with. The Pudneys had behaved shockingly, but that was no excuse. Base ingratitude, gross indecency—one had one's choice only of such formulas as that the more they fitted the less they gave one rest. These are dead aches now, and I am under no obligation, thank heaven, to be definite about the business. There are things which if I had had to tell them—well, I wouldn't have told my story.

I went abroad for the general election, and if I don't know how much, on the Continent, I forgot, I at least know how much I missed, him. At a distance, in a foreign land, ignoring, abjuring, unlearning him, I discovered what he had done for me. I owed him, oh unmistakably, certain noble conceptions; I had lighted my little taper at his smoky lamp, and lo, it continued to twinkle. But the light it gave me just showed me how much more I wanted. I was pursued of course by letters from Mrs Saltram, which I didn't scruple not to read, though I was duly conscious that her embarrassments would now be of the

gravest. I sacrificed to propriety by simply putting them away,
and this is how, one day as my absence drew to an end, my
eye, as I rummaged in my desk for another paper, was caught
by a name on a leaf that had detached itself from the packet.
The allusion was to Miss Anvoy, who, it appeared, was engaged to be married to Mr George Gravener; and the news
was two months old. A direct question of Mrs Saltram's had
thus remained unanswered—she had inquired of me in a post-
script what sort of man this Mr Gravener might be. This Mr
Gravener had been triumphantly returned for Clockborough,
in the interest of the party that had swept the country, so that
I might easily have referred Mrs Saltram to the journals of the
day. But when I at last wrote to her that I was coming home
and would discharge my accumulated burden by seeing her,
I remarked in regard to her question that she must really put it
to Miss Anvoy.

VI

I HAD almost avoided the general election, but some of its
consequences, on my return, had smartly to be faced. The
season, in London, began to breathe again and to flap its folded
wings. Confidence, under the new Ministry, was understood
to be reviving, and one of the symptoms, in the social body,
was a recovery of appetite. People once more fed together, and
it happened that, one Saturday night, at somebody's house, I
fed with George Gravener. When the ladies left the room I
moved up to where he sat and offered him my congratulation.
"On my election?" he asked after a moment; whereupon I
feigned, jocosely, not to have heard of his election and to be
alluding to something much more important, the rumour of
his engagement. I daresay I coloured, however, for his political
victory had momentarily passed out of my mind. What was

present to it was that he was to marry that beautiful girl; and yet his question made me conscious of some discomposure—I had not intended to put that before everything. He himself indeed ought gracefully to have done so, and I remember thinking the whole man was in this assumption that in expressing my sense of what he had won I had fixed my thoughts on his "seat." We straightened the matter out, and he was so much lighter in hand than I had lately seen him that his spirits might well have been fed from a double source. He was so good as to say that he hoped I should soon make the acquaintance of Miss Anvoy, who, with her aunt, was presently coming up to town. Lady Coxon, in the country, had been seriously unwell, and this had delayed their arrival. I told him I had heard the marriage would be a splendid one; on which, brightened and humanised by his luck, he laughed and said: "Do you mean for *her?*" When I had again explained what I meant he went on: "Oh, she's an American, but you'd scarcely know it; unless, perhaps," he added, "by her being used to more money than most girls in England, even the daughters of rich men. That wouldn't in the least do for a fellow like me, you know, if it wasn't for the great liberality of her father. He really has been most kind, and everything is quite satisfactory." He added that his eldest brother had taken a tremendous fancy to her and that during a recent visit at Coldfield she had nearly won over Lady Maddock. I gathered from something he dropped later that the free-handed gentleman beyond the seas had not made a settlement, but had given a handsome present and was apparently to be looked to, across the water, for other favours. People are simplified alike by great contentments and great yearnings, and whether or no it was Gravener's directness that begot my own I seem to recall that in some turn taken by our talk he almost imposed it on me as an act of decorum to ask if Miss Anvoy had also by chance expectations from her aunt. My inquiry drew out that Lady Coxon, who was the oddest of women, would have in any

contingency to act under her late husband's will, which was
odder still, saddling her with a mass of queer obligations complicated with queer loopholes. There were several dreary
people, Coxon cousins, old maids, to whom she would have
more or less to minister. Gravener laughed, without saying no,
when I suggested that the young lady might come in through
a loophole; then suddenly, as if he suspected that I had turned
a lantern on him, he exclaimed quite dryly: "That's all rot—
one is moved by other springs!"

A fortnight later, at Lady Coxon's own house, I understood
well enough the springs one was moved by. Gravener had
spoken of me there as an old friend, and I received a gracious
invitation to dine. The knight's widow was again indisposed
—she had succumbed at the eleventh hour; so that I found
Miss Anvoy bravely playing hostess, without even Gravener's
help, inasmuch as, to make matters worse, he had just sent up
word that the House, the insatiable House, with which he supposed he had contracted for easier terms, positively declined
to release him. I was struck with the courage, the grace and
gaiety of the young lady left to deal unaided with the possibilities of the Regent's Park. I did what I could to help her to
keep them down, or up, after I had recovered from the confusion of seeing her slightly disconcerted at perceiving in the
guest introduced by her intended the gentleman with whom
she had had that talk about Frank Saltram. I had at that
moment my first glimpse of the fact that she was a person who
could carry a responsibility; but I leave the reader to judge of
my sense of the aggravation, for either of us, of such a burden
when I heard the servant announce Mrs Saltram. From what
immediately passed between the two ladies I gathered that the
latter had been sent for post-haste to fill the gap created by the
absence of the mistress of the house. "Good!" I exclaimed,
"she will be put by *me;*" and my apprehension was promptly
justified. Mrs Saltram taken in to dinner, and taken in as a
consequence of an appeal to her amiability, was Mrs Saltram

9:K

with a vengeance. I asked myself what Miss Anvoy meant by doing such things, but the only answer I arrived at was that Gravener was verily fortunate. She had not happened to tell him of her visit to Upper Baker Street, but she would certainly tell him to-morrow; not indeed that this would make him like any better her having had the simplicity to invite such a person as Mrs Saltram on such an occasion. I reflected that I had never seen a young woman put such ignorance into her cleverness, such freedom into her modesty; this, I think, was when, after dinner, she said to me frankly, with almost jubilant mirth: "Oh, you don't admire Mrs Saltram?" Why should I? This was truly an innocent maiden. I had briefly to consider before I could reply that my objection to the lady in question was the objection often formulated in regard to persons met at the social board—I knew all her stories. Then, as Miss Anvoy remained momentarily vague, I added: "About her husband."

"Oh yes, but there are some new ones."

"None for me. Oh, novelty would be pleasant!"

"Doesn't it appear that of late he has been particularly horrid?"

"His fluctuations don't matter," I replied, "for at night all cats are grey. You saw the shade of this one the night we waited for him together. What will you have? He has no dignity."

Miss Anvoy, who had been introducing with her American distinctness, looked encouragingly round at some of the combinations she had risked. "It's too bad I can't see him."

"You mean Gravener won't let you?"

"I haven't asked him. He lets me do everything."

"But you know he knows him and wonders what some of us see in him."

"We haven't happened to talk of him," the girl said.

"Get him to take you some day out to see the Mulvilles."

"I thought Mr Saltram had thrown the Mulvilles over."

"Utterly. But that won't prevent his being planted there again, to bloom like a rose, within a month or two."

Miss Anvoy thought a moment. Then, "I should like to see them," she said with her fostering smile.

"They're tremendously worth it. You mustn't miss them."

"I'll make George take me," she went on as Mrs Saltram came up to interrupt us. The girl smiled at her as kindly as she had smiled at me and, addressing the question to her, continued: "But the chance of a lecture—one of the wonderful lectures? Isn't there another course announced?"

"Another? There are about thirty!" I exclaimed, turning away and feeling Mrs Saltram's little eyes in my back. A few days after this I heard that Gravener's marriage was near at hand—was settled for Whitsuntide; but as I had received no invitation I doubted it, and presently there came to me in fact the report of a postponement. Something was the matter; what was the matter was supposed to be that Lady Coxon was now critically ill. I had called on her after my dinner in the Regent's Park, but I had neither seen her nor seen Miss Anvoy. I forget to-day the exact order in which, at this period, certain incidents occurred and the particular stage at which it suddenly struck me, making me catch my breath a little, that the progression, the acceleration was for all the world that of a drama. This was probably rather late in the day, and the exact order doesn't matter. What had already occurred was some accident determining a more patient wait. George Gravener, whom I met again, in fact told me as much, but without signs of perturbation. Lady Coxon had to be constantly attended to, and there were other good reasons as well. Lady Coxon had to be so constantly attended to that on the occasion of a second attempt in the Regent's Park I equally failed to obtain a sight of her niece. I judged it discreet under the circumstances not to make a third; but this didn't matter, for it was through Adelaide Mulville that the side-wind of the comedy, though I was at first unwitting, began to reach me. I went to Wimbledon at times because Saltram was there, and I went at others because he was not. The Pudneys, who had taken him to Birmingham, had already got rid of him, and we had a horrible consciousness of his wandering roofless, in dishonour, about the smoky Midlands, almost as the injured Lear wandered on the storm-lashed heath. His room, upstairs, had been lately done up (I could hear the crackle of the new chintz) and the difference only made his smirches and bruises, his splendid tainted genius, the more tragic. If he wasn't barefoot in the mire he was sure to be unconventionally shod. These were the things Adelaide and I, who were old enough friends to stare at each other in silence, talked about when we didn't speak. When we spoke it was only about the brilliant girl George Gravener was to marry, whom he had brought out the other Sunday. I could see that this presentation had been happy, for Mrs Mulville commemorated it in the only way in which she ever expressed her confidence in a new relation. "She likes me—she likes me": her native humility exulted in that measure of success. We all knew for ourselves how she liked those who liked her, and as regards Ruth Anvoy she was more easily won over than Lady Maddock.

VII

ONE of the consequences, for the Mulvilles, of the sacrifices they made for Frank Saltram was that they had to give up their carriage. Adelaide drove gently into London in a one-horse greenish thing, an early Victorian landau, hired, near at hand, imaginatively, from a broken-down jobmaster whose wife was in consumption—a vehicle that made people turn round all the more when her pensioner sat beside her in a soft white hat and a shawl, one of her own. This was his position and I daresay his costume when on an afternoon in July she went to return Miss Anvoy's visit. The wheel of fate had now revolved, and amid silences deep and exhaustive, compunctions and con-donations alike unutterable, Saltram was reinstated. Was it in pride or in penance that Mrs Mulville began immediately to drive him about? If he was ashamed of his ingratitude she might have been ashamed of her forgiveness; but she was in-corrigibly capable of liking him to be seen strikingly seated in the landau while she was in shops or with her acquaintance. However, if he was in the pillory for twenty minutes in the Regent's Park (I mean at Lady Coxon's door, while her com-panion paid her call) it was not for the further humiliation of any one concerned that she presently came out for him in per-son, not even to show either of them what a fool she was that she drew him in to be introduced to the clever young American. Her account of the introduction I had in its order, but before that, very late in the season, under Gravener's auspices, I met Miss Anvoy at tea at the House of Commons. The member for Clockborough had gathered a group of pretty ladies, and the Mulvilles were not of the party. On the great terrace, as I strolled off a little with her, the guest of honour immediately exclaimed to me: "I've seen him, you know—I've seen him!" She told me about Saltram's call.

"And how did you find him?"

"Oh, so strange!"

"You didn't like him?"

"I can't tell till I see him again."

"You want to do that?"

She was silent a moment. "Immensely."

We stopped; I fancied she had become aware Gravener was looking at us. She turned back toward the knot of the others, and I said: "Dislike him as much as you will—I see you are bitten."

"Bitten?" I thought she coloured a little.

"Oh, it doesn't matter!" I laughed; "one doesn't die of it."

"I hope I sha'n't die of anything before I've seen more of

Mrs Mulville." I rejoiced with her over plain Adelaide, whom she pronounced the loveliest woman she had met in England; but before we separated I remarked to her that it was an act of mere humanity to warn her that if she should see more of Frank Saltram (which would be likely to follow on any increase of acquaintance with Mrs Mulville) she might find herself flattening her nose against the clear, hard pane of an eternal question—that of the relative importance of virtue. She replied that this was surely a subject on which one took everything for granted; whereupon I admitted that I had perhaps expressed myself ill. What I referred to was what I had referred to the night we met in Upper Baker Street—the importance relative (relative to virtue) of other gifts. She asked me if I called virtue a gift—as if it were handed to us in a parcel on our birthday; and I declared that this very inquiry showed me the problem had already caught her by the skirt. She would have help, however, help that I myself had once had, in resisting its tendency to make one cross.

"What help do you mean?"

"That of the member for Clockborough."

She stared, smiled, then exclaimed: "Why, my idea has been to help *him!*"

She *had* helped him—I had his own word for it that at Clockborough her bedevilment of the voters had really put him in. She would do so doubtless again and again, but I heard the very next month that this fine faculty had undergone a temporary eclipse. News of the catastrophe first came to me from Mrs Saltram, and it was afterwards confirmed at Wimbledon: poor Miss Anvoy was in trouble—great disasters in America had suddenly summoned her home. Her father, in New York, had had reverses—lost so much money that it was really provoking as showing how much he had had. It was Adelaide who told me that she had gone off alone at less than a week's notice.

"Alone? Gravener has permitted that?"

"What will you have? The House of Commons!"

I'm afraid I cursed the House of Commons: I was so much interested. Of course he would follow her as soon as he was free to make her his wife; only she mightn't now be able to bring him anything like the marriage-portion of which he had begun by having the virtual promise. Mrs Mulville let me know what was already said: she was charming, this American girl, but really these American fathers! What was a man to do? Mr Saltram, according to Mrs Mulville, was of opinion that a man was never to suffer his relation to money to become a spiritual relation, but was to keep it wholesomely mechanical. "*Moi pas comprendre!*" I commented on this; in rejoinder to which Adelaide, with her beautiful sympathy, explained that she supposed he simply meant that the thing was to use it, don't you know? but not to think too much about it. "To take it, but not to thank you for it?" I still more profanely inquired. For a quarter of an hour afterwards she wouldn't look at me, but this didn't prevent my asking her what had been the result, that afternoon in the Regent's Park, of her taking our friend to see Miss Anvoy.

"Oh, so charming!" she answered, brightening. "He said he recognised in her a nature he could absolutely trust."

"Yes, but I'm speaking of the effect on herself."

Mrs Mulville was silent an instant. "It was everything one could wish."

Something in her tone made me laugh. "Do you mean she gave him something?"

"Well, since you ask me!"

"Right there—on the spot?"

Again poor Adelaide faltered. "It was to me of course she gave it."

I stared; somehow I couldn't see the scene. "Do you mean a sum of money?"

"It was very handsome." Now at last she met my eyes, though I could see it was with an effort. "Thirty pounds."

"Straight out of her pocket?"

"Out of the drawer of a table at which she had been writing. She just slipped the folded notes into my hand. He wasn't looking; it was while he was going back to the carriage. Oh," said Adelaide reassuringly, "I dole it out!" The dear practical soul thought my agitation, for I confess I was agitated, had reference to the administration of the money. Her disclosure made me for a moment muse violently, and I daresay that during that moment I wondered if anything else in the world makes people so indelicate as unselfishness. I uttered, I suppose, some vague synthetic cry, for she went on as if she had had a glimpse of my inward amaze at such episodes. "I assure you, my dear friend, he was in one of his happy hours."

But I wasn't thinking of that. "Truly, indeed, these Americans!" I said. "With her father in the very act, as it were, of swindling her betrothed!"

Mrs Mulville stared. "Oh, I suppose Mr Anvoy has scarcely failed on purpose. Very likely they won't be able to keep it up, but there it was, and it was a very beautiful impulse."

"You say Saltram was very fine?"

"Beyond everything. He surprised even me."

"And I know what *you've* heard." After a moment I added: "Had he peradventure caught a glimpse of the money in the table-drawer?"

At this my companion honestly flushed. "How can you be so cruel when you know how little he calculates?"

"Forgive me, I do know it. But you tell me things that act on my nerves. I'm sure he hadn't caught a glimpse of anything but some splendid idea."

Mrs Mulville brightly concurred. "And perhaps even of her beautiful listening face."

"Perhaps even! And what was it all about?"

"His talk? It was à *propos* of her engagement, which I had told him about: the idea of marriage, the philosophy, the poetry, the sublimity of it." It was impossible wholly to restrain one's mirth at this, and some rude ripple that I emitted again caused my companion to admonish me. "It sounds a little stale, but you know his freshness."

"Of illustration? Indeed I do!"

"And how he has always been right on that great question."

"On what great question, dear lady, hasn't he been right?"

"Of what other great men can you equally say it? I mean that he has never, but *never*, had a deviation?" Mrs Mulville exultantly demanded.

I tried to think of some other great man, but I had to give it up. "Didn't Miss Anvoy express her satisfaction in any less diffident way than by her charming present?" I was reduced to inquiring instead.

"Oh yes, she overflowed to me on the steps while he was getting into the carriage." These words somehow brushed up a picture of Saltram's big shawled back as he hoisted himself into the green landau. "She said she was not disappointed," Adelaide pursued.

I meditated a moment. "Did he wear his shawl?"

"His shawl?" She had not even noticed.

"I mean yours."

"He looked very nice, and you know he's really clean. Miss Anvoy used such a remarkable expression—she said his mind is like a crystal!"

I pricked up my ears. "A crystal?"

"Suspended in the moral world—swinging and shining and flashing there. She's monstrously clever, you know."

I reflected again. "Monstrously!"

VIII

GEORGE GRAVENER didn't follow her, for late in September, after the House had risen, I met him in a railway-carriage. He was coming up from Scotland, and I had just quitted the abode of a relation who lived near Durham. The current of travel back to London was not yet strong; at any rate on entering the compartment I found he had had it for some time to himself. We fared in company, and though he had a blue-book in his lap and the open jaws of his bag threatened me with the white teeth of confused papers, we inevitably, we even at last sociably conversed. I saw that things were not well with him, but I asked no question until something dropped by himself made, as it had made on another occasion, an absence of curiosity invidious. He mentioned that he was worried about his good old friend Lady Coxon, who, with her niece likely to be detained some time in America, lay seriously ill at Clockborough, much on his mind and on his hands.

"Ah, Miss Anvoy's in America?"

"Her father has got into a horrid hole, lost no end of money."

I hesitated, after expressing due concern, but I presently said: "I hope that raises no objection to your marriage."

"None whatever; moreover it's my trade to meet objections. But it may create tiresome delays, of which there have been too many, from various causes, already. Lady Coxon got very bad, then she got much better. Then Mr Anvoy suddenly began to totter, and now he seems quite on his back. I'm afraid he's really in for some big reverse. Lady Coxon is worse again, awfully upset by the news from America, and she sends me word that she *must* have Ruth. How can I give her Ruth? I haven't got Ruth myself!"

"Surely you haven't lost her?" I smiled.

"She's everything to her wretched father. She writes me every post—telling me to smooth her aunt's pillow. I've other things to smooth; but the old lady, save for her servants, is really alone. She won't receive her Coxon relations, because she's angry at so much of her money going to them. Besides, she's hopelessly mad," said Gravener very frankly.

I don't remember whether it was this, or what it was, that

made me ask if she had not such an appreciation of Mrs Saltram as might render that active person of some use.

He gave me a cold glance, asking me what had put Mrs Saltram into my head, and I replied that she was unfortunately never out of it. I happened to remember the wonderful accounts she had given me of the kindness Lady Coxon had shown her. Gravener declared this to be false; Lady Coxon, who didn't care for her, hadn't seen her three times. The only foundation for it was that Miss Anvoy, who used, poor girl, to chuck money about in a manner she must now regret, had for an hour seen in the miserable woman (you could never know what she would see in people) an interesting pretext for the liberality with which her nature overflowed. But even Miss Anvoy was now quite tired of her. Gravener told me more about the crash in New York and the annoyance it had been to him, and we also glanced here and there in other directions; but by the time we got to Doncaster the principal thing he had communicated was that he was keeping something back. We stopped at that station, and, at the carriage-door, some one made a movement to get in. Gravener uttered a sound of impatience, and I said to myself that but for this I should have had the secret. Then the intruder, for some reason, spared us his company; we started afresh, and my hope of the secret returned. Gravener remained silent, however, and I pretended to go to sleep; in fact, in discouragement, I really dozed. When I opened my eyes I found he was looking at me with an injured air. He tossed away with some vivacity the remnant of a cigarette and then he said: "If you're not too sleepy I want to put you a case." I answered that I would make every effort to attend, and I felt it was going to be interesting when he went on: "As I told you a while ago, Lady Coxon, poor dear, is a maniac." His tone had much behind it—was full of promise. I inquired if her ladyship's misfortune were a feature of her malady or only of her character, and he replied that it was a product of both. The case he wanted to put to me was a matter on which it would interest him to have the impression—the judgment, he might also say—of another person. "I mean of the average intelligent man," he said; "but you see I take what I can get." There would be the technical, the strictly legal view; then there would be the way the question would strike a man of the world. He had lighted another cigarette while he talked, and I saw he was glad to have it to handle when he brought out at last, with a laugh slightly artificial: "In fact it's a subject on which Miss Anvoy and I are pulling different ways."

"And you want me to pronounce between you? I pronounce in advance for Miss Anvoy."

"In advance—that's quite right. That's how I pronounced when I asked her to marry me. But my story will interest you only so far as your mind is not made up." Gravener puffed his cigarette a minute and then continued: "Are you familiar with the idea of the Endowment of Research?"

"Of Research?" I was at sea for a moment.

"I give you Lady Coxon's phrase. She has it on the brain."

"She wishes to endow——?"

"Some earnest and disinterested seeker," Gravener said. "It was a sketchy design of her late husband's, and he handed it on to her; setting apart in his will a sum of money of which she was to enjoy the interest for life, but of which, should she eventually see her opportunity—the matter was left largely to her discretion—she would best honour his memory by determining the exemplary public use. This sum of money, no less than thirteen thousand pounds, was to be called the Coxon Fund; and poor Sir Gregory evidently proposed to himself that the Coxon Fund should cover his name with glory—be universally desired and admired. He left his wife a full declaration of his views, so far at least as that term may be applied to views vitiated by a vagueness really infantine. A little learning is a dangerous thing, and a good citizen who happens to have been an ass is worse for a community than bad sewerage. He's worst of all when he's dead, because then he can't be stopped. However, such as they were, the poor man's aspirations are now in his wife's bosom, or fermenting rather in her foolish brain: it lies with her to carry them out. But of course she must first catch her hare."

"Her earnest, disinterested seeker?"

"The flower that blushes unseen for want of the pecuniary independence necessary to cause the light that is in it to shine upon the human race. The individual, in a word, who, having the rest of the machinery, the spiritual, the intellectual, is most hampered in his search."

"His search for what?"

"For Moral Truth. That's what Sir Gregory calls it."

I burst out laughing. "Delightful, munificent Sir Gregory! It's a charming idea."

"So Miss Anvoy thinks."

"Has she a candidate for the Fund?"

"Not that I know of; and she's perfectly reasonable about it. But Lady Coxon has put the matter before her, and we've naturally had a lot of talk."

"Talk that, as you've so interestingly intimated, has landed you in a disagreement."

"She considers there's something in it," Gravener said.

"And you consider there's nothing?"

"It seems to me a puerility fraught with consequences inevitably grotesque and possibly immoral. To begin with, fancy the idea of constituting an endowment without establishing a tribunal—a bench of competent people, of judges."

"The sole tribunal is Lady Coxon?"

"And any one she chooses to invite."

"But she has invited you."

"I'm not competent—I hate the thing. Besides, she hasn't. The real history of the matter, I take it, is that the inspiration was originally Lady Coxon's own, that she infected him with it, and that the flattering option left her is simply his tribute to her beautiful, her aboriginal enthusiasm. She came to England forty years ago, a thin transcendental Bostonian, and even her odd, happy, frumpy Clockborough marriage never really materialised her. She feels indeed that she has become very British—as if that, as a process, as a *Werden*, were conceivable; but it's precisely what makes her cling to the notion of the 'Fund'—cling to it as to a link with the ideal."

"How can she cling if she's dying?"

"Do you mean how can she act in the matter?" my companion asked. "That's precisely the question. She can't! As she has never yet caught her hare, never spied out her lucky impostor (how should she, with the life she has led?), her husband's intention has come very near lapsing. His idea, to do him justice, was that it *should* lapse if exactly the right person, the perfect mixture of genius and chill penury, should fail to turn up. Ah! Lady Coxon's very particular—she says there must be no mistake."

I found all this quite thrilling—I took it in with avidity. "If she dies without doing anything, what becomes of the money?" I demanded.

"It goes back to his family, if she hasn't made some other disposition of it."

"She may do that, then—she may divert it?"

"Her hands are not tied. The proof is that three months ago she offered to make it over to her niece."

"For Miss Anvoy's own use?"

"For Miss Anvoy's own use—on the occasion of her prospective marriage. She was discouraged—the earnest seeker required so earnest a search. She was afraid of making a mistake; every one she could think of seemed either not earnest enough or not poor enough. On the receipt of the first bad news about Mr Anvoy's affairs she proposed to Ruth to make the sacrifice for her. As the situation in New York got worse she repeated her proposal."

"Which Miss Anvoy declined?"

"Except as a formal trust."

"You mean except as committing herself legally to place the money?"

"On the head of the deserving object, the great man frustrated," said Gravener. "She only consents to act in the spirit of Sir Gregory's scheme."

"And you blame her for that?" I asked with an excited smile.

My tone was not harsh, but he coloured a little and there was a queer light in his eye. "My dear fellow, if I 'blamed' the young lady I'm engaged to, I shouldn't immediately say so even to so old a friend as you." I saw that some deep discomfort, some restless desire to be sided with, reassuringly, approvingly mirrored, had been at the bottom of his drifting so far, and I was genuinely touched by his confidence. It was inconsistent with his habits; but being troubled about a woman was not, for him, a habit: that itself was an inconsistency. George Gravener could stand straight enough before any other combination of forces. It amused me to think that the combination he had succumbed to had an American accent, a transcendental aunt and an insolvent father; but all my old loyalty to him mustered to meet this unexpected hint that I could help him. I saw that I could from the insincere tone in which he pursued: "I've criticised her of course, I've contended with her, and it has been great fun." It clearly couldn't have been such great fun as to make it improper for me presently to ask if Miss Anvoy had nothing at all settled upon herself. To this he replied that she had only a trifle from her mother—a mere four hundred a year, which was exactly why it would be convenient to him that she shouldn't decline, in the face of this total change in her prospects, an accession of income which would distinctly help them to marry. When I inquired if there were no other way in which so rich and so affectionate an aunt could cause the weight of her benevolence to be felt, he answered that Lady Coxon was affectionate indeed, but was scarcely to be called rich. She could let her project of the Fund lapse for her niece's benefit, but she couldn't do anything else. She had been accustomed to regard her as tremendously provided for, and she was up to her eyes in promises to anxious Coxons. She was a woman of an inordinate conscience, and her conscience was now a distress to her, hovering round her bed in irreconcilable forms of resentful husbands, portionless nieces and undiscoverable philosophers.

We were by this time getting into the whirr of fleeting platforms, the multiplication of lights. "I think you'll find," I said with a laugh, "that your predicament will disappear in the very fact that the philosopher *is* undiscoverable."

He began to gather up his papers. "Who can set a limit to the ingenuity of an extravagant woman?"

"Yes, after all, who indeed?" I echoed, as I recalled the extravagance commemorated in Mrs Mulville's anecdote of Miss Anvoy and the thirty pounds.

IX

THE thing I had been most sensible of in that talk with George Gravener was the way Saltram's name kept out of it. It seemed to me at the time that we were quite pointedly silent about him; but afterwards it appeared more probable there had been on my companion's part no conscious avoidance. Later on I was sure of this, and for the best of reasons—the simple reason of my perceiving more completely that, for evil as well as for good, he said nothing to Gravener's imagination. Gravener was not afraid of him; he was too much disgusted with him. No more was I, doubtless, and for very much the same reason. I treated my friend's story as an absolute confidence; but when before Christmas, by Mrs Saltram, I was informed of Lady Coxon's death without having had news of

Miss Anvoy's return, I found myself taking for granted that we should hear no more of these nuptials, in which I now recognised an element incongruous from the first. I began to ask myself how people who suited each other so little could please each other so much. The charm was some material charm, some affinity exquisite doubtless, yet superficial; some surrender to youth and beauty and passion, to force and grace and fortune, happy accidents and easy contacts. They might dote on each other's persons, but how could they know each other's souls? How could they have the same prejudices, how could they have the same horizon? Such questions, I confess, seemed quenched but not answered when, one day in February, going out to Wimbledon, I found our young lady in the house. A passion that had brought her back across the wintry ocean was as much of a passion as was necessary. No impulse equally strong indeed had drawn George Gravener to America; a circumstance on which, however, I reflected only long enough to remind myself that it was none of my business. Ruth Anvoy was distinctly different, and I felt that the difference was not simply that of her being in mourning. Mrs Mulville told me soon enough what it was: it was the difference between a handsome girl with large expectations and a handsome girl with only four hundred a year. This explanation indeed did not wholly content me, not even when I learned that her mourning had a double cause—learned that poor Mr Anvoy, giving way altogether, buried under the ruins of his fortune and leaving next to nothing, had died a few weeks before.

"So she has come out to marry George Gravener?" I demanded. "Wouldn't it have been prettier of him to have saved her the trouble?"

"Hasn't the House just met?" said Adelaide. Then she added: "I gather that her having come is exactly a sign that the marriage is a little shaky. If it were certain, a self-respecting girl like Ruth would have waited for him over there."

9:L

I noted that they were already Ruth and Adelaide, but what I said was: "Do you mean that she has returned to make it a certainty?"

"No, I mean that I figure she has come out for some reason independent of it." Adelaide could only figure as yet, and there was more, as we found, to be revealed. Mrs Mulville, on hearing of her arrival, had brought the young lady out in the green landau for the Sunday. The Coxons were in possession of the house in Regent's Park, and Miss Anvoy was in dreary lodgings. George Gravener was with her when Adelaide called, but he had assented graciously enough to the little visit at Wimbledon. The carriage, with Mr Saltram in it but not mentioned, had been sent off on some errand from which it was to return and pick the ladies up. Gravener left them together, and at the end of an hour, on the Saturday afternoon, the party of three drove out to Wimbledon. This was the girl's second glimpse of our great man, and I was interested in asking Mrs Mulville if the impression made by the first appeared to have been confirmed. On her replying, after consideration, that of course with time and opportunity it couldn't fail to be, but as yet she was disappointed, I was sufficiently struck with her use of this last word to question her further.

"Do you mean that you're disappointed because you judge that Miss Anvoy is?"

"Yes; I hoped for a greater effect last evening. We had two or three people, but he scarcely opened his mouth."

"He'll be all the better this evening," I added after a moment. "What particular importance do you attach to the idea of her being impressed?"

Adelaide turned her mild, pale eyes on me as if she were amazed at my levity. "Why, the importance of her being as happy as *we* are!"

I'm afraid that at this my levity increased. "Oh, that's a happiness almost too great to wish a person!" I saw she had

not yet in her mind what I had in mine, and at any rate the
visitor's actual bliss was limited to a walk in the garden with
Kent Mulville. Later in the afternoon I also took one, and I
saw nothing of Miss Anvoy till dinner, at which we were
without the company of Saltram, who had caused it to be
reported that he was indisposed, lying down. This made us,
most of us—for there were other friends present—convey to
each other in silence some of the unutterable things which in
those years our eyes had inevitably acquired the art of expressing. If an American inquirer had not been there we would
have expressed them otherwise, and Adelaide would have pretended not to hear. I had seen her, before the very fact, abstract
herself nobly; and I knew that more than once, to keep it
from the servants, managing, dissimulating cleverly, she had
helped her husband to carry him bodily to his room. Just
recently he had been so wise and so deep and so high that I
had begun to get nervous—to wonder if by chance there was
something behind it, if he were kept straight for instance by
the knowledge that the hated Pudneys would have more to
tell us if they chose. He was lying low, but unfortunately it
was common wisdom with us that the biggest splashes took
place in the quietest pools. We should have had a merry life
indeed if all the splashes had sprinkled us as refreshingly as the
waters we were even then to feel about our ears. Kent Mulville
had been up to his room, but had come back with a face that
told as few tales as I had seen it succeed in telling on the
evening I waited in the lecture-room with Miss Anvoy. I said
to myself that our friend had gone out, but I was glad that the
presence of a comparative stranger deprived us of the dreary
duty of suggesting to each other, in respect of his errand,
edifying possibilities in which we didn't ourselves believe. At
ten o'clock he came into the drawing-room with his waistcoat
much awry but his eyes sending out great signals. It was precisely with his entrance that I ceased to be vividly conscious of
him. I saw that the crystal, as I had called it, had begun to

swing, and I had need of my immediate attention for Miss Anvoy.

Even when I was told afterwards that he had, as we might have said to-day, broken the record, the manner in which that attention had been rewarded relieved me of a sense of loss. I had of course a perfect general consciousness that something great was going on: it was a little like having been etherised to hear Herr Joachim play. The old music was in the air; I felt the strong pulse of thought, the sink and swell, the flight, the poise, the plunge; but I knew something about one of the listeners that nobody else knew, and Saltram's monologue could reach me only through that medium. To this hour I'm of no use when, as a witness, I'm appealed to (for they still absurdly contend about it) as to whether or no on that historic night he was drunk; and my position is slightly ridiculous, for I have never cared to tell them what it really was I was taken up with. What I got out of it is the only morsel of the total experience that is quite my own. The others were shared, but this is incommunicable. I feel that now, I'm bound to say, in even thus roughly evoking the occasion, and it takes something from my pride of clearness. However, I shall perhaps be as clear as is absolutely necessary if I remark that she was too much given up to her own intensity of observation to be sensible of mine. It was plainly not the question of her marriage that had brought her back. I greatly enjoyed this discovery and was sure that had that question alone been involved she would have remained away. In this case doubtless Gravener would, in spite of the House of Commons, have found means to rejoin her. It afterwards made me uncomfortable for her that, alone in the lodging Mrs Mulville had put before me as dreary, she should have in any degree the air of waiting for her fate; so that I was presently relieved at hearing of her having gone to stay at Coldfield. If she was in England at all while the engagement stood the only proper place for her was under Lady Maddock's wing. Now that she was unfortunate and

relatively poor, perhaps her prospective sister-in-law would
be wholly won over. There would be much to say, if I had
space, about the way her behaviour, as I caught gleams of it,
ministered to the image that had taken birth in my mind, to
my private amusement, as I listened to George Gravener in the
railway-carriage. I watched her in the light of this queer
possibility—a formidable thing certainly to meet—and I was
aware that it coloured, extravagantly perhaps, my interpretation of her very looks and tones. At Wimbledon for instance
it had seemed to me that she was literally afraid of Saltram, in
dread of a coercion that she had begun already to feel. I had
come up to town with her the next day and had been convinced
that, though deeply interested, she was immensely on her
guard. She would show as little as possible before she should
be ready to show everything. What this final exhibition might
be on the part of a girl perceptibly so able to think things out I
found it great sport to forecast. It would have been exciting to
be approached by her, appealed to by her for advice; but I
prayed to heaven I mightn't find myself in such a predicament.
If there was really a present rigour in the situation of which
Gravener had sketched for me the elements she would have to
get out of her difficulty by herself. It was not I who had
launched her and it was not I who could help her. I didn't fail
to ask myself why, since I couldn't help her, I should think so
much about her. It was in part my suspense that was responsible for this; I waited impatiently to see whether she wouldn't
have told Mrs Mulville a portion at least of what I had learned
from Gravener. But I saw Mrs Mulville was still reduced to
wonder what she had come out again for if she hadn't come as
a conciliatory bride. That she had come in some other character
was the only thing that fitted all the appearances. Having for
family reasons to spend some time that spring in the west of
England, I was in a manner out of earshot of the great oceanic
rumble (I mean of the continuous hum of Saltram's thought)
and my uneasiness tended to keep me quiet. There was

something I wanted so little to have to say that my prudence surmounted my curiosity. I only wondered if Ruth Anvoy talked over the idea of the Coxon Fund with Lady Maddock, and also somewhat why I didn't hear from Wimbledon. I had a reproachful note about something or other from Mrs Saltram, but it contained no mention of Lady Coxon's niece, on whom her eyes had been much less fixed since the recent untoward events.

<h1 style="text-align:center">X</h1>

ADELAIDE'S silence was fully explained later; it was practically explained when in June, returning to London, I was honoured by this admirable woman with an early visit. As soon as she appeared I guessed everything, and as soon as she told me that darling Ruth had been in her house nearly a month I exclaimed: "What in the name of maidenly modesty is she staying in England for?"

"Because she loves me so!" cried Adelaide gaily. But she had not come to see me only to tell me Miss Anvoy loved her: that was now sufficiently established, and what was much more to the point was that Mr Gravener had now raised an objection to it. That is he had protested against her being at Wimbledon, where in the innocence of his heart he had originally brought her himself; in short he wanted her to put an end to their engagement in the only proper, the only happy manner.

"And why in the world doesn't she do so?" I inquired.

Adelaide hesitated. "She says you know." Then on my also hesitating she added: "A condition he makes."

"The Coxon Fund?" I cried.

"He has mentioned to her his having told you about it."

"Ah, but so little! Do you mean she has accepted the trust?"

"In the most splendid spirit—as a duty about which there can be no two opinions." Then said Adelaide after an instant: "Of course she's thinking of Mr Saltram."

I gave a quick cry at this, which, in its violence, made my visitor turn pale. "How very awful!"

"Awful?"

"Why, to have anything to do with such an idea oneself."

"I'm sure you needn't!" Mrs Mulville gave a slight toss of her head.

"He isn't good enough!" I went on; to which she responded with an ejaculation almost as lively as mine had been. This made me, with genuine, immediate horror, exclaim: "You haven't influenced her, I hope!" and my emphasis brought back the blood with a rush to poor Adelaide's face. She declared while she blushed (for I had frightened her again) that she had never influenced anybody and that the girl had only seen and heard and judged for herself. *He* had influenced her, if I would, as he did every one who had a soul: that word, as we knew, even expressed feebly the power of the things he said to haunt the mind. How could she, Adelaide, help it if Miss Anvoy's mind was haunted? I demanded with a groan what right a pretty girl engaged to a rising M.P. had to *have* a mind; but the only explanation my bewildered friend could give me was that she was so clever. She regarded Mr Saltram naturally as a tremendous force for good. She was intelligent enough to understand him and generous enough to admire.

"She's many things enough, but is she, among them, rich enough?" I demanded. "Rich enough, I mean, to sacrifice such a lot of good money?"

"That's for herself to judge. Besides, it's not her own money; she doesn't in the least consider it so."

"And Gravener does, if not *his* own; and that's the whole difficulty?"

"The difficulty that brought her back, yes: she had absolutely to see her poor aunt's solicitor. It's clear that by

Lady Coxon's will she may have the money, but it's still clearer to her conscience that the original condition, definite, intensely implied on her uncle's part, is attached to the use of it. She can only take one view of it. It's for the Endowment or it's for nothing."

"The Endowment is a conception superficially sublime, but fundamentally ridiculous."

"Are you repeating Mr Gravener's words?" Adelaide asked.

"Possibly, though I've not seen him for months. It's simply the way it strikes me too. It's an old wife's tale. Gravener made some reference to the legal aspect, but such an absurdly loose arrangement has no legal aspect."

"Ruth doesn't insist on that," said Mrs Mulville; "and it's, for her, exactly this technical weakness that constitutes the force of the moral obligation."

"Are you repeating her words?" I inquired. I forget what else Adelaide said, but she said she was magnificent. I thought of George Gravener confronted with such magnificence as that, and I asked what could have made two such people ever suppose they understood each other. Mrs Mulville assured me the girl loved him as such a woman could love and that she suffered as such a woman could suffer. Nevertheless she wanted to see me. At this I sprang up with a groan. "Oh, I'm so sorry!—when?" Small though her sense of humour, I think Adelaide laughed at my tone. We discussed the day, the nearest it would be convenient I should come out; but before she went I asked my visitor how long she had been acquainted with these prodigies.

"For several weeks, but I was pledged to secrecy."

"And that's why you didn't write?"

"I couldn't very well tell you she was with me without telling you that no time had even yet been fixed for her marriage. And I couldn't very well tell you as much as that without telling you what I knew of the reason of it. It was not till a day or two ago," Mrs Mulville went on, "that she asked me to ask you if you wouldn't come and see her. Then at last she said that you knew about the idea of the Endowment."

I considered a little. "Why on earth does she want to see me?"

"To talk with you, naturally, about Mr Saltram."

"As a subject for the prize?" This was hugely obvious, and I presently exclaimed: "I think I'll sail to-morrow for Australia."

"Well then—sail!" said Mrs Mulville, getting up.

"On Thursday at five, we said?" I frivolously continued. The appointment was made definite and I inquired how, all this time, the unconscious candidate had carried himself.

"In perfection, really, by the happiest of chances: he has been a dear. And then, as to what we revere him for, in the most wonderful form. His very highest—pure celestial light. You *won't* do him an ill turn?" Adelaide pleaded at the door.

"What danger can equal for him the danger to which he is exposed from himself?" I asked. "Look out sharp, if he has lately been decorous. He'll presently take a day off, treat us to some exhibition that will make an Endowment a scandal."

"A scandal?" Mrs Mulville dolorously echoed.

"Is Miss Anvoy prepared for that?"

My visitor, for a moment, screwed her parasol into my carpet. "He grows bigger every day."

"So do you!" I laughed as she went off.

That girl at Wimbledon, on the Thursday afternoon, more than justified my apprehensions. I recognised fully now the cause of the agitation she had produced in me from the first—the faint foreknowledge that there was something very stiff I should have to do for her. I felt more than ever committed to my fate as, standing before her in the big drawing-room where they had tactfully left us to ourselves, I tried with a smile to string together the pearls of lucidity which, from her chair, she successively tossed me. Pale and bright, in her monotonous mourning, she was an image of intelligent purpose, of the passion of duty; but I asked myself whether any girl had ever had so charming an instinct as that which permitted her to laugh out, as if in the joy of her difficulty, into the priggish old room. This remarkable young woman could be earnest without being solemn, and at moments when I ought doubtless to have cursed her obstinacy I found myself watching the unstudied play of her eyebrows or the recurrence of a singularly intense whiteness produced by the parting of her lips. These aberrations, I hasten to add, didn't prevent my learning soon enough why she had wished to see me. Her reason for this was as distinct as her beauty: it was to make me explain what I had meant, on the occasion of our first meeting, by Mr Saltram's want of dignity. It wasn't that she couldn't imagine, but she desired it there from my lips. What she really desired of course was to know whether there was worse about him than what she had found out for herself. She hadn't been a month in the house with him, that way, without discovering that he wasn't a man of monumental bronze. He was like a jelly without a mould, he had to be embanked; and that was precisely the source of her interest in him and the ground of her project. She put her project boldly before me: there it stood in its preposterous beauty. She was as willing to take the humorous view of it as I could be: the only difference was that for her the humorous view of a thing was not necessarily prohibitive, was not paralysing.

Moreover she professed that she couldn't discuss with me the primary question—the moral obligation: that was in her own breast. There were things she couldn't go into—injunctions, impressions she had received. They were a part of the closest intimacy of her intercourse with her aunt, they were absolutely clear to her; and on questions of delicacy, the interpretation of a fidelity, of a promise, one had always in the last resort to make up one's mind for oneself. It was the idea of the application to the particular case, such a splendid one at last, that troubled her, and she admitted that it stirred very deep things. She didn't pretend that such a responsibility was a simple matter; if it had been she wouldn't have attempted to saddle me with any portion of it. The Mulvilles were sympathy itself; but were they absolutely candid? Could they indeed be, in their position—would it even have been to be desired? Yes, she had sent for me to ask no less than that of me—whether there was anything dreadful kept back. She made no allusion whatever to George Gravener—I thought her silence the only good taste and her gaiety perhaps a part of the very anxiety of that discretion, the effect of a determination that people shouldn't know from herself that her relations with the man she was to marry were strained. All the weight, however, that she left me to throw was a sufficient implication of the weight that he had thrown in vain. Oh, she knew the question of character was immense, and that one couldn't entertain any plan for making merit comfortable without running the gauntlet of that terrible procession of interrogation-points which, like a young ladies' school out for a walk, hooked their uniform noses at the tail of governess Conduct. But were we absolutely to hold that there was never, never, never an exception, never, never, never an occasion for liberal acceptance, for clever charity, for suspended pedantry—for letting one side, in short, outbalance another? When Miss Anvoy threw off this inquiry I could have embraced her for so delightfully emphasising her unlikeness to Mrs Saltram. "Why not have the courage of one's forgiveness," she asked, "as well as the enthusiasm of one's adhesion?"

"Seeing how wonderfully you have threshed the whole thing out," I evasively replied, "gives me an extraordinary notion of the point your enthusiasm has reached."

She considered this remark an instant with her eyes on mine, and I divined that it struck her I might possibly intend it as a reference to some personal subjection to our fat philosopher, to some aberration of sensibility, some perversion of taste. At least I couldn't interpret otherwise the sudden flush that came into her face. Such a manifestation, as the result of any word of mine, embarrassed me; but while I was thinking how to re-assure her the flush passed away in a smile of exquisite good-nature. "Oh, you see, one forgets so wonderfully how one dislikes him!" she said; and if her tone simply extinguished his strange figure with the brush of its compassion, it also rings in my ear to-day as the purest of all our praises. But with what quick response of compassion such a relegation of the man himself made me privately sigh, "Ah, poor Saltram!" She instantly, with this, took the measure of all I didn't believe, and it enabled her to go on: "What can one do when a person has given such a lift to one's interest in life?"

"Yes, what can one do?" If I struck her as a little vague it was because I was thinking of another person. I indulged in another inarticulate murmur—"Poor George Gravener!" What had become of the lift *he* had given that interest? Later on I made up my mind that she was sore and stricken at the appearance he presented of wanting the miserable money. This was the hidden reason of her alienation. The probable sincerity, in spite of the illiberality, of his scruples about the particular use of it under discussion didn't efface the ugliness of his demand that they should buy a good house with it. Then, as for *his* alienation, he didn't, pardonably enough, grasp the lift Frank Saltram had given her interest in life. If a mere spectator could ask that last question, with what rage in his heart the man himself might! He was not, like her, I was to see, too proud to show me why he was disappointed.

XI

I WAS unable, this time, to stay to dinner: such, at any rate, was the plea on which I took leave. I desired in truth to get away from my young lady, for that obviously helped me not to pretend to satisfy her. How *could* I satisfy her? I asked myself—how could I tell her how much had been kept back? I didn't even know, and I certainly didn't desire to know. My own policy had ever been to learn the least about poor Saltram's weaknesses—not to learn the most. A great deal that I had in fact learned had been forced upon me by his wife. There was something even irritating in Miss Anvoy's crude conscientiousness, and I wondered why, after all, she couldn't have let him alone and been content to entrust George Gravener with the purchase of the good house. I was sure he would have driven a bargain, got something excellent and cheap. I laughed louder even than she, I temporised, I failed her; I told her I must think over her case. I professed a horror of responsibilities and twitted her with her own extravagant passion for them. It was not really that I was afraid of the scandal, the moral discredit for the Fund; what troubled me most was a feeling of a different order. Of course, as the beneficiary of the Fund was to enjoy a simple life-interest, as it was hoped that new beneficiaries would arise and come up to new standards, it would not be a trifle that the first of these worthies should not have been a striking example of the domestic virtues. The Fund would start badly, as it were, and the laurel would, in some respects at least, scarcely be greener from the brows of the original wearer. That idea, however, was at that hour, as I have hinted, not the source of anxiety it ought perhaps to have been, for I felt less the irregularity of Saltram's getting the money than that of this exalted young woman's giving it up. I wanted her to have it for herself, and I told her so before I went away. She looked graver at this than she had looked at all, saying she hoped such a preference wouldn't make me dishonest.

It made me, to begin with, very restless—made me, instead of going straight to the station, fidget a little about that many-coloured Common which gives Wimbledon horizons. There was a worry for me to work off, or rather keep at a distance, for I declined even to admit to myself that I had, in Miss Anvoy's phrase, been saddled with it. What could have been clearer indeed than the attitude of recognising perfectly what a world of trouble the Coxon Fund would in future save us, and of yet liking better to face a continuance of that trouble than see, and in fact contribute to, a deviation from attainable bliss in the life of two other persons in whom I was deeply interested? Suddenly, at the end of twenty minutes, there was projected across this clearness the image of a massive, middle-aged man seated on a bench, under a tree, with sad, far-wandering eyes and plump white hands folded on the head of a stick—a stick I recognised, a stout gold-headed staff that I had given him in throbbing days. I stopped short as he turned his face to me, and it happened that for some reason or other I took in as I had perhaps never done before the beauty of his rich blank gaze. It was charged with experience as the sky is charged with light, and I felt on the instant as if we had been overspanned and conjoined by the great arch of a bridge or the great dome of a temple. Doubtless I was rendered peculiarly sensitive to it by something in the way I had been giving him up and sinking him. While I met it I stood there smitten, and I felt myself responding to it with a sort of guilty grimace. This brought back his attention in a smile which expressed for me a cheerful, weary patience, a bruised, noble gentleness. I had told Miss Anvoy that he had no dignity, but what did he seem to me, all unbuttoned and fatigued as he waited for me to come up, if he didn't seem unconcerned with small things,

didn't seem in short majestic? There was majesty in his mere
unconsciousness of our little conferences and puzzlements
over his maintenance and his reward.

After I had sat by him a few minutes I passed my arm over
his big soft shoulder (wherever you touched him you found
equally little firmness) and said in a tone of which the sup-
pliance fell oddly on my own ear: "Come back to town with
me, old friend—come back and spend the evening." I wanted
to hold him, I wanted to keep him, and at Waterloo, an hour
later, I telegraphed possessively to the Mulvilles. When he
objected, as regards staying all night, that he had no things, I
asked him if he hadn't everything of mine. I had abstained
from ordering dinner, and it was too late for preliminaries at a
club; so we were reduced to tea and fried fish at my rooms—
reduced also to the transcendent. Something had come up
which made me want him to feel at peace with me, which was
all the dear man himself wanted on any occasion. I had too
often had to press upon him considerations irrelevant, but it
gives me pleasure now to think that on that particular evening
I didn't even mention Mrs Saltram and the children. Late into
the night we smoked and talked; old shames and old rigours
fell away from us; I only let him see that I was conscious of
what I owed him. He was as mild as contrition and as abun-
dant as faith; he was never so fine as on a shy return, and even
better at forgiving than at being forgiven. I daresay it was a
smaller matter than that famous night at Wimbledon, the night
of the problematical sobriety and of Miss Anvoy's initiation;
but I was as much in it on this occasion as I had been out of it
then. At about 1.30 he was sublime.

He never, under any circumstances, rose till all other risings
were over, and his breakfasts, at Wimbledon, had always been
the principal reason mentioned by departing cooks. The coast
was therefore clear for me to receive her when, early the next
morning, to my surprise, it was announced to me that his wife
had called. I hesitated, after she had come up, about telling her

Saltram was in the house, but she herself settled the question, kept me reticent by drawing forth a sealed letter which, looking at me very hard in the eyes, she placed, with a pregnant absence of comment, in my hand. For a single moment there glimmered before me the fond hope that Mrs Saltram had tendered me, as it were, her resignation and desired to embody the act in an unsparing form. To bring this about I would have feigned any humiliation; but after my eyes had caught the superscription I heard myself say with a flatness that betrayed a sense of something very different from relief: "Oh, the Pudneys!" I knew their envelopes though they didn't know mine. They always used the kind sold at post-offices with the stamp affixed, and as this letter had not been posted they had wasted a penny on me. I had seen their horrid missives to the Mulvilles, but had not been in direct correspondence with them.

"They enclosed it to me, to be delivered. They doubtless explain to you that they hadn't your address."

I turned the thing over without opening it. "Why in the world should they write to me?"

"Because they have something to tell you. The worst," Mrs Saltram dryly added.

It was another chapter, I felt, of the history of their lamentable quarrel with her husband, the episode in which, vindictively, disingenuously as they themselves had behaved, one had to admit that he had put himself more grossly in the wrong than at any moment of his life. He had begun by insulting the matchless Mulvilles for these more specious protectors, and then, according to his wont at the end of a few months, had dug a still deeper ditch for his aberration than the chasm left yawning behind. The chasm at Wimbledon was now blessedly closed; but the Pudneys, across their persistent gulf, kept up the nastiest fire. I never doubted they had a strong case, and I had been from the first for not defending him—reasoning that if they were not contradicted they would perhaps subside. This was above all what I wanted, and I so far prevailed that I did arrest the correspondence in time to save our little circle an infliction heavier than it perhaps would have borne. I knew, that is I divined, that their allegations had gone as yet only as far as their courage, conscious as they were in their own virtue of an exposed place in which Saltram could have planted a blow. It was a question with them whether a man who had himself so much to cover up would dare his blow; so that these vessels of rancour were in a manner afraid of each other. I judged that on the day the Pudneys should cease for some reason or other to be afraid they would treat us to some revelation more disconcerting than any of its predecessors. As I held Mr Saltram's letter in my hand it was distinctly communicated to me that the day had come—they had ceased to be afraid. "I don't want to know the worst," I presently declared.

"You'll have to open the letter. It also contains an enclosure."

I felt it—it was fat and uncanny. "Wheels within wheels!" I exclaimed. "There is something for me too to deliver."

"So they tell me—to Miss Anvoy."

I stared; I felt a certain thrill. "Why don't they send it to her directly?"

Mrs Saltram hesitated. "Because she's staying with Mr and Mrs Mulville."

"And why should that prevent?"

Again my visitor faltered, and I began to reflect on the grotesque, the unconscious perversity of her action. I was the only person save George Gravener and the Mulvilles who was aware of Sir Gregory Coxon's and of Miss Anvoy's strange bounty. Where could there have been a more signal illustration of the clumsiness of human affairs than her having complacently selected this moment to fly in the face of it? "There's the chance of their seeing her letters. They know Mr Pudney's hand."

Still I didn't understand; then it flashed upon me. "You

9:M

mean they might intercept it? How can you imply anything so base?" I indignantly demanded.

"It's not I; it's Mr Pudney!" cried Mrs Saltram with a flush. "It's his own idea."

"Then why couldn't he send the letter to *you* to be delivered?"

Mrs Saltram's embarrassment increased; she gave me another hard look. "You must make that out for yourself."

I made it out quickly enough. "It's a denunciation?"

"A real lady doesn't betray her husband!" this virtuous woman exclaimed.

I burst out laughing, and I fear my laugh may have had an effect of impertinence.

"Especially to Miss Anvoy, who's so easily shocked? Why do such things concern *her?*" I asked, much at a loss.

"Because she's there, exposed to all his craft. Mr and Mrs Pudney have been watching this: they feel she may be taken in."

"Thank you for all the rest of us! What difference can it make when she has lost her power to contribute?"

Again Mrs Saltram considered; then very nobly, "There are other things in the world than money," she remarked. This hadn't occurred to her so long as the young lady had any; but she now added, with a glance at my letter, that Mr and Mrs Pudney doubtless explained their motives. "It's all in kindness," she continued as she got up.

"Kindness to Miss Anvoy? You took, on the whole, another view of kindness before her reverses."

My companion smiled with some acidity. "Perhaps you're no safer than the Mulvilles!"

I didn't want her to think that, nor that she should report to the Pudneys that they had not been happy in their agent; and I well remember that this was the moment at which I began, with considerable emotion, to promise myself to enjoin upon Miss Anvoy never to open any letter that should come to her in one of those penny envelopes. My emotion and I fear I must add my confusion quickly deepened; I presently should have been as glad to frighten Mrs Saltram as to think I might by some diplomacy restore the Pudneys to a quieter vigilance.

"It's best you should take *my* view of my safety," I at any rate soon responded. When I saw she didn't know what I meant by this I added: "You may turn out to have done, in bringing me this letter, a thing you will profoundly regret." My tone had a significance which, I could see, did make her uneasy, and there was a moment, after I had made two or three more remarks of studiously bewildering effect, at which her eyes followed so hungrily the little flourish of the letter with which I emphasised them that I instinctively slipped Mr Pudney's communication into my pocket. She looked, in her embarrassed annoyance, as if she might grab it and send it back to him. I felt, after she had gone, as if I had almost given her my word I wouldn't deliver the enclosure. The passionate movement, at any rate, with which, in solitude, I transferred the whole thing, unopened, from my pocket to a drawer which I double-locked would have amounted for an initiated observer to some such promise.

XII

MRS SALTRAM left me drawing my breath more quickly and indeed almost in pain—as if I had just perilously grazed the loss of something precious. I didn't quite know what it was—it had a shocking resemblance to my honour. The emotion was the livelier doubtless in that my pulses were still shaken with the rejoicing with which, the night before, I had rallied to the rare analyst, the great intellectual adventurer and pathfinder. What had dropped from me like a cumbersome garment as Saltram appeared before me in the afternoon on the heath was the disposition to haggle over his value. Hang it, one had to choose, one had to put that value somewhere; so I would put it really high and have done with it. Mrs Mulville drove in for him at a discreet hour—the earliest she could suppose him to have got up; and I learned that Miss Anvoy would also have come had she not been expecting a visit from Mr Gravener. I was perfectly mindful that I was under bonds to see this young lady, and also that I had a letter to deliver to her; but I took my time, I waited from day to day. I left Mrs Saltram to deal as her apprehensions should prompt with the Pudneys. I knew at last what I meant—I had ceased to wince at my responsibility. I gave this supreme impression of Saltram time to fade if it would; but it didn't fade, and, individually, it has not faded even now. During the month that I thus invited myself to stiffen again, Adelaide Mulville, perplexed by my absence, wrote to me to ask why I *was* so stiff. At that season of the year I was usually oftener with them. She also wrote that she feared a real estrangement had set in between Mr Gravener and her sweet young friend—a state of things only partly satisfactory to her so long as the advantage accruing to Mr Saltram failed to disengage itself from the merely nebulous state. She intimated that her sweet young friend was, if anything, a trifle too reserved; she also intimated that there might now be an opening for another clever young man. There never was the slightest opening, I may here parenthesise, and of course the question can't come up to-day. These are old frustrations now. Ruth Anvoy has not married, I hear, and neither have I. During the month, toward the end, I wrote to George Gravener to ask if, on a special errand, I might come to see him, and his answer was to knock the very next day at my door. I saw he had immediately connected my inquiry with the talk we had had in the railway carriage, and his promptitude showed that the ashes of his eagerness were not yet cold. I told him there was something I thought I ought in candour to let him know—I recognised the obligation his friendly confidence had laid upon me.

"You mean that Miss Anvoy has talked to you? She has told me so herself," he said.

"It was not to tell you so that I wanted to see you," I replied; "for it seemed to me that such a communication would rest wholly with herself. If however she did speak to you of our conversation she probably told you I was discouraging."

"Discouraging?"

"On the subject of a present application of the Coxon Fund."

"To the case of Mr Saltram? My dear fellow, I don't know what you call discouraging!" Gravener exclaimed.

"Well I thought I was, and I thought she thought I was."

"I believe she did, but such a thing is measured by the effect. She's not discouraged."

"That's her own affair. The reason I asked you to see me was that it appeared to me I ought to tell you frankly that decidedly I can't undertake to produce that effect. In fact I don't want to!"

"It's very good of you, damn you!" my visitor laughed, red and really grave. Then he said: "You would like to see that fellow publicly glorified—perched on the pedestal of a great complimentary fortune?"

"Taking one form of public recognition with another, it seems to me on the whole I could bear it. When I see the compliments that *are* paid right and left, I ask myself why this one shouldn't take its course. This therefore is what you're entitled to have looked to me to mention to you. I have some evidence that perhaps would be really dissuasive, but I propose to invite Miss Anvoy to remain in ignorance of it."

"And to invite me to do the same?"

"Oh, you don't require it—you've evidence enough. I speak of a sealed letter which I've been requested to deliver to her."

"And you don't mean to?"

"There's only one consideration that would make me."

Gravener's clear, handsome eyes plunged into mine a minute, but evidently without fishing up a clue to this motive—a failure by which I was almost wounded. "What does the letter contain?"

"It's sealed, as I tell you, and I don't know what it contains."

"Why is it sent through you?"

"Rather than you?" I hesitated a moment. "The only explanation I can think of is that the person sending it may have imagined your relations with Miss Anvoy to be at an end —may have been told this is the case by Mrs Saltram."

"My relations with Miss Anvoy are not at an end," poor Gravener stammered.

Again, for an instant, I deliberated. "The offer I propose to make you gives me the right to put you a question remarkably direct. Are you still engaged to Miss Anvoy?"

"No, I'm not," he slowly brought out. "But we're perfectly good friends."

"Such good friends that you will again become prospective husband and wife if the obstacle in your path be removed?"

"Removed?" Gravener anxiously repeated.

"If I give Miss Anvoy the letter I speak of she may drop her project."

"Then for God's sake give it!"

"I'll do so if you're ready to assure me that her dropping it would now presumably bring about your marriage."

"I'd marry her the next day!" my visitor cried.

"Yes, but would she marry you? What I ask of you of course is nothing less than your word of honour as to your conviction of this. If you give it me," I said, "I'll engage to hand her the letter before night."

Gravener took up his hat; turning it mechanically round, he stood looking a moment hard at its unruffled perfection. Then, very angrily, honestly and gallantly: "Hand it to the devil!" he broke out; with which he clapped the hat on his head and left me.

"Will you read it or not?" I said to Ruth Anvoy, at Wimbledon, when I had told her the story of Mrs Saltram's visit.

She reflected for a period which was probably of the briefest, but which was long enough to make me nervous. "Have you brought it with you?"

"No indeed. It's at home, locked up."

There was another great silence, and then she said: "Go back and destroy it."

I went back, but I didn't destroy it till after Saltram's death, when I burnt it unread. The Pudneys approached her again pressingly, but, prompt as they were, the Coxon Fund had already become an operative benefit and a general amaze: Mr Saltram, while we gathered about, as it were, to watch the manna descend, was already drawing the magnificent income. He drew it as he had always drawn everything, with a grand abstracted gesture. Its magnificence, alas, as all the world now knows, quite quenched him; it was the beginning of his decline. It was also naturally a new grievance for his wife, who began to believe in him as soon as he was blighted, and who at this hour accuses us of having bribed him, on the whim of a meddlesome American, to renounce his glorious office, to become, as she says, like everybody else. The very day he found himself able to publish he wholly ceased to produce. This deprived us, as may easily be imagined, of much of our occupation, and especially deprived the Mulvilles, whose want of self-support I never measured till they lost their great inmate. They have no one to live on now. Adelaide's most frequent reference to their destitution is embodied in the remark that dear far-away Ruth's intentions were doubtless good. She and Kent are even yet looking for another prop, but no one presents a true sphere of usefulness. They complain that people are self-sufficing. With Saltram the fine type of the child of adoption was scattered, the grander, the elder style. They have got their carriage back, but what's an empty carriage? In short I think we were all happier as well as poorer before; even including George Gravener, who, by the deaths of his brother and his nephew, has lately become Lord Maddock. His wife, whose fortune clears the property, is criminally dull; he hates being in the upper House, and he has not yet had high office. But what are these accidents, which I should perhaps apologise for mentioning, in the light of the great eventual boon promised the patient by the rate at which the Coxon Fund must be rolling up?

A GUIDE TO FURTHER READING

(i) Bibliographies

A Bibliography of Henry James, The Soho Bibliographies, edited by Leon Edel and Dan H. Laurence and revised with the assistance of James Rambeau (New York, 1957; third edition, Clarendon Press, Oxford and New York, 1982).

Henry James, 1917-1959: A Reference Guide, A Reference Publication in Literature (Hall, Boston, Mass., 1979), compiled by Kristian P. McColgan.

Henry James, 1960-1974: A Reference Guide, A Reference Publication in Literature (Hall, Boston, Mass., 1979), compiled by Dorothy M. Scura.

(ii) Letters

The Letters of Henry James, 2 vols., edited by Percy Lubbock (Macmillan, London and New York, 1920).

Henry James Letters, vol. I-, edited by Leon Edel (Belknap Press, Cambridge Mass., and Macmillan, London, 1974-).

(iii)   Autobiography and Biography

Henry James: Autobiography, edited with an introduction by Frederick W. Dupee (W.H. Allen, London, 1956); this comprises Henry James, *A Small Boy and Others* (1913), *Notes of a Son and a Brother* (1914), and *The Middle Years* (1917).

F.O. Matthiessen, *The James Family* (Alfred A. Knopf, New York, 1947; reprinted, Random House, New York, 1980).

Leon Edel, *The Life of Henry James*, 2 vols. (Peregrine Books, London, 1977). This is a revised and condensed version of his five-volume biography.

(iv)   Tales

The Complete Tales of Henry James, edited with an introduction by Leon Edel, 12 vols. (Rupert Hart-Davis, London, and J.B. Lippincott, Philadelphia and New York, 1962-4).

The Tales of Henry James, edited with an introduction by Maqbool Aziz, vol.I- (Clarendon Press, Oxford, 1973-).

(v)   Other Writings

The Complete Plays of Henry James, edited with an introduction and notes by Leon Edel (Rupert Hart-Davis, London, and J.B. Lippincott, Philadelphia and New York, 1949).

The Notebooks of Henry James, edited with an introduction and notes by F.O. Matthiessen and Kenneth B. Murdock (Oxford University Press, New York, 1947; reprinted, the University of Chicago Press, Chicago and London, 1981).

The Art of the Novel: Critical Prefaces by Henry James, with an introduction by Richard P. Blackmur (Scribner's, New York, 1934, and London, 1935).

Henry James Selected Literary Criticism, edited by Morris Shapira (Heinemann Educational, London, 1963; reprinted, Cambridge University Press, Cambridge, 1981).

(vi)   Background

Ian Fletcher (ed.), *Decadence and the 1890s*, Stratford-Upon-Avon Studies 17 (Edward Arnold, London, 1979).

Wendell V. Harris, *British Short Fiction in the Nineteenth Century: A Literary and Bibliographical Guide* (Wayne State University Press, Detroit, 1979).

Holbrook Jackson, *The Eighteen Nineties* (Grant Richards, London, 1913; reprinted, Harvester Press, Brighton, 1976).

Valerie Shaw, *The Short Story: A Critical Introduction* (Longman, London and New York, 1983).

Eric Warner and Graham Hough (eds.), *Strangeness and Beauty: An Anthology of Aesthetic Criticism, 1840-1910*, 2 vols. (Cambridge University Press, Cambridge, 1983).

(vii) Criticism

Wayne C. Booth, *The Rhetoric of Fiction* (University of Chicago Press, Chicago and London, 1961; second edition, 1983).

F.W. Dupee, *Henry James*, The American Men of Letters Series (Methuen, London and New York, 1951).

Laurence Bedwell Holland, *The Expense of Vision: Essays on the Craft of Henry James* (Princeton University Press, Princeton, 1964; reprinted John Hopkins University Press, Baltimore and London, 1982).

F.O. Matthiessen, *Henry James: The Major Phase* (London and New York, 1944). This concentrates on the later novels and tales; still the best book on James.

Tzvetan Todorov, 'The Structural Analysis of Literature: the Tales of Henry James', in *Structuralism: an Introduction,* edited by David Robey (Oxford, 1973), pp.73-103.

NOTE ON THE TEXTS

The complicated publishing history of Henry James' tales indicates the extent of the opportunity he took to be, like Dencombe in 'The Middle Years', 'a passionate corrector, a fingerer of style'. The introduction to volume I of Maqbool Aziz's *The Tales of Henry James*, (Clarendon Press, Oxford, 1973) together with his ' "Four Meetings": A Caveat for James Critics' in *Essays in Criticism*, XVIII (July, 1968), pp. 258-74 are useful initiations into this contentious area of textual criticism. All but nine of the 112 tales originally appeared in periodicals and eighty-seven of these, mostly revised, were published in various collections in book form. The most considerable revisions were made for the twenty-four volumes of *The Novels and Tales of Henry James*, New York Edition (New York, 1907-9; London, 1908-9) and in which James included only fifty-five of his tales. The degree and nature of the revisions at each stage shift enormously and, following the usual editorial practice, the text of James' work most widely available is often that, if included in that edition, of his revision for the New York Edition. One of the problems with this policy is that it is difficult to develop a sense of James' changing style over the six decades of his writing career. And the perspective on his work inevitably becomes that of the late period, particularly from the vantage point of 1907-9, with its characteristically more involuted mode. For these reasons the text here is that of the first authorised book edition, often corrected at this stage instead of radically revised, and not that of its periodical publication nor, where available, New York Edition.

'Brooksmith' first appeared in *Harper's Weekly*, XXXV (2 May 1891), pp.321-3 and simultaneously in *Black and White*, I (2 May 1891), pp.417-20,22. It was reprinted in *The Lesson of the Master* (1892) and later revised for volume XVIII of the New York Edition.

'The Chaperon' and 'Nona Vincent' were both included by James in a volume of tales entitled *The Real Thing and Other Tales* (1893). 'The Chaperon' was originally published in *Atlantic Monthly*, LXVIII (November-December, 1891), pp. 659-70, 721-35 and 'Nona Vincent' in *English Illustrated Magazine*, IX (February-March, 1892) pp.365-76, 491-502. 'The Chaperon' was collected in the New York Edition (volume X) but 'Nona Vincent' was excluded.

Two of the stories in this volume from *Terminations* (1895) were initially contributed to the *Yellow Book*: 'The Death of the Lion', I (April, 1894), pp.7-52 and 'The Coxon Fund', II (July, 1894), pp.290-360. (For a sense of the *Yellow Book* and its contents see *The Yellow Book: An Anthology*, selected and introduced by Fraser Harrison, The Boydell Press, Woodbridge, Suffolk, 1982.) 'The Death of the Lion' and 'The Coxon Fund' are in volume XV of the New York Edition.

'The Middle Years' was originally published in *Scribner's Magazine*, XIII (May, 1893), pp.609-20 and collected in book form first in *Terminations* and then in volume XVI of the New York Edition.